I0633841

YARDIE AND THE ALIENS

TANYA R CHAMBERS

A NOVEL

YARDIE AND THE ALIENS

YARDIE AND THE ALIENS

TANYA R CHAMBERS

DAN SERIES
BOOK 1 of 3

OLD MAN TREE PRESS

OLD MAN TREE PRESS

This book is a work of fiction. Some names, characters, places and incidents are the products of the author's imagination, and are used fictitiously. Resemblance to any actual events, locations, persons, living or dead, is coincidental.

Copyright © 2024 by TANYA R CHAMBERS

YARDIE AND THE ALIENS

All rights reserved.
Paperback

Cover art by Anike Gold of ANIKE GOLD GRAPHIC DESIGN
Cover art by Tanya Chambers of LGSS-P&T LLC
Cover design by Tanya Chambers of LGSS-P&T LLC
Cover by Tanya Chambers of LGSS-P&T LLC
Editing: Yaya Oluwubarunla

This is the paperback edition of YARDIE AND THE ALIENS published by Old Man Tree Press. Old Man Tree Press is an imprint of LAZY GAL SWOFIYAH SELF PUBLISHING & THINGS LLC.
PO Box 60392, Rochester, NY 14606

Published and printed in the United States Of America

Old Man Tree Press.
www.oldmantreepress.com

No part of this publication may be reproduced, stored in a retrieval system or transmitted in any form or by any means, electronically, mechanically, photocopying, recording, or otherwise without the prior written consent of the author/Press

Designed by Lazy Gal Swofiyah Self-Publishing & Things LLC

Library of Congress Cataloging-in-Publication Data is available

ISBN 979-8-9916668-4-8

Library of Congress Control Number: 2024950287

To my sister Karen, to my wonderful friend Kim, and to Delroy.
Thank you all.

TABLE OF CONTENT

PROLOGUE

Dan stood under the flickering light post at the busy intersection of Genesee Street and Plymouth Avenue, intently observing her as she moved. She was slowly making her way into the CVS Pharmacy, her expression appeared a bit pensive and she was lost in thought. He didn't need to ask her if she was okay, for he already knew well how she felt, but he asked anyway, savoring the sound of her voice echoing in his head.

"How are you feeling today?"

"I'm not sure. I think I'm feeling a little anxious," she replied, glancing over her shoulder.

"Not sure, or feeling anxious?" he prompted, gently.

"I don't know. I really hate it when I get like this. Nothing seems to make sense," she admitted, her brows furrowing in frustration.

Hmm, that's more like it. She had been quiet for what felt like ten minutes—ten minutes too long for him to endure her silence. Their internal dialogue was the only meaningful connection he had with her at that moment. She, on the other hand, simply thought she was having a conversation with herself while navigating her own internal chaos.

He watched her intently as she moved slowly and deliberately from aisle to aisle, each step marked by a hesitance that tugged at his heart in ways he had long thought were impossible. He knew she was going to be in there for quite a while, carefully sifting through the myriad of choices, but when it came to her, he felt he had all the time in the world.

A couple of teenage boys, tall and athletically built, sporting long locs that swayed with their movements, shouted and laughed while chasing each other at high speed. They were heading straight for him in a blur of youthful energy. He swiftly moved out of their way, acutely aware of the potential chaos that would ensue if they were to collide with him. He watched them as they ran past the newly built stores on Genesee Street, projecting an aura of happiness and carefree joy that seemed so innocent.

It was quiet, yet there lingered that palpable fear in the air as a lingering consequence of the afflictions humanity was experiencing in these troubled times.

The boys seemed blissfully immune to the heavy energy that weighed down on others, or perhaps they were just so thrilled to be out and about that they actively chose to ignore it altogether. But no matter the reason, he firmly reminded himself that he was not here to get involved in the fleeting drama of humanity crisis.

He was an ethereal immortal being, one who had existed long before the very creation of time itself.

They both were, but she had inexplicably forgotten these truths, embracing her mortal guise and limitations. He watched her as she searched the aisles, reaching for human items she didn't even know she didn't need. His other senses alerted him to the human male who was stalking her from a distance. The male was a student at the University of Rochester, where she also attended, and he had been attempting to get her attention for some time now, but with each effort, he was thwarted and left feeling disappointed.

Dan could feel the excitement radiating from the human male at the sight of her in the store — so far from the campus and its demanding atmosphere. He listened closely to the rapid beating of the male's heart as he tried to muster the courage to approach her and introduce himself.

Dan was filled with the sensation of displeasure. He didn't like it at all. It angered him deeply when human males tried to draw her attention, driven by motives he couldn't help but mistrust.

Materializing in the aisle she was about to enter, he casually picked up a bottle of Oral B mouth rinse and then proceeded towards her with a leisurely gait, gently bouncing into her the very moment she turned around. In a playful manner, he pretended to drop the mouth rinse. The plastic bottle made a loud, startling noise on the floor, echoing through the quiet store.

"I am so sorry," she apologized, bending down to pick up the fallen bottle and handing it to him with an apologetic smile. "Sorry," she said again, her voice trailing off as she walked off, appearing very preoccupied with her thoughts.

He wasn't disappointed by her distracted demeanor; he had already anticipated the outcome. He turned to the human male, who was still stalking her through the aisles, and caught his eyes. The male suddenly forgot what he was planning to do, as if a spell had been cast upon him. He stopped for a moment to try to remember, shrugged his shoulders when he couldn't, and walked right out of the store.

YARDIE AND THE ALIENS

1

THE LOTTO TICKETS

My mother didn't know how incredibly correct she was when she repeatedly called me derogatory names like "duppy," "demons," or other similar, equally hurtful derivatives. It was her way of unleashing her pent-up anger and frustration, and I was usually the easiest target, the forgiving idiot who took the brunt of her rage. Her insensitive words, inevitably followed by physical abuse, always forced me to escape my body and disappear into a safer space, elsewhere.

Today was no different in this cycle of hurt. Last night, after the Lotto results were broadcasted, she was absolutely jubilated, convinced that she had gotten five out of the six winning Lotto numbers. That triumphant feeling filled her with the hope that the winnings would offer her enough money to make a down payment on one of the houses they were building near Doncaster Drive, which was conveniently located right by the sea.

Ever since she discovered the development taking place, she had been dreaming of a beautiful waterfront view.

This morning, she got up bright and early, eager to purchase a Thursday newspaper to confirm her supposed fortune. When she returned, she had grabbed her well-worn exercise book that meticulously contained all the Lotto numbers she had ever purchased painstakingly written down in it, along with a plastic bag that was almost as old as my earthly existence. The bag was filled with old Lotto tickets, organized painstakingly by months and carefully banded together. It had holes all over it, and some of the banded tickets were threatening to escape.

They were all collected atop her makeshift table — a two by two piece of half-inch plywood board — that she usually propped up on her knees and balanced precariously between the creases of her bulging, fatty belly.

A big, lit spliff dangled precariously from her mouth, and she was sucking on it deeply, expertly sending thick clouds of smoke through her nostrils. With her relaxed demeanor and blissful expression, she resembled the rolling calves one might encounter in the myriad spirit realms. I paused for a moment, captivated by the familiar scene, and wondered, if she wasn't bound by her human form, what ethereal shape would she have automatically assumed in that twilight space where reality and fantasy blurred?

Earlier that day, I had risen before dawn, around four, and diligently washed down the expansive slab. we called a veranda, with a mix of lime and water. It was just one of the many chores I was accustomed to. But getting up that early was more than just fulfilling daily responsibilities; it served as a necessary excuse. I needed to check on my grandmother, my cherished soul sister. She hadn't been herself lately, and I felt a strong compulsion to keep a watchful eye on her.

As I observed my mother, she settled her somewhat obese frame onto the worn, dirty red velvet ottoman that had clearly seen better days. This particular area of the house was typically regarded as hers, so we all naturally avoided it. She appeared unusually happy, filled with an air of anticipation.

The evening before, she had spent hours meticulously studying the Lotto numbers, deliberating over the ones she would ultimately decide to purchase. It made me wonder what might have transpired had she devoted that same level of effort into her school assignments and books when she was younger. Who would she have become had her priorities been different?

Suddenly, she broke the quiet lull with a loud proclamation, "All a oonuu come kiss me raas," directed at no one in particular.

We had long since grown accustomed to this type of erratic behavior from her—something the neighbors were familiar with as well. We all had already come to terms with her eccentricity, so I continued to water the yard that I had just finished sweeping, while discreetly observing her from my peripheral vision.

The sun was slowly rising over the hill as she picked up a ticket that I assumed was from last night's drawing, then opened up the Gleaner to the Lotto section. I watched as she scrolled down the page with focused intensity until she finally arrived at the area she was most interested in, her eyes gleaming with hope and excitement.

"Yes, Puppa Jesas!" she shouted out once more, taking another long, indulgent draw from the now half-finished spliff, exhaling it in a cloud through both her nostrils and her mouth, sending a thick plume of smoke gathering around her head, where it slowly began to dissipate as it floated upward into the hot air.

Once the haze cleared, she returned to studying the numbers printed on the ticket, meticulously matching them with the corresponding numbers in the Gleaner. A wave of happiness washed over me as I thought about her potential win. If she actually won, perhaps she wouldn't feel the urge to beat us quite so often, and she might finally have other things to occupy her restless mind and keep her distracted. I truly wanted her to win.

Just then, in a fit of frustration, she lifted her makeshift plywood tabletop and hurled it onto the concrete slab with force.

"Cho bloodclaat, me is a idiot!" she berated herself, her voice laced with anger. "Me have the bumboclaat number dem and me neva buy dem."

My heart sank. It meant she had not won anything, and she was going be in a foul mood until Saturday rolled around again.

"Over two million me woulda win, cho bloodclaat," she repeated, hissing the few teeth she had left, her anger boiling over as she abruptly got up from her spot and stepped off the veranda, disappearing from sight in a storm of frustration.

~~~~~~~~~~~~~

Swofiyah's spirit slowly emerged from the house, rubbing her sleepy eyes as they adjusted to the early morning sun now basking us all. Her material body remained nestled in bed, probably lost in the depths of a dream, completely unaware of what was transpiring.

"Where Netty gone?" she asked curiously.

I shrugged my shoulders, placing the pan down on the clean, sunlit veranda as I stepped up, eager to discover why Netty believed she had won. I made my way to the spot where she had unceremoniously discarded her belongings and picked up the ten tickets that had been carelessly tossed upon the ground. Using my otherworldly eyes, I quickly scanned the tickets, along with the numbers published in the Gleaner. To my surprise, the numbers she thought she had won belonged to last Saturday's draw, and she hadn't bothered to repurchase those particular tickets.

I carefully replaced the tickets in the exact positions I found them. Netty wasn't fond of us touching her personal belongings; she considered us mere crosses, poking our noses into matters that did not concern us.

"Klam, where Netty gone?" Swofiyah asked again, her tone growing anxious.

I turned to look at her spirit, which appeared to be from the black and white spirit realm, hovering in an incomplete form. It had yet to fully solidify into its true essence. The spirit seemed to resemble a child around six years old, destined to remain that age for the entirety of her material existence. Additionally, two delicate little wings jutted from its back like coco plants sprouting from the fertile ground, sure to grow and evolve according to how her mind adapted in this realm. At this moment, I was the only one able to perceive her.

"I don't...," Klam began, preparing to explain the predicament. We certainly weren't prepared for the unexpected return of Netty so soon. My soul instinctively jumped out the moment it felt her heavy hand slapping Klam's small, fragile body.

"Duppy, a who tell yuh to touch me things dem?" she asked, her big hefty right foot rising threateningly. I didn't stick around to see the end of that confrontation; I was already in my grandmother's house, desperately rushing to her bedside.

"Roboliac, a yuh dat?" she asked pitifully, her voice barely a whisper as she remained too weak to even open her eyes.

"*Yes, Jalaniac, it's me,*" I responded softly, gently taking her outstretched right hand, while kneeling beside her frail form.

Granny was dying. It was absolutely not her time to leave us yet, so we had been tirelessly searching for any way to heal her. The task was incredibly difficult, especially for someone with an eight-year-old body that lacked the necessary sensibilities and a mother from the material realm who possessed the brain of a tiki tiki fish.

I glanced over at Laliac, tall and strikingly blue, with her three-inch length hair sticking defiantly out of her head. Each strand was the size of a medium sewing needle and just as sharp at the ends. Her eyebrows dramatically met together in the middle, framing her face, while her lashes were all spiked out, adorned with the same blue-coloured, needle-like hair. Her eyes, mesmerizing and deep, mirrored the colour of the sea at midday, with pupil-less irises that seemed to gaze into the very souls of humans. Curiously, they changed colours depending on her emotions, shifting like the tides. Her skin, smooth and perfect, was as flawless as that of a one-year-old Earthling toddler.

On the golden planet, situated hundreds of thousands of light years away, she was considered a...

"Don't say it," she warned firmly, turning her back on us with determination, and gracefully gliding over to the window to admire the sprawling expanse of the many ackee trees that Granny had lovingly planted over the years.

Golealm, as our kind were referred to, possessed an intense love for ackee in the material realm we called Earth. It was the only edible source of sustenance we could consume. However, unlike the humans in this material realm, we could only indulge in it when it was prepared in a very specific way. Unfortunately, the humans would not allow the precious fruit to reach that perfect stage of ripeness, which compelled Granny to fill up her yard with an abundance of ackee trees.

I turned back to face Jalaniac, my human grandmother, and found her gazing intently at me with a mix of hope and concern. I knew she couldn't see me clearly through her aging eyes, so I gently squeezed her hand. It was a gesture that her soul recognized well and cherished deeply.

"Jalaniac, I promise we are close to finding a cure for you, just hang on a little while longer," I reassured her softly.

Her vessel was riddled with the burdens of human sickness—cancer, arthritis, the trials of old age, and diabetes. Her soul had to endure residing in it until she reached the age of ninety Earth years. It couldn't simply hop out and leave. In fact, her soul was trapped, unable to travel while held in this fragile state. Should she die now, her soul would return to its origin and start the entire cycle from the beginning. And I would—we would—have to embark on the arduous searching process all over again.

It had taken Laliac and me nearly two hundred long years to locate her. We were not about to lose her again. Just then, Laliac appeared before me, reaching out and holding our hands tightly.

"No, we're not going to lose her, again," her words reverberated in my mind like a haunting echo, resonating deeply within my thoughts.

We both focused our attention intently on our eldest triplet, when I was suddenly and unexpectedly forced back into my small, insignificant earthly body, feeling every ounce of its limitation. Swofiyah's tiny, suck fingers were stuffed into Klam's mouth, while her other hand was gently twirling Klam's silky hair, creating a soothing rhythm. They were both lying on the so-called veranda, a place that felt simultaneously serene and chaotic, head nestled together, sharing warmth and comfort.

"Yuh wake up, Klam?" she asked softly, her voice a sweet melody that broke the silence as she released the braided hair she was twirling, immediately sensing her sister's distress when Klam moaned.

Klam's little body felt like it was being squished from opposite sides by two oversized boulders, each one pressing against her with a weight that seemed insurmountable. She sat up suddenly, crying in a flood of emotion. She couldn't help it; she was engulfed in excruciating pain, and crying was a natural human response that came automatically whenever she felt sad, hurt, frustrated, or even happy, sometimes, overwhelming her senses.

Swofiyah sat up beside her, instinctively putting her left arm around Klam's shoulders, providing a sense of security, then she began rocking us gently from side to side. The movement was so blissfully comforting that I could feel the pain easing from Klam's body as the tears slowly began to subside. It was a strange, almost magical feeling, this calming energy I was receiving from her. It reached deep down to the very soles of Klam's tiny feet, making me wonder how she intuitively knew how to do that. I turned to her, Klam's head bent to the right, allowing me to look at her through my Golealm eyes, but to my dismay, I couldn't see her anymore; she was shrouded in an enigmatic mist.

Interesting, indeed.

I knew deep down that I was not the same person, but that left me wondering, what exactly was she? I had always thought she hailed from the mysterious black and white realm, a place I could scarcely comprehend. Hmm!

~~~~~~~~~

We got up and Klam promptly retrieved the pan she had been using to water the ground, skillfully restoring it to its proper place under the table located in the far left-hand corner of the veranda. Netty was nowhere in sight, and there was absolutely no indication of breakfast being made, which left us feeling a bit perplexed. Klam ventured into the house with Swofiyah following closely behind her.

"Weh Netty gone?" Klam inquired curiously, glancing around the table in the one-room house for something edible to prepare for breakfast.

"A don't know," Swofiyah responded nonchalantly, her fingers stuffed in her mouth and another one poking up her nostril.

Klam began to search through the box under the kitchen table inside the modest house and was pleased to find some dried-out salt-fish and flour. She also spotted some onions, colorful peppers, and ripe tomatoes, along with a bottle of homemade coconut oil and a jar filled with sugar. All the ingredients for a delicious dish of salt-fish fritters and refreshing mint tea were right at her fingertips. The mint, as they both remembered, was growing vibrantly in the garden outside.

After they managed to prepare and eat breakfast, the two of them set about cleaning the house, washing the dishes, and then tackling their laundry. By the time they finished with their chores, it was well past two o'clock, just in time for Netty's return.

She walked in, carrying two large bags, which suggested she had gone to the market for supplies.

Klam then disappeared to the back of the house to water the flowers and the vegetables that lined the garden. As she tended to the plants, I noticed the little fairies flitting from one transparent fungus to another, creating a delightful spectacle. It seemed to be a small community of them that had taken refuge in the garden, and I felt relieved that Netty didn't possess the curiosity to investigate the fungi, as it allowed these small beings to live safely, at least until the sun dried out the fungi and altered their home.

2

THE SHAMAN'S VESSEL

This human world, in which we unexpectedly found ourselves, was so uniquely strange, so liquidy and noisy, so hot and cold, so vibrant with green and lush landscapes, yet at times, so dry and barren, and often enveloped in shadows and darkness. Yet, despite these extremes, it was undeniably majestic. There existed a magnetic allure to Earth and all her multifaceted mysteries that made it incredibly easy to understand why so many diverse space creatures were choosing to call this planet their home.

As beings from a distant realm, our kind, who were known to be borrowers of human bodies, had no choice but to embrace the good along with the inevitable bad and the deeply mysterious aspects of life here. My soul, or rather what those from Materealm referred to as 'spirit,' was a traveler, originating from a vibrant and captivating planet known as the Golden Realm—Golealm for short. When Golealm's curious travelers first discovered

Earth, we quickly learned that in order to remain grounded and connected, we had to occupy living matter. While humans were the preferred vessels, we discovered that we could also survive within various forms of animals, insects, and even the resilient plants and trees. Anything that we could attach ourselves to became a potential host for our spirits. Living on Earth for any extended period of time without an appropriate matter could be incredibly detrimental to our well-being, potentially sending us back to our original beginnings. And without a doubt, no Golealm resident ever wanted that.

The bodies we occupied—be they humans or animals—were typically those that had no chance of surviving beyond the first month of birth. Consequently, their natural souls would not form an alliance or bond with them. For those of us who found ourselves inhabiting animal matter, our earthly lives were, unfortunately, quite short-lived. However, there was a silver lining: our lifespan was boundless and entirely limitless.

~~~~~~~

I gained earthly matter more than nine hundred Earth years ago, which is more than half a day in Golealm time. During the first three hundred years of my existence on this planet, I essentially lived in the bodies of every different kind of animal and mammal that roamed the Earth. Among all the creatures, I absolutely loved being a gorilla, as they possessed the most unique perspective on the world around them. The tigers and the lions imparted important lessons about fierceness and survival; without understanding that fierce nature, my own survival would have surely been doomed. The gluttonous snakes posed a significant temptation during this time, and they were almost the end of me. I made it a point to steer clear of their deceptive charms. Living in the body of an eagle was probably the most fulfilling existence I experienced while being matter on Earth. In fact, I spent more time in the form of an eagle than in any other animal form, which offered me unparalleled freedom and perspective.

The time spent living as animals taught me valuable lessons about the diverse characteristics and behaviors exhibited by different species that inhabit my adopted planet. While I was immersed in the lives of animals, I was simultaneously busy observing the humans of the lands. I couldn't help but notice that they were the most fierce of all the living creatures on Earth, yet paradoxically, they were also the least humble. This contradiction drew me in, and I watched them intently, fascinated by the elaborate ways they structured their societies, which bore similarities to our own. However, each different land harbored its own unique cultures, along with varying ways of doing and perceiving things. Through these observations, I was gaining a profound understanding of their characteristics, behaviors, and habits.

I realized that although humans appeared to be more civilized than the animal creatures I had embodied, they were not fundamentally different at all.

After living in so many various animal forms, it took quite a while for me to fully adjust to being human, but eventually, I did find my footing.

The first human vessel I occupied was that of a young shaman residing in the stunningly beautiful Miombo woodland jungle of Tanzania. He was diligently cutting plants in the dense jungle when he first noticed me. Having encountered some of my kind before, he graciously offered me room and board in his vessel, recognizing the unique bond we could share.

Because he was such a calm and restful soul, I had absolutely no problem sharing vessel with him for a couple of decades. This arrangement also allowed him to function normally when I was off visiting my beloved sisters in the vibrant Caribbean Island of Jamaica.

During the many decades of sharing this intimate space with another soul, the vessel sired many sons. As a result, I never lacked for human material to experience life through. After a hundred years of living in human form in that particular region of Africa, I became caught up in humanity troubles—

something Laliac had strongly advised me against. It was incredibly difficult to remain detached when I was living as one of them.

The bodies I had occupied for so long had multiplied and spread out across the entire eastern region of Africa, creating a web of interconnected lives and stories that I couldn't ignore.

~~~~~~~~~~

When the Europeans first arrived, the indigenous people were completely oblivious to their true characteristics and intentions, and I was unable to foresee the impending intrusion. I had no way to warn them of the dire consequences that would come from falling for the facade of their altruism and seemingly jovial demeanor. During this tumultuous time, I was living in the deepest, most secluded part of the jungle with my beloved tribe, blissfully unaware of the unfolding devastating situation until nearly fifty years had elapsed. By that time, it was far too late to alter the course of events, and tragically, most of my offspring had been sold into the horrors of slavery or killed in desperate battles against the unyielding chains that bound them.

When I finally learned of the catastrophic events taking place, I was devastated to discover that one of my immediate sons had already gotten carried away into their cruel world. His mother, heartbroken and inconsolable, sent me out to bring our son back home, but I, unfortunately, fell into their grasp.

For the next century, I endured a harrowing existence as a human, living in abject poverty, alongside depravity, degradation, and profound shame. The body I inhabited, along with those of the children I had sired, were deemed undesirable. From the perspective of the dominant human society, we were not considered human beings and were consequently treated with utter contempt.

The families I had helped bring into the world were forced to endure lives of bondage and were often regarded as less than animals. However, the choice was already made, and thus it was a burden that had to be accepted and lived with. As one generation passed, I leaped to the next, always assuming the form of a male. I repeated this cycle for another half-century, continually taking on the male form to navigate through the complexities of existence.

Alas! The last of the family I had sired met their tragic end, and I narrowly escaped the final male body I had ever assumed, mere moments before it was engulfed in a catastrophic explosion caused by dynamite planted in particularly unsavory locations.

I found myself in the beautiful Caribbean, with the vibrant colors of the sea and sky surrounding me, and Laliac, my soul triplet, guiding me towards Jalaniac, our eldest triplet. As I brushed aside the memories of that tedious and wicked past life, determined to forget that I had ever lived such experiences, I welcomed the comforting thought of seeing my eldest sister again. It filled my heart with warmth, especially since we hadn't had the opportunity to reunite in quite some time, and I longed to reconnect with her.

~~~~~~~~~~

Slavery was widespread, and the tropics had indeed had its share of this horrific practice. When I was finally able to visit Jalaniac, she did not recognize us at all. It took an entire century for her to trust us enough to believe in our good intentions. By that time, her family had grown to such an extensive degree that they spread far and wide across the land. It would take many generations, possibly a few hundred years, to eradicate the remnants of her lineage completely.

At first, Jalaniac made several attempts to get rid of both Laliac and me, as she viewed us as a threat. Laliac, occupied with far more important matters in another solar system more than two million light years away from this Earth, left me behind to "deal with this little issue" on my own. I did not relish the thought of reliving the traumatic experiences I had suffered over the past two hundred years, so I decided that becoming an animal would be the safest way to go. I transformed into Jalaniac's racing horse, a magnificent thoroughbred that was not only strong but incredibly fast as well. For almost a century, I raced tirelessly, helping to build her wealth and producing more outstanding thoroughbreds the likes of which the Arabians had never seen before.

In the meantime, Laliac and I did everything we could to assist our triplet in regaining her lost memories. It was quite a monotonous and painstaking task, especially since we were operating within the constraints of human time. Eventually, something miraculous occurred, and she suddenly remembered who I was and what we had shared.

For the next two hundred years, after the return of her memories, she made it up to me by allowing me to take on the cherished role of her daughter. During the many years spent playing the roles of both daughter and granddaughter within our complex family dynamic, our human family blossomed and spread out extensively. We became truly inseparable throughout this profound journey together.

~~~~~~~~~

It was in the twenty-first century, a seemingly peaceful time that was subtly threatened by deep-seated political turbulences in various areas of the globe. Three hundred and eighty years after finding Jalaniac, I found myself once again seeking another human form, who, by an intriguing twist of fate, just so happened to be the daughter of Netty, Jalaniac's human child who was now pregnant.

Klam was supposed to have tragically expired at merely three months inside her mother's womb. Her once vibrant natural soul had already deserted her, thus affording me a long-awaited opportunity to acquire a new vessel. The palpable desperation in Netty's voice as she fervently prayed to the Ancient One could be felt resonating far and wide. It drew me to her like a moth to a flame. I was beside her in less than a millisecond, hoping against hope that I was the only being paying attention to her desperate plight.

She instinctively sensed that something was dreadfully wrong with the fetus inside her. She was discharging far too heavily.

The very idea of having to tell the father that she had miscarried sent her spiraling into a frantic praying frenzy.

"Lawd Jesas nuh mek no'ting happen to mi baby, please," she begged pitifully, rubbing her trembling hands together in desperation. Sweat soaked through her clothes, which clung to her shaking body. Her tears, like a river of sorrow, rolled down her cheeks, meeting the sweat as it coursed down her neck. Blood and water had begun pooling around her kneeling form on the floor, creating a stark reminder of the life that hung perilously in the balance.

How was she ever going to find the words to tell the father that she had tragically lost his child? The harrowing thought of him leaving her, never to return and perhaps harboring feelings of anger or betrayal, sent her spiraling into another desperate praying frenzy.

"Lawd, mi a beg yuh," she hollered across the dimly lit room, not caring in the slightest if the neighbors were listening to her anguished pleas. She was in excruciating pain, but the overwhelming fear that gripped her like a vice was far more crippling. It radiated from every cell of her frail being. She instinctively held on to her belly, a slight curve hardly noticeable due to her obesity, and cried out, "Lawd Jesas, mi a beg yuh," before giving one final, heart-wrenching, pitiful cry that echoed in the stillness of the night before she fainted in her own liquid, feeling utterly lost.

~~~~~~~~~~

It was the perfect opportunity, and I seized it with both hands, fully aware of the transformative power I was about to embrace. The moment I entered the delicate body, time seemed to cease existing in the same way I had always known it. This was merely the first step in an unexpected journey. My soul slowly began the intricate process of adapting to Earth's rhythm once again. I could feel the tiny heart within me starting to thump softly, its pulse growing stronger as nourishment flowed from the mother into the fragile little being. Relieved and hopeful, I settled myself into the frail package, ready to wait and experience this new existence. However, as I waited patiently, I was suddenly seized and hoisted from the minute vessel with cruel force. My complete absorption in Netty's world had prevented me from noticing another being's unwelcome interest in my new form. Taken by surprise and nearly sent back to my beginning, I felt an urgent need to fight back.

I sensed the new body spasming in response, instinctively trying to protect itself from the perceived threat. Yet, I had already begun to weaken since the first merging process had initiated. I was drained, and the other being pursuing my vessel was far too strong.

Panic surged as I sensed the vessel's heart contracting—this was never a good sign. It was fighting with all its might, but a chilling thought crept into my mind: what if there was no hope for it? Gritting my teeth, I tried to summon every ounce of strength and resolve to fight harder.

Goddammit! This was my vessel, my new beginning, and I was not going to surrender it without a battle. The thought ignited a flicker of determination within me, but still, it felt like a futile endeavor against such overwhelming odds.

I positioned myself firmly between the strange being and my beloved vessel, desperately trying to maintain my stance amidst the chaos. The being, whom I could hardly see through the haze of the moment, was clearly not having any of it. With a sudden and violent motion, it punched me with a jolt of electric shock emanating from a rubber-like fist. I lost my balance entirely, tumbling backward into the cramped confines of the small vessel. In that moment, I could feel my precious prize slipping away from me.

As I prepared to relinquish the lifeless body to the being—who was insidiously tugging at my aluminum hair, dragging me towards a fate I dreaded—I sensed a change in the atmosphere.

Just when I thought all was lost, Jalaniac surged onto the scene and expertly thrust the creature away from us. Laliac, standing valiantly beside her, swung her sword with precision, cutting through the empty space that surrounded us.

Suddenly, a snake of extraordinary size materialized, consuming half of the room with its immense form. I left the two sisters to deal with the monstrous being while I re-positioned myself within Netty's uterus, the warmth of her body engulfing me. I waited patiently for my vessel to warm up fully while I focused intently on locating the blood circulating around its heart. Yes, it was still warm and flowing steadily—a good sign amidst so much turmoil. I breathed deeply, and in response, the vessel breathed alongside me as if to confirm our connection.

Yes, indeed, this was a good sign. I had never felt such immense joy or relief as I did when I laid my eyes upon my sisters that fateful day.

Eight long months of Klam gestating in the mother's womb had led me to another moment of despair, where once again, I thought we might be separated forever. The baby wasn't doing too well this time; the mother was smoking heavily, and we struggled to breathe in the toxic air surrounding us. It was surprisingly simple for Jalaniac to squeeze Netty's heart—just enough to send a shock through her system and instill some urgency. It worked far too well, however, as we were forced to exit the womb prematurely.

In my weakened state, I felt utterly helpless to aid the body I inhabited, and unfortunately, the baby became lodged in Netty's passage. Some clueless nurse then made the questionable decision to use a metal clamp to pull us out, which only served to further damage the head and the frontal lobe of my vessel. The sudden pain hit me with an intensity that was almost unbearable, driving me to flee from the body momentarily, granting it the much-needed flexibility to be extracted. The instant the body was out, appearing half-dead and devoid of life, I immediately returned, giving it everything it needed to take its very first breath.

3

THE HEALING POTION

Had it not been for my sisters, I wouldn't be here standing now. It was finally my time to find a way to save Jalaniac back, to restore what had been lost. These were the swirling thoughts that occupied my mind as we walked home from the basic school we were attending on Briden Street, in Kingston. Netty didn't even bother to come to pick us up today; she was probably somewhere knocked out cold from her THC stupor, or perhaps engaging in a binge session with White Rum. Using my ethereal eyes— since Klam's eyes were not strong enough to see what I could—I carefully watched Swofiyah skipping ahead of us, seemingly carefree.

I continued to observe her after the strangeness she had exhibited nearly a month ago, which had left all of us perplexed. Suddenly, I watched as she tripped and fell onto the gravelled sidewalk. She sat up crying, tears were streaming down her face, but not for long. Klam was aching to rush to her aid, but I held her back with a firm grip, wanting to see what would unfold next.

As we drew closer to her, I could smell the unmistakable scent of blood escaping from her bruised knee. It was a lot more than I had anticipated. I had long established that Swofiyah's body was chronically anaemic, which only made the situation worse, and yet there was nothing we could do about it if she was to grow up and lead a normal life like any other child.

As I got closer to her, I found myself becoming increasingly fascinated with her unique presence. I watched intently as the child placed a finger to the red blood running down her delicate ankle, then brought it up to her mouth, curious and perhaps oblivious to the meaning of it all. She scrunched up her face like she was tasting a particularly sour orange, a reaction that both amused and alarmed me. Suddenly, in an astonishing turn of events, her entire body began to disintegrate, transforming into a pile of dirt right there on the spot where she had been standing.

The dirt quickly became moist, then saturated, eventually being covered over with clear water. To my surprise, a few birds flew down to the spot, hesitantly beginning to drink the water and peck at the freshly disturbed dirt. In that instant, the patch of ground started to burst forth with vibrant green grass. I watched on in stunned fascination as the grassy dirt swirled up to Swofiyah's original height, slowly and miraculously reforming her before my very eyes.

Astonishingly, all of this took less than two minutes. I nearly jumped out of Klam's skin. With my heart racing against my chest, I quickly glanced around to see if anyone else was witnessing this extraordinary spectacle, and I felt a wave of relief wash over me when I realized that we were utterly alone.

It was the year two thousand and nineteen, the year of the millennials, and the day was beautifully serene. The sun was shining down brilliantly upon us, and the sudden rustling of the many surrounding trees grew louder as a gentle wind swept through the area.

We found ourselves now stooping in front of her. Much to my astonishment, she appeared completely back to normal. I was surprised to see the cut had vanished completely, along with all traces of blood. Even the evidence had been erased from her pink sock, leaving no indication of what had just transpired.

"Yuh awwight?" Klam asked, gently pulling her to her feet with a concerned look in her eyes.

"Yea," Swofiyah nodded her head, though her voice was barely a whisper.

"Look how yuh dooty. Netty a guh beat yuh," Klam warned, her tone filled with a mix of empathy and frustration.

Swofiyah started to cry, black tears with sparkles twinkling in the sunlight rolling down her cheeks. I was even more shocked by the sight. I could feel Klam's body trembling from my soul's reaction to the extraordinary sight of those tears.

Klam stretched out her right pointy finger toward Swofiyah's face, letting the peculiar black sparkly liquid run onto it. She quickly retrieved the lollypop wrapper that she had shoved into her pocket during lunch, carefully collecting the strange teardrops that had dried and transformed into small shiny pieces resembling obsidian pebbles upon it.

I was still looking around, scanning the area to see if we were being observed. There were no humans or domestic animals in sight, but the rustling of the trees and the loud hawking of the birds told me they were watching everything unfold.

I pushed my soul out of Klam and spoke to them in Golealm. They all instantly quieted down, eerily attentive. When I was sure we had collected every teardrop that had fallen, Klam methodically wiped away all traces of the black hardened debris from her face, restoring a semblance of normalcy in our unusual circumstances.

We continued to walk down the familiar path. Klam's arm was warmly wrapped around her little sister's shoulders as we strolled along, sharing whispers and giggles. I couldn't contain my excitement and eagerness to reach Netty's house.

Suddenly, Klam shifted her arms from around Swofiyah's neck and took her hand instead. With a playful tug, she pulled Swofiyah very swiftly, then stopped just as suddenly, prompting a burst of laughter from Swofiyah. The sound of her laughter was evolving, becoming even more delightful. I couldn't help myself; the joyous melody of her laughter filled my heart with a happiness I hadn't felt in ages, and I joined in, laughing along with them.

Klam repeated her playful action, and Swofiyah laughed even harder this time, so much so that she had to clutch her belly with both hands. The laughter was so enchanting that even the curious birds perched nearby flew closer, while the trees seemed to sway and bend toward us, as if captivated by the joyful sound. In that moment, my soul felt like the happiest it had ever been since my arrival on this earthly realm, and Klam let out a hearty laugh, which only added to the magic of the moment.

I knew that the laughter would have to eventually be quelled, but deep down, I didn't want it to end; it was simply too magical to let go. Klam wrapped her arm around Swofiyah's shoulders once more, and we all continued to walk toward the house while still chuckling softly. A few brave birds decided to follow closely behind us, attempting to capture the last remnants of that magically enchanting sound.

When we finally arrived home, we found Netty sprawled out in deep slumber on the floor, blocking the doorway entirely. The remnants of spliff tails were and collected in an old, well-worn ashtray, while two small flasks of empty White Rum bottles sat beside it, suggesting that she wouldn't be conscious for another few hours. I watched as Swofiyah carefully squeezed past our mother, making sure not to walk over her head in her haste. I followed suit, treading lightly.

We both dropped our little school bags unceremoniously at Netty's big feet, then went to nestle comfortably by her side. With Klam's body curled close to Netty's, and Swofiyah nestled next to Klam, I observed as the ethereal soul left Swofiyah's body, still very much shrouded in mystery, then quietly disappeared.

Interesting!

~~~~~~~~~~

"Today the little one had a lot of surprises," I enthusiastically threw the thought at them while entering Jalaniac's brightly lit bedroom.

"What kind of surprises?" Laliac inquired with curiosity as I materialized before her. I eagerly showed her the special items, and she promptly darted off to the kitchen to fetch a glass of vibrant red sorrel juice on a beautifully adorned tray. When she returned, she held the thick, blood-red liquid that served as vital medicine for both the material body and the ethereal Golealm soul. I then presented her with the shiny, obsidian, pebble-like dried teardrops, which she delicately placed into the glass of sorrel. We watched in fascination as the murky hue transformed into a brilliant bright purple and then shifted to an enchanting blue.

Without hesitation, Laliac carefully brought the liquid to Jalaniac's mouth, pouring as much as she could down her throat, diligently trying not to let it spill too much in the process. It was crucial for Jalaniac to consume the liquid as quickly and thoroughly as possible to feel its restorative effects. Once all the medicine had been consumed, Laliac gently placed the tray with the empty glass on the bedside table. Then we waited in anticipation.

We didn't wait for very long; within just ten minutes, she was awakened, sitting upright in her bed with her legs crossed. We were mesmerized as we watched an extraordinary phenomenon—something that a lot of people on Earth would kill for—unfold before our eyes. Jalaniac's vessel began to age backwards, regressing into youth with each passing second. Her Materealm body transformed, cycling through the ages until she briefly appeared as a radiant sixteen-year-old, then transitioned back to fifty. Laliac and I couldn't hold back our laughter at the wondrous spectacle.

"Why didn't you stay at sixteen?" we both asked her in unison, our voices echoing softly in the spacious room.

"And what would I say to my children? That I was their bastard sister? You know that would never work. They are already suspicious of me as it is. Fifty is a good age, and I can cleverly use the new man as a convenient excuse for looking twenty years younger," she retorted sharply, gazing at us through her Golealm's mesmerizing eyes, while nimbly getting off her plush bed with an agility and elegance we hadn't witnessed in decades.

In that moment, I felt a rush of happiness — we were genuinely happy for her. We followed her down the hidden stairs to the magnificent underground palace that no one else knew existed, captivated as we watched her move gracefully to the expansive bathroom, which was as large as the entire house above.

"How did you come by the obsidian teardrops?" she inquired, letting the luxurious white silk sheet that she had wrapped around her body slip carelessly to the floor as she stepped into the oversized grey whirlpool bathtub, which was filled to the brim with steaming hot water. I focused my thoughts and showed her the vivid images in my head, observing as she closed her eyes in concentration. A soft moan escaped her lips as the soothing hot water enveloped her human form, cascading down her skin.

We understood then that we wouldn't be getting anything more out of her for the time being, not until she had completed her luxurious bath. With a sense of comfort, we settled into the lush gold chaise lounge chairs that adorned the oversized bathroom and sipped on the refreshing ackee cocktail that had been thoughtfully provided, patiently waiting for our eldest sister to satisfy her human needs in peace.

"She's an Ancient," Jalaniac said, sedately, forty-five minutes later, still looking at us through her Golealm's eyes.

"An Ancient?" Laliac and I both asked at the same time, coming down from our ackee cocktail high, the lingering effects slowly dissipating from our senses.

Ackee had a unique way of affecting Golealm, stimulating them much like how drugs and passion invigorate humans, but in a positive manner, free from the negative consequences.

"Yes, she's a Powerful. The longer you are around her, the more energy she will draw from you, and the greater power she will manifest. You will need to take Klam with you and come here."

"Bu..."

I was abruptly hurled forcefully back into Klam, a sensation that felt both unsettling and strange.

"Don't trouble Klam!" Swofiyah was shouting at our mother, her voice filled with urgency as she shot an angry look from her small yet fierce expression, her little dark brown face already glistening with sweat from the intense emotion that was bubbling inside her.

We watched in horror as Netty stepped backwards onto the bags we had carelessly discarded at her feet and tumbled to the ground, landing awkwardly on her back on the unforgiving concrete floor, hitting her head with a dull thud. She went limp and passed out.

"Don't trouble Klam," Swofiyah said again, softly now, pushing out her little lips in a pout and blowing air into her cheeks as if trying to release the tension.

I was looking at her through my Golealm eyes, and I was utterly awed by her presence. She was glowing intensely in shades of gold and red, and a deep, unsettling fear gripped my soul in a way it never had before. Klam's body started trembling involuntarily as a result of the overwhelming emotions swirling around us all.

4

THE DEPARTURE

K lam made her way over to Swofiyah and gently wrapped her arms around her neck in a comforting embrace. Swofiyah, caught in her own distress, stuck her fingers in her mouth, her gaze still fixed on Netty's unresponsive, overweight body, which lay sprawled out and helplessly on the floor.

"Hotts Swopia, don't mind har, she going to be awwight," Klam reassured, her voice trembling slightly with worry.

Just then, Jalaniac and Laliac appeared, as if they were gliding through an invisible door that only they had the power to perceive. I stepped out of Klam's body, determined to show them the alarming events that had just unfolded. Jalaniac nodded her head in acknowledgment of what she witnessed.

Meanwhile, little Swofiyah continued to watch us, her expression surprisingly unfazed. We waited in hopeful anticipation to see if her spirit would emerge to greet us, but we guessed it wasn't quite ready yet.

Or perhaps it felt it didn't need to make an appearance at this moment.

"Laliac, put Netty on her bed," Jalaniac instructed firmly.

Almost instantly, Netty was placed gently in her bed, despite Laliac remaining completely still in her position. Suddenly, the calm was shattered as Swofiyah's body began to convulse violently, her eyes transforming into a startling gold color while froth emerged at the corners of her mouth. Klam's arms, still wrapped tightly around Swofiyah's neck, struggled to hold on, but with me having vacated her body, Klam's form slumped to the floor like an abandoned rag doll.

"We have to go," stated Jalaniac, her voice firm and edged with urgency, still watching Swofiyah with a frown firmly etched on her face. I quickly returned to Klam's body, and she immediately stood up, instinctively wrapping her arms back around her sister, seeking comfort and reassurance.

We all watched in silent relief as Swofiyah's eyes gradually returned to their natural warm brown colors, and the convulsion that had gripped her body finally ceased.

Klam gently took the tip of her uniform skirt and tenderly wiped away the froth that had begun to trickle down her sister's smooth chin. The atmosphere shifted as we observed her begin to push her fingers into her mouth, gently rocking back and forth, a gesture that created a sense of comfort. The calm that suddenly stole over everyone in the room was so profound and enveloping that it felt as though we had all just been doused in a bucket of rich ackee cocktail.

With pursed lips and a determined expression, Jalaniac turned her back on us and disappeared from sight, Laliac following closely behind her, barely a second later.

~~~~~~~~

I gently pulled Swofiyah with us towards our bed and sank down onto the floor next to it, feeling the cool surface beneath me. We were sitting there comfortably with our backs resting against the warm bed when Netty woke up abruptly. She blinked a couple of times, looking utterly puzzled, and then her gaze shifted upward to Swofiyah as if some fleeting memory had just brushed past her, yet the recollections remained frustratingly out of reach. She seemed to have nothing substantial to accuse us of in her confused state.

"Yuh, ugly gal! Get ready to guh to yuh granny!" Netty commanded with a hint of irritation in her voice.

"Swopia a come to?" Klam asked innocently, her lisped baby voice breaking the tension.

"No ask me nuh raas question and guh get ready!" Netty snapped back, holding her head and groaning in apparent discomfort. Klam got up and made her way over to the big cardboard box where she kept all her clothing. She was in the process of taking off her school uniform when Netty ordered sternly, "Nuh bother tek dem off, just pack some clothes in a plastic bag and come out a me house!"

In a moment of dramatic flair, she started moaning once more, loudly this time, as if she was experiencing excruciating pain that seemed to radiate from deep within her. I looked over at Swofiyah and noticed that the mesmerizing golden hue had returned, illuminating the small space around us. Meanwhile, Netty's eyes were tightly closed, unaware of the beautiful glow surrounding her.

Klam went to the kitchen and picked up an overripe banana from the fruit basket that Netty kept prominently displayed on the table. She walked over to Swofiyah, peeling the banana carefully, and then she stuffed it directly into her sister's mouth. The instant the banana touched her tongue, the golden hue disappeared as though it had never existed.

I watched as Swofiyah sighed in relief while she chewed, simultaneously releasing Netty from her pain. The wave of relief that washed over Netty's face was unmistakable; she fell back onto her bed, surrendering to comfort and letting out a contented sigh.

Klam went back to busily arranging her bag, ensuring everything was just right. She didn't need much for just a short trip; after all, she was only going for the weekend. However, as she packed her few essential items, her mind was flooded with worries about Swofiyah. Despite her concerns, she consoled herself with the reassuring thought that the weekend would pass by quickly and everything would be fine.

"No, no, no, no! Pack up all a yuh clothes dem. Yuh a guh live with yuh granny!" Netty exclaimed loudly, rising from the bed with a slight grunt. The bed squeaked audibly under her heft, sounding almost as if it were protesting her movement.

"That blasted Jalaniac yuh see mon," I muttered explosively in Jamaican tongue under my breath, feeling the frustration bubble within me. "That blue being son of a worm hole planted the thought in her head, good," I sighed deeply, trying to maintain a semblance of calm.

I could hear a laughter echoing in my mind, and I struggled hard to keep my soul in check.

"Hurry up, bloodclaat monkey!" Netty yelled.

Feeling the urgency rise within her. It was clear that Jalaniac had planted that troublesome thought deep in her mind. As I wrestled with the desire to escape from Klam's presence, the sight of Swofiyah's golden hue returning, along with a bright red tint around her limbus, kept me focused and striving to maintain my composure.

"Swopia, bing the plaksik bag par me," Klam requested, her voice tinged with a hint of anxiety now.

Swofiyah sprang to her feet, hastily shoving the last piece of ripe banana into her mouth, her vibrant colors rapidly fading into nothingness.

"A wope a nuh me bloodclaat banana she a nyam, cause she never asked me for it," Netty cursed loudly, completely oblivious to the fact that I was working tirelessly to save her from this utterly chaotic situation.

It was the final straw. Swofiyah's body suddenly erupted with energy. She grew taller and taller, stretching upward until her head touched the ceiling, glowing golden from head to toe. She was shining brightly like the sun, with her glowing black and white sisterlocks cascading thick, long, and voluminous around her. Her uniform lay tattered in shreds at her feet, a testament to her transformation.

The sight of her unleashed a powerful shockwave through us. Netty appeared as though she was on the verge of having a heart attack.

The dazzling Swofiyah strode over to Netty, looked down at her with an intimidating air, and declared, "Listen, monkey mother, if you don't start treating your children them better, I'm going to roast you like a shish kabob and eat you for dinner. Understand?"

The mischief dancing playfully in the enchanting eyes of the golden being was completely lost on Netty, who, in that moment, fainted dramatically, collapsing softly onto the ground beneath her. Shinny

Swofiyah then turned to me with a playful wink that held a world of unspoken meaning and mystery.

"Yuh better hurry up and go; your sisters are eagerly waiting for you. Don't worry about Swofiyah; she'll be perfectly fine," she reassured me, her voice light yet compelling.

The golden being, who obviously did not originate from our familiar world of Golealm, exhibited an incredible ability to read my thoughts as if they were an open book. How in the world was that even possible? Only a Golealm had ever been known to read another Golealm's thoughts. It can truly read my mind?

"Yes, and every other being on this planet and beyond, now hurry up and go before monkey mother wakes up from her slumber. Your grandmother has thoughtfully sent you a taxi to help you," she added with urgency.

Shinny Swofiyah smiled down at me, and the brilliance of her smile was so luminous that I almost fainted from the sheer beauty radiating from her presence. Klam's heart felt like it was going to explode from her chest in a rush of overwhelming emotion that threatened to drown her. I needed to work incredibly hard at controlling myself because little Klam couldn't handle this kind of intense and powerful emotion.

With a few deep, controlled breaths to steady my racing heart and calm my spirit, I returned to my packing with renewed determination. When I turned again to get another fleeting glimpse, it was just little Swofiyah sitting there, completely naked, with her tiny fingers in her mouth, looking utterly innocent and cherubic. I took out a pair of shorts and a matching T-shirt, ready to dress her, fully aware of the numerous challenges that lay ahead in our unfolding adventure.

~~~~~~~~~

I was tightly hugging Swofiyah when the taxi man unexpectedly and rather abruptly came onto the veranda, brazenly interrupting our precious moment.

"A which one a yuh name Klam?" he asked in a sharply demanding tone that sent a chill down my spine.

Swofiyah, sensing the tension, pointed directly at me, and then he added impatiently, "A where yuh things dem? Yuh granny said a must bring everything with you."

We quickly showed him the two plastic bags we had meticulously prepared, and he swiftly picked them up with a practiced motion that suggested this was not his first time overseeing such matters.

"Come," he ordered firmly, without even glancing back to see if we were following closely behind him.

I waved a reluctant farewell to Swofiyah, who walked out with me, her tiny fingers lodged in her mouth, looking every bit like an ordinary little girl lost in her own quaint world of thoughts and imagination.

I watched her closely as she sat down on the so-called veranda, still sucking on her fingers with that innocent expression that seemed so pure and untainted, while her other small hand waved at us in a soft, gentle goodbye. Klam—I was crying. It was a natural, deeply human emotional reaction that felt almost compulsory in that poignant moment. I couldn't help it, no matter how hard I tried to suppress the tears that threatened to spill over.

5

THE MERGING SOUL

K lam was fast asleep when the taxi finally pulled up in front of Granny's cozy yard on Little Lane, situated in the heart of Central Village, Spanish Town. Little Lane was one of the few quiet and serene lanes in the bustling town of Spanish Town. Granny's charming house stood directly in front of a large football field, which was securely fenced off with tall, sturdy brick walls, offering a sense of privacy to her lush property.

"Pickney, yuh reach, wake up!" The driver called out loudly, breaking the tranquility of the early evening.

Klam stretched her arms wide before sitting up, a bit disoriented, while the driver stepped out to open her door for her. She climbed out of the taxi, albeit a bit clumsily, but with an enormous smile lighting up her face at the sight of her grandmother standing at the gate, eagerly waiting for her arrival.

"But Myry, how you look so young? Every time I see yuh, yuh look different! Is what yuh eating suh?" the driver exclaimed, utterly shocked at her youthful appearance.

"A di new face cream me new man buy me. You want to give it a try?" She responded playfully, giving him a conspiratorial wink and a soft chuckle, while holding her arms out wide to embrace Klam.

Filled with excitement, Klam ran towards her grandmother joyfully, almost tripping on a small stone in her path.

"Good ebening, Gwanny," she exclaimed with warmth in her voice.

"Good evening me dear," she responded warmly, bending down gracefully to pick her up. Klam shrieked with delight, her laughter ringing out clearly in the cool evening air like a sweet melody.

She absolutely adored it when granny performed that little act of affection, and it filled her tiny heart with joy.

"Is how yuh so lite? Yuh mother not feeding yuh?" Granny inquired playfully, a teasing little frown dancing across her face while she simultaneously fished out some cash from her purse to pay the taxi driver. He took the money with a slight smirk, gave her a suggestive, lingering look, and then sauntered back to his vehicle with an air of confidence, leaving her to shake her head in exasperation. As she entered her cozy yard, the cool, refreshing breeze rustled playfully around her, and she locked the gate securely behind her, all the while still effortlessly carrying Klam alongside the heavy bags in her arms.

~~~~~~~~

Jalaniac's human form stood as a strapping five feet, ten inches tall, her dark brown skin radiating warmth, framed by long, curly hair cascading elegantly down her back. She bore a striking resemblance to an Australian Aboriginal woman, exuding a no-nonsense demeanor that commanded attention and respect.

As she walked, each step was imbued with grace and a palpable confidence that earned her admiration from her family, friends, and the neighbors who lived nearby.

She glanced affectionately at her granddaughter, her light brown eyes gleaming with warmth. Unable to resist the moment, she playfully rubbed the tip of her nose against Klam's, eliciting another delighted chuckle from her.

"Yuh hungry?" she inquired gently, as they arrived at the side door that led directly into her cozy kitchen. Granny carefully helped Klam settle into one of the plush velvet chairs surrounded by the elegant cherrywood dining table, which was located conveniently near the open floor plan of the compact kitchen.

With practiced ease, she took the two plastic bags and placed them neatly inside a cabinet in the laundry area across from the kitchen.

Her footsteps were soft and graceful on the shiny, cream-colored ceramic tile flooring that extended throughout the entirety of her charming three-bedroom house.

Granny's home was one of those enduring brick houses, built long before the lamentable days of slavery. The interior was beautifully decorated, exuding an air of warmth, while the exterior remained well-maintained and inviting.

Her soul had inhabited this space for an astounding seven hundred and twenty years, always returning in a new vessel as soon as the old one perished. Her human family, encompassing a rich tapestry of ethnicities, had spread out across the vibrant regions of St. Catherine and Clarendon.

"Yuh hungry?" she asked again, her voice warm as she headed towards the spotless kitchen, which gleamed with its stainless steel appliances reflecting the soft light of the room.

"Yets Gwanny, me bewy, bewy hunguy," Klam replied, her voice shy and tentative as she looked up at her.

"Well then, I'll get to it," said Myry, offering a soft smile that was full of fondness for the little one in front of her.

The love that Klam had never truly received from her daughter shined brightly through her light brown eyes, illuminating her face as all the stress and worry from being around Netty faded away momentarily. She let out a long, deep sigh that echoed her relief.

"Me really sorry yuh suffering so much under my idiot daughter; she took everything from her father. I just can't understand how she come to be like dat."

"It awwight, Gwanny, me just was thinkin' bout Swopia, but the Shinny Swopia said she was going to be okay," Klam reassured her, a hint of hope in her voice.

"Shinny Swopia?" Granny asked, her brow furrowing in puzzlement.

The experience of being a Golealm spirit in a human form in Materealm was quite limited. I observed Myry turn off the stove and then gracefully walk over to the dining table, where she took a seat directly in front of my vessel. I tried with all my might to exit my form to show Jalaniac the scene that had unfolded earlier today, but a strange feeling of disorientation suddenly washed over me. I watched her human form slouched over, as I willed myself to mimic that movement, but I found I couldn't. It felt as though I was stuck in place, observing from a distance. I then noticed Jalaniac approach Klam, inspecting her with a curious gaze.

I realized with a jolt that I could see everything quite clearly through Klam's eyes now, a stark contrast to my inability to do so less than two hours ago.

Jalaniac transformed back into her human form and sat there quietly, gazing intently at Klam as if she was meant to say something important, but the words just wouldn't come to her mind.

"Hmm, Shinny Swofiyah, why do you call your sister Shinny Swofiyah?"

Klam responded with a shrug, "A don't know," as she bounced herself up and down enthusiastically in the comfy chair, a shy smile forming on her face as she glanced over at her grandmother.

"How was school today?" Jalaniac inquired, eager for details.

"Owkay, me and Swopia piay skipping," Klam replied, her tone shifting as she seemed to grow more agitated. I was attempting to extract my soul from Klam, turning and twisting this way and that, but it was absolutely futile.

"Oh my God! Did Shinny Swofiyah lock me in here? Is that what this is?" I exclaimed, frustration creeping into my voice.

"Gwanny!" Klam interjected. "Yes, Sweetie," came the calm response. "Sumpting intide me a scueem."

"What? Oh, okay. Mek me hurry and get yuh something to eat, then yuh can guh lay down for a bit," Granny answered, trying to soothe her.

"Okay, Gwanny," Klam chirped, still bouncing excitedly in the chair.

"What? No, I'm not screaming!" I protested, raising my voice slightly, feeling overwhelmed by the situation.

"Gwanny."

"Yes, sweetie," Myry said, a bit distractedly, her attention drifting in and out.

"Sumpting intide me a scueem." I watched as my grandmother, or rather, my sister, exited her human form and moved gracefully over to me.

"Hush dawling, don't cry," she told Klam, soothingly, her voice gentle and warm like a comforting blanket. Then she turned her gaze back to me and added, "Roboliac, stop scaring the child. We will see what's going on in another hour. Just be patient."

I nodded my head in agreement through Klam's perspective, slowly starting to relax as the tension eased within me. I watched as Jalaniac assumed her human form once more and returned to the task of cooking, her movements fluid and confident. As I observed her, it dawned on me that I had never truly taken the time to bond with the child on an emotional level; instead, I had merely used her body as if it were a piece of clothing. Shinny Swofiyah must have noticed this disconnection and decided it was time to act. I probably should have been angry about this revelation, but deep down, I realized I likely deserved it all.

I sighed softly, coming to the realization that I needed to take better care of Klam and nurture the connection between us a little more lovingly.

~~~~~~~~~

It was with this profound thought that my soul truly began the intricate process of merging with Klam's mind. This moment was the final merging, a milestone that very few Golealm had ever achieved throughout history. When a Golealm reached the ultimate final stage of merging with a human, the earthly form would take on all the remarkable characteristics of the Golealm, and the Golealm soul would verifiably become one with the human mind. Every aspect of the Golealm would manifest within the human, leading even the physical features of the human to undergo a transformation.

I started seeing everything through Klam's eyes with such clarity that it felt as though I was still observing the world through the lenses of my own Golealm eyes. I found myself accessing that deep subconscious area of my brain—I couldn't readily tap into when we were separated—granting me the ability to reach a profoundly deeper level of human understanding. As I looked at Myry, my beloved grandmother, it felt like I was truly seeing her for the very first time. She was stunningly beautiful, radiating a glow that I had never noticed before.

"Grandmother, you are so beautiful," I exclaimed, filled with admiration.

She looked at me with her eyes and mouth wide open in surprise. After a moment, she snapped her mouth shut, turned her head to the side, and stared intently at me, using her own Golealm eyes while stirring the pot on the stove.

I gently got off the chair and walked over to the towering bookshelf that lined one of the four walls of the cozy room. As I approached, I noticed for the very first time just how extensive and diverse my grandmother's book collections truly were, each volume proudly displayed. I began scrolling through the titles, absorbing the variety they offered, until I stumbled upon a section that particularly piqued my interest. It was filled with memoirs and nonfiction works, each promising a unique story. I carefully selected one book with a rather captivating title and decided it would be my very first read from my grandmother's cherished collection: "Idiotism And Yardie Life."

I made my way back to my chair, eagerly scrolling through the pages at the headings and subheadings, while the intriguing names mentioned in the book captured my attention, drawing me deeper into this literary adventur

6

MY DECISION

By the time Grandmother placed a steaming plate of dinner in front of me, I was completely absorbed, a hundred and fifty pages deep into the book, and tears were streaming down my face uncontrollably. There were moments when I laughed so hard that I nearly toppled off the chair in pure amusement. As I immersed myself in the narrative, I realized that the story bore an uncanny similarity to my own life experiences, almost as if the author had drawn from my personal history. Even the names and characters felt familiar, stirring an odd sense of connection within me. It was quite weird and mesmerizing.

"Grandmother, have you read this book?" I asked enthusiastically, momentarily putting the book down —after carefully marking my page—to finally enjoy my dinner.

I hadn't truly realized how hungry I was until I savored a piece of boiled dumpling paired with the delectable ackee and saltfish.

"Oh my gosh, this is absolutely wonderful!" I exclaimed, chomping on the food as if I had never tasted anything quite like it before.

Grandmother, noticing my delight, got up and gracefully came over to me. She took my face gently in her hands and turned me toward her with care. Positioning the back of her hand against my temple, she took my temperature in that old-fashioned, affectionate way that only she could manage.

"Yuh don't have a tempichu. Look at me, child." It wasn't Grandmother speaking, but rather the deep-seated wisdom that came from her years of experience.

"How are you feeling?" Jalaniac inquired softly.

"I feel wonderful, truly wonderful. I feel like this has been my first day on earth, breathing in all this beauty. It's so lovely," I confirmed, feeling an immense wave of happiness wash over me while still chewing on my food.

She returned to her place at the table and resumed her meal with an air of contentment.

"Grandmother."

"Yes, Sweetie?"

"I want to go back home."

"What? Yuh don't like it here nuh more?"

Grandmother looked at me with such profound disappointment in her eyes; I almost felt compelled to retract my words. But I had to stay resolute—Swofiyah needed me.

"No, Grandmother, I love it here very much, but I have to go look after Swofiyah," I explained to her truthfully, trying to convey the urgency of my feelings.

Jalaniac pushed her head out and regarded me thoughtfully for a minute, her gaze intense, then she returned to aligning herself with my grandmother. She seemed to be weighing my words.

As I continued to eat, I kept stealing glances at her. I felt a twinge of guilt, realizing that I was hurting her feelings, yet the overwhelming need to return to Netty was pressing down on my heart. I watched her thoughts flicker across her face for a moment, then sighed heavily, knowing the decision I had to make.

"If yuh must go then a can't do nothing bout that, but make sure you come here on the weekends," she said, rising from her seat and taking her empty dish with her to the kitchen sink. With a fluid motion, she poured some refreshing sorrel into two glasses and then brought them over to the table we often shared. She carefully laid one glass on the brightly colored place mat in front of me.

As I brought the glass to my lips, I drank the sorrel as if I was experiencing it for the very first time, savoring its unique flavors. When I finished, I picked up my book and settled in to read once again.

"It's time for yuh shower and bed, young lady. We have so much to duh together tomorrow," Grandmother said gently, taking my dish with the spoon and my empty glass. I took the book to my cozy room, laid it down on my inviting bed, and then prepared myself for my bath.

Grandmother came in to help bathe me, even though I wanted to assert that I was a big girl and could bathe myself just fine. However, I remembered how I had hurt her feelings before, so I decided to let her continue our little ritual. After my warm bath, she lovingly dressed me in one of the many new bedgowns she had purchased for me, carefully tucking me in. She kissed my forehead tenderly, turned down the light, and bid me goodnight as she quietly walked out, leaving the door half turned, the comforting glow from the hallway spilling gently into my room.

"Goodnight, Grandmother," I told her softly, my voice barely above a whisper, as I watched her slowly exit my room, her silhouette gradually fading into the dimly lit hallway.

I got up with deliberate slowness, my feet shuffling as I made my way to the door, turning the handle just enough to almost shut it completely, ensuring that the quietude of the night remained undisturbed. I reached for the book I had been engrossed in earlier, its pages filled with memories and stories that comforted me. With a long, deep sigh, I climbed back into bed, pulling the covers up snugly to my chin, seeking warmth and solace. That night, I went to sleep with tears streaming silently down my face, a clear reflection of my inner turmoil, feeling an overwhelming sense of loss and more convinced than ever that going back to Netty was indeed the right thing for me to do.

~~~~~~~~

The next morning, when I woke up and made my way to use the bathroom, I carefully climbed up onto the little foot stool that grandmother had lovingly placed in front of the bathroom sink just for me. It was my designated spot to stand on while I washed my hands. As I gazed into the mirror at my reflection, I couldn't help but notice some subtle, yet distinct, structural changes to my features. Curiously, I turned my face this way and that, observing each angle, but at only eight years old, I eventually lost interest in my appearance. I quickly brushed my teeth and washed my face, eager to start the day, before rushing off to the kitchen in search of breakfast. I was famished and my stomach growled with anticipation.

I found grandmother lounging back on the sofa, her eyes closed in a peaceful slumber. The delicious smell of fried plantains sizzling alongside eggs and the rich aroma of chocolate tea filled the room, creating a warm atmosphere that felt like home. When I glanced over at the dining table, I was delighted to see that breakfast was indeed ready and waiting for me. I hurried to the table, lifted the covers, and admired the spread before me; everything looked absolutely mouthwatering. Turning my gaze to where she was napping, I called out with gratitude, "Thank you, Grandmother," before eagerly starting to dig into my meal.

Just then, Jalaniac and Laliac appeared at the table, one on each side of me, their eyes searching my face for something. They looked at me with curiosity, clearly trying to decipher my thoughts, but I was equally perplexed and struggling to read theirs as well. Jalaniac's mouth began to move, but I found myself unable to hear or comprehend what she was saying, leaving me feeling a bit lost.

Laliac looked at me, perplexed. I shrugged my shoulders to let them know I couldn't hear their conversation and continued eating my breakfast. I chewed hungrily on my food while watching them watch me with a mixture of curiosity and confusion. It felt so strange, this new embodied me, navigating the reality that I now had two ghosts sitting beside me with whom I could no longer converse. So strange indeed.

"Are you two going to be my invisible friends?" I asked finally, slowly chewing on the last of my fried plantains, savoring the warm and crispy taste while simultaneously staring them down. Jalaniac pursed her lips in contemplation, and Laliac rolled her eyes —a gesture that was the most human expression I had ever seen her make.

They both departed in the same manner in which they had arrived, and I shrugged my shoulders again, stood up, and took my utensils to the kitchen sink for Grandmother to wash. I then returned to my room to dress and tidied up the familiar space I had grown comfortable with. After I placed the book where it belonged, I found my Grandmother at the kitchen sink, diligently cleaning up. She was moving her hips to the rhythm of her favorite singer, Beres Hammond, as she worked, bringing joy to the morning routine.

"Good morning, Grandmother," I greeted her warmly, feeling a sense of comfort wash over me.

"Good morning, sweetie," she responded cheerfully as she continued to move her waistline to the rhythm.

Grandmother absolutely adored dancing, but more than anything else, she especially cherished dancing to the lyrics of her favorite singers.

I wandered back to her extensive and impressive book collection to find another captivating book to read. It was well after one o'clock when she strolled over to the plush sofa where I was comfortably laying, deeply engrossed in my reading.

"Yuh not hungry, love?" she asked with a hint of concern in her voice.

"Yes, Grandmother, I'm very, very hungry," I told her earnestly.

She looked at me strangely for a brief moment, processing my reply, then went to set the table for our lunch. Lunch was a delightful, simple affair, comprising a vibrant fruit salad made of ripe mangoes, sweet bananas, tangy pineapples, juicy papayas, and zesty oranges, all accompanied by a glass of refreshing melon juice.

After we were finished with our meal, she busily cleaned the kitchen while I returned to my book.

"Grandmother, may I take some of your wonderful books back with me to Netty's?" I asked hopefully.

"Of course, yuh know yuh don't have to ask. I won't ask yuh to take care of them, because I know yuh will," she assured me with a warm smile.

"Thank you," I replied gratefully.

It was a very hot and humid Saturday, the kind of day that made you feel sticky and lethargic. I must have fallen asleep during my reading. When I woke up, I was greeted by an almost eerie silence permeated the air. I stretched my arms wide, looked around, and noticed, to my surprise, that I was completely alone in the big, quiet, open space surrounding me. I got up to use the bathroom in my room, feeling a bit disoriented as I made my way there. Once in front of the sink, I went to wash my hands, and I realized with a smile that I no longer needed to climb on the stool. I had grown a whole foot! My hair had also transformed; it had become longer and curlier, cascading beautifully down my shoulders. I absolutely loved the new look. I turned this way and that, shaking my head side to side to let the feathery locks swing gracefully with every movement. I was beginning to look more and more like my Golealm self, and I felt genuinely pleased with that evolution.

After leaving the bathroom to go search for my grandmother. I approached her bedroom...hoping she would be there. Her door was wide open, but no sign of her. As I walked in, I was struck by the fact that her room was the biggest in the house, and it radiated an unexpected loveliness. For an older home, the space felt remarkably clutter-free and impressively up to date. I began to move from place to place, taking in the stunning collection of expensive perfumes and beautiful designer jewelry that adorned her dresser. My curiosity then led me to her closet, where I marveled at her lovely clothing. Finally, I made my way to her bathroom, which was not only a lot bigger than mine but also even more impressive in its design and elegance.

I loved her house and wished that Netty's house was more like it, but it seemed that Netty didn't care much for material things, nor did she show any willingness to work hard for them. As long as she had a comfortable place to sleep, food to eat, and her spliff to smoke, she was perfectly happy and content with her life.

I eventually grew bored of snooping around my grandmother's space and decided to head back to my previous activity of reading. It was another full hour before I saw her again. She walked in with the three large shopping bags she normally took with her to the market, all filled to the brim with various items of food.

"Klam, I have to guh take care of some things. I'm not sure when I'll come back, suh I'm going to have the same taxi driver who took you here yesterday come back to take you home." She said this matter-of-factly while putting her things away in the kitchen.

"Okay, Grandmother," I replied, feeling a mix of emotions. I was really looking forward to returning to Netty's house.

"Just stay out of yuh mother's way, and yuh'll be awright," she reassured me with a gentle smile.

"Okay, Grandmother. I will," I told her, although I felt less convinced than I sounded. I watched her as she hurriedly packed my belongings, including the many bright pieces of new clothing she had bought for me.

She was moving at such a brisk pace; if I didn't know better, I would have thought she couldn't wait to get rid of me. I watched for a couple more minutes, pondering silently what was going on.

Knowing that I wasn't capable of helping her with anything at the moment, I shrugged my shoulders in resignation and returned to the living room to continue reading the new book I had just started, hoping to lose myself in the pages.

Since I had received permission to borrow as many books as I wanted, I diligently packed all the books I intended to read. Among them were a few rare first edition psychology books that piqued my interest. Maybe, just maybe, they would provide me with the insights I needed to better decipher the complexities of Netty's character.

~~~~~~~~~

I had never once questioned Klam's apparent lack of reading ability when I was merely wearing her body, but now that I'm fully inhabiting her, I have come to the realization that it wasn't so much Klam's absence of ability, but rather my own lack of genuine interest in the world of books. To my astonishment, I discovered that I now wanted to read everything I could get my hands on, and seemingly, nothing could bore me in the least.

Just then, the loud sound of a horn, blowing impatiently outside the gate, indicated the arrival of the taxi. The driver's voice sounded rushed, as if he had somewhere urgent to be. Grandmother entered the living room with that faraway look still etched in her eyes, a sign of her preoccupation with thoughts that seemed to pull her away from the present moment.

I had a strong sense that if she weren't so mentally distracted, she would have felt very sad to see me go. But for the moment, I supposed she felt relieved that she would be able to tackle the problem at hand without having to feel too badly about me. After all, it was I who wanted to leave.

"The taxi man is here, just take what yuh can manage, him will come for the rest," she instructed with a calm yet urgent tone.

I closed the book I had been engrossed in and made my way over to her to give her a warm hug. I was growing fast, but not quite fast enough; I could only manage to hug her around her hips. She bent down and picked me up just like she normally did, squeezing me tightly and rocking me gently while she sniffed softly at my neck, a gesture that felt comforting and familiar.

"Mi sorry mi child, sometimes things like this happened, and I had to get with it as it comes," she apologized cryptically, her voice tinged with both love and sadness.

Maybe if I hadn't wanted to return home so desperately, I would have tried to engage further in our situation. But all that occupied my mind was the thought of going home.

"It's okay, Grandmother. Things will be fine," I said, hoping against hope that I was indeed correct. "By next week, everything should be back to normal, and I'll get to see you again."

The taxi driver blew his horn, once again, his impatience evident in the sharpness of the sound.

Grandmother quickly put me down and picked up one of my suitcases, her expression one of urgency and irritation.

"Come before dat idiat give me a headache with him noise," she said, her tone mirroring the familiar cadence of her voice, as she grasped my right hand firmly and began walking towards the door.

As we moved, I noticed that she appeared increasingly agitated while approaching the taxi that was parked just outside her gate. I had never seen her in such a state before, and it made me feel uneasy. I really wished there was something I could do to ease her discomfort; however, I was at a loss for how to help, so I decided to leave that thought for Laliac. I was sure she would be more than capable of addressing the matter at hand.

"Tell the little girl to hurry up, me on a schedule," the taxi driver shouted loudly to my grandmother, the irritation dripping from each word.

For a moment, I found myself confused about who exactly he was referring to as "little girl," until it dawned on me that I was the one he meant; my transformation seemed to have occurred so rapidly that perhaps he didn't even recognize me anymore.

"A dis a di one yuh going to take back," Grandmother told him firmly, offering no additional explanation.

"Suh, where is the other one? She not going back tuh?" he asked, his tone both curious and critical.

"No bother youself bout her, this is the one me a pay yuh to drive round," she snapped at him, clearly trying her utmost to maintain her composure and a semblance of normalcy in a rather chaotic moment. I had never witnessed this side of her before, which only deepened my concern and made me wonder all the more about what was actually unfolding around us.

"The rest of her things in the kitchen, guh get them," she commanded curtly, her impatience boiling over.

He left quietly and headed to the kitchen to retrieve the other pieces of luggage without uttering another word, while she kindly escorted me to the taxi and opened the door for me with a gentle gesture.

"If everything works out well, we will see each other again next week," she promised enthusiastically as she carefully placed the suitcase into the taxi right beside me. "Be good and do your best to stay out of Netty's way."

"Okay, Grandmother, I will certainly try my absolute best," I assured her, solemnly and with earnest sincerity.

The driver soon returned, dragging my other belongings behind him, which included the travel bag filled to the brim with all the books I had borrowed.

"Bye, Grandmother. I'll see you soon," I waved at her as the driver began to pull away from the gate. She waved back at me, managing to muster a warm smile. Once the driver turned the corner, she went back inside and locked the gate behind her with resolve.

I sighed deeply, feeling a mix of emotions. Looking up, I noticed the driver watching me closely through the rearview mirror, curiosity evident in his eyes. I then pulled out the book I had been reading, intentionally ignoring the question he was clearly eager to ask.

CHANGING

The driver reached Netty's modest one-room house exactly one and a half hours later. It was now just after five in the evening, and the heat was still intense and suffocating. I had been anticipating seeing Netty comfortably seated in her usual spot, so I felt a wave of relief wash over me when I noticed that she wasn't there.

The driver, whom I had been deliberately ignoring throughout the journey, appeared slightly disappointed as he realized I had yet to engage with him. He continued to chat away while I was engrossed in my book, seemingly undeterred by my silence. Eventually, I decided to close the book and feigned sleep in hopes of ending the conversation. He wanted to confirm that I was indeed the same person he had picked up on Friday, but he struggled to affirm my identity.

"Just leave them there," I ordered when he finally brought my bags onto the veranda, feeling a sense of irritation creeping in. "Thank you."

The driver stood there for a moment, looking a bit uncertain, as if unsure of what to do next. He glanced at me, and in an instant, he seemed eager to exit the situation as quickly as possible. He stepped off the veranda and was so preoccupied that he almost miscalculated his step.

The door was left ajar. Netty often believed she had nothing of value for anyone to steal, which was why she typically left the door wide open. I found myself pulling the hefty suitcases inside with significant effort, feeling the weight in every muscle. The bag filled with books was particularly heavy, and when I finally managed to get it inside, I realized I was sweating profusely, as if I had just come in from a grueling workout.

I left the suitcases by the bed that Swofiyah and I shared, then made my way over to the dresser that held a large mirror. Curiosity propelled me to see what changes had taken place in my appearance that could possibly have shocked the taxi driver, earlier. Upon gazing at my reflection in the mirror, I was taken aback and realized I didn't even recognize myself anymore. Instead of the familiar black shoulder-length afro curls I sported that very morning, my hair had transformed into a striking shiny silver, with a hint of vibrant blue at the tips. It was now puffy and had grown astonishingly longer, to the middle of my back. It was a remarkable change. The hue seemed to reflect my original Golealm color.

As I examined further, I noticed that my skin mirrored the unusual color of my hair, but the most astonishing features were undoubtedly my eyes. They were now an incredible silver color, except for the unsettling red pupils that contrasted sharply. I nearly fainted upon seeing myself fully in human form. No wonder the taxi driver had reacted as if he had seen something out of this world. I let out a sigh, trying very hard not to imagine what Swofiyah or anyone else might think, especially Netty.

Where was Swofiyah, anyway? I stepped away from the mirror and exited the cramped one-room house just as Netty was entering. We collided at the door.

"Look weh yuh a bloodclaat guh nuh dutty gal!" she snapped, her tone making it clear she was not in the best of moods.

"I'm really sorry, Mother," I sincerely apologized, momentarily forgetting that she had strongly instructed us not to call her 'mother,' 'mummy,' or any such expressions of affection that she deemed too soft or sentimental.

"A who yuh?" she asked, her sharp, crazed eyes locking onto mine as if trying to pierce through the layers of my identity.

"It's me, Mother. Klam." I feigned surprise and innocence, acting as if it were truly shocking that she did not recognize me.

"Klam, no, yuh a nuh Klam, Klam gone to her granny," she declared, her voice laced with fear and disbelief, her gaze darting around as if searching for an unseen threat.

"No, Netty, it's me. Grandmother had to take care of an urgent matter, so she sent me back a little early," I explained, hoping to bridge the gap of confusion between us.

She scrutinized me closely, shaking her head in disbelief, her demeanor growing increasingly frantic.

"No, no, yuh a no Klam. Yuh a demons like the other one. The two yuh a demons. Come out a me house!" She finished with a loud shout, her voice echoing in the dimly lit room, and then she began chanting Psalms while making the sign of the cross vigorously across her chest.

If she wasn't looking so wild and unstable, I might have found her antics amusing. But the signs of her unraveling mental state were painfully apparent, visible in the trembling of her hands and the alarming twitching of her head.

"Mother, where is Swofiyah?" I asked her, desperately seeking some clue as to her whereabouts.

"Don't bloodclaat call me mother. Me look like yuh mother? Come out a me bloodclaat house and guh look fi yuh mother, demons!" She grabbed for a cigarette with fingers shaking so badly the pack fell from her.

I didn't want to agitate her further, so I chose to quietly leave the room.

"Yes, gwon! All of a bumboclaat sudden, demons a tek me up. Nuh bother come back yah a bloodclaat, bout mother," she railed angrily, slamming the door with a fierce force behind me.

~~~~~~~~

I went searching for Swofiyah, anxiously wondering where in the world she could have gone. I made my way to Aunty Norma's cozy cottage, which was just two blocks away from our house, located on the other side of the road. Sometimes, Swofiyah would escape and seek refuge there, but to my disappointment, neither Aunty Norma nor her son was at home. Feeling reluctant to return to Netty's, I decided to take a stroll to the bottom of Doncaster Drive, where the beach awaited. Directly across the road from the beach was the vast development site that stretched all the way to Rae Town.

It was Saturday evening, and the atmosphere had settled into a peaceful quiet; things had calmed down at the construction site as well, and most of the beachgoers had already left the sandy shores to prepare for their evening activities.

My stomach growled loudly, reminding me that I hadn't smelled any cooking aromas wafting from

Netty's kitchen. I pondered whether she had decided to cook early today. The thought of indulging in a warm bowl of Saturday pea soup for dinner only intensified my hunger.

Where could Swofiyah be, I wondered?

I shifted my focus away from food and found a place to sit down on a large, weathered rock.

Swofiyah didn't have many friends to spend time with, and considering it was not a school day, it was unlikely that she could have gone off to school. Where on earth could she have possibly wandered off to?

I was momentarily distracted by the captivating sight of a large red snapper fish unexpectedly leaping out of the water, soaring gracefully into the air before splashing back down into the inviting depths. The thrill of the action had me unwinding more than I had anticipated, and I found myself gratefully thanking the fish in my head for this delightful distraction.

As I settled into the moment, I began to relish the beautiful sun creating exquisite diamond sparkles on the calm, blue sea. A cool breeze waved past, enhancing the soothing feeling while pleasantly cooling me down. I sat there in quiet reflection for a little while longer, soaking in the harmonious sounds of the seagulls and the gentle lapping of the water against the shore. It was indeed a wonderfully serene moment. This was, after all, the first occasion I had visiting the beach on my own.

Circumstances had shifted since my final merger, and as a result, there was going to be a multitude of firsts for me to experience. I sat there deep in thought, trying to figure out how I was going to navigate through this challenging phase of my life. How was I going to get through this? The uncertainty loomed over me like a shadow.

I had never encountered anyone in my situation before. I didn't quite know what to expect, nor did I possess any clear idea about what steps I should take next. Laliac and Jalaniac had appeared just as clueless as I felt. I sighed heavily and decided to get up. I might as well return to Netty's, even if I wasn't particularly looking forward to her raucous rants and unpredictable madness. Nonetheless, I felt I had little choice in the matter. I sighed again, feeling the weight of my dilemma.

Walking through the vast and somewhat eerie property of Bellevue Mental Hospital, which stretched across many acres of unkempt land, was undeniably the quickest, albeit the most perilous route one could take to reach Netty's house. Although the evening was surprisingly quiet and calm, I found myself feeling particularly cautious. Mental illness can often render individuals unpredictable, which is precisely why no one with a sound mind would dare to tread this path at such a late hour. To ease my anxiety, I was relying heavily on the vigilant presence of the birds and the rustling trees, hoping they would provide an early warning of any lurking danger.

Perspiration was collecting beneath my Barbie dread cap, which I had fashioned to conceal my voluminous hair. This unique hairstyle wasn't typical for someone my age; in fact, it was considered too mature and sophisticated according to societal standards, and surely it would attract unwanted attention. The vibrant colour of my hair was also an obvious point of interest, not to mention my striking silver-tinted skin, which, fortunately, was mostly obscured by the long-sleeved T-shirt and jeans I had chosen to wear. Meanwhile, the Barbie sunglasses I wore were common enough to help shield my eyes, but anyone who chose to look a little closer would find me to be quite the curious character, indeed.

8

THE TWO OSPREYS

Returning to Netty's after my much-needed relaxation bout at the beach certainly wasn't the smartest decision I could have made — not after witnessing her unexpected and rather hurtful reaction towards me. Feeling a mix of confusion and disappointment, I decided it was best to head back to my aunt's house to check if Swofiyah was there. But to my dismay, she wasn't there. I found myself at a loss, questioning where Swofiyah could have disappeared to?

I searched for her with little success, and as I made my way back home, a heaviness of dejection settled in my heart. Then it struck me that I should probable spend more time practicing my Golealm skills. After all, I was still the same person inside, just taking on a human form.

When I finally reached Netty's house, I discovered that the door was locked. Fortunately, I had the key tucked away on a piece of fishnet thread that I always kept hanging around my neck, allowing me to open it.

As I stepped inside, I was immediately hit with the realization that I was absolutely famished. It felt as if an eternity had passed since I last had a meal. I supposed this overwhelming hunger was simply the result of my recent growth spurt that seemed to have come out of nowhere.

When I entered, the house didn't smell of pea soup, which honestly made me feel a bit disappointed. I trudged over to the little kitchen area and began searching for something, anything, other than just fruits to fill my empty stomach. After rummaging through the fridge, I discovered some leftover boiled dumplings and boiled green bananas, and a small container of curry chicken still sitting there. I decided to start eating whatever I could find. If my mother was going to be mean today, she might as well have something tangible to be mean about, I thought.

When that small meal didn't quite satiate my hunger, I reached for a perfectly ripe banana and an orange sitting on the counter. I cut the orange in two without even bothering to peel it first. I squeezed the juice into a large cup and added a bit of sugar along with some water, then gave it a good stir. After that, I eagerly drank the refreshing orange juice and quickly chugged down the banana. I felt significantly better.

I tried to relax and enjoy Netty's absence by grabbing a book from my stash and disappearing under her bed. It turned out that under there was much more spacious than under our bed.

It was getting a little dark, but there was still enough daylight filtering in for me to read without straining my eyes too much. I must have dozed off, because the sudden sound of a giant walking onto the veranda and then stumbling into the house startled me awake. For a moment, I thought I was still dreaming, but the earth-shaking echo of the giant's footsteps coming towards me sent my heart racing in panic. I reflexively did the scared little girl thing and squeezed my eyes shut tightly, hoping that whatever was happening would somehow just go away. The sound grew increasingly deafening as the heavy footsteps drew closer to Netty's bed. My body was shaking uncontrollably with fright, but I couldn't keep my eyes closed any longer. I had to know what was lurking just beyond my vision. The shocking sight of what I was confronted with sent my body into spasms, and in an instant, I lost consciousness.

When I finally opened my eyes again, it was morning, and I found myself lying on the familiar bed I shared with Swofiyah. A warm feeling of happiness infused my body from head to toe, filling me with a sense of peace, I stretched lazily. It felt like it was going to be a truly wonderful day. As I turned to stretch again, I noticed Swofiyah stooping over me, her fingers stuck in her mouth. She seemed to be waiting patiently for me to awaken, her eyes bright with interest.

I sat up abruptly, suddenly remembering the cacophonous noise of the giant's footsteps and the immense fright and shock I experienced at the sight of that terrifying thing. The residual feeling of fear was intense, but for the life of me, I couldn't recall exactly what I had seen in that moment. I rubbed my eyes vigorously, shaking off the lingering feeling of dread that threatened to settle in again. Looking around for Netty, I wondered if she was the one who had thoughtfully put me to bed, but I didn't see her anywhere.

"Yuh wake up for real this time?" Swofiyah asked, her fingers still stuck in her mouth, an innocent expression on her face.

"Where is mother?" I asked, swinging my legs off the bed and preparing to seek her out.

I started staring at Swofiyah as if she were a two-headed stranger, utterly perplexed by the dramatic transformation she had undergone. Her changes were nothing short of bewildering. She no longer resembled the familiar sister I once knew and cherished. Her hair had grown extravagantly longer— much longer than I had ever before. It swathed her entire body in the stooping position she had assumed, flowing down and trailing elegantly on the bed behind her. The hair was expertly parted down the middle; the left side was an intense, jet black, while the right side gleamed in a striking solid gold hue. This golden section transitioned into shimmering silver, then into a stunning platinum shade, before finally cascading into an ethereal white and a deep mesmerizing blue. The left side of her head seemed to have developed a life all its own, each strand dancing freely as if delighted by its own beauty. I found myself utterly mesmerized by this spectacle, and the compelling urge to reach out and touch it was so overwhelming that I instinctively began to stretch my hand towards her. But in that moment, she stood up gracefully and stepped off the bed, revealing another startling revelation — she had grown taller — remarkably taller than I remembered. Her beautiful dark brown skin was now radiating a warm, golden glow, reminiscent of the ignited brilliance of Shinny Swofiyah, though perhaps not quite as rich. Her eyes, which previously exuded warmth, now appeared to be solid gold, except for a striking ring of fire that danced around the limbus. They presented a strange, yet wondrous, sight to behold — she embodied both strangeness and wonder.

Curiously unaware of her own ethereal stunningness, she was still absentmindedly sucking on her fingers when she reached over with her other hand and gently touched my long curls that I could feel hanging down my back. Where her fingers made contact sparked with energy, yet it did not blaze.

"Netty gone, she not coming back," she said softly, releasing my hair and turning unexpectedly towards the door, which she opened with a grace that left me breathless.

The fresh and invigorating smell of early morning rushed into the room, bringing with it a wave of happiness that enveloped me once again. I eagerly followed her out the door onto the so called veranda, where I watched as she raised her head to the vast, cloudless blue sky, filled with promise. Above us, two small specks began to appear, soaring high amidst the gentle morning breeze. She remained fixated on the sky, compelling me to divert my gaze upward alongside her. As the two birds flew overhead, they gradually grew larger, their presence becoming more pronounced as they glided closer to where we stood. The sounds they created, a harmonious blend of nature's music, added a certain surreal quality to the already enchanting beauty of the morning.

She extended her right hand, while keeping her other hand still stuck in her mouth, a gesture that made me watch in astonishment. I couldn't believe my eyes as the two magnificent birds descended, their sizes becoming more impressive the nearer they approached. One gracefully landed on the slender arm she had outstretched, while the other settled itself softly at her feet. With a gentle turn, she began to walk back inside, carrying the unusually large osprey that she had perched upon her hand. The other bird, equally magnificent, followed closely behind her, with me trailing along in awe behind them, back into the house.

Inside, the two remarkable birds vanished, transformed into two breathtakingly beautiful Nubian males who stood by her side like ethereal guardian angels. In all my years on earth, I had never once witnessed such a remarkable display of male beauty. I yearned to ask her what on earth was happening, but deep down, I sensed that it was simply not the right moment for such inquiries.

The sound of someone stepping onto the veranda had us instinctively turning our attention towards the door. Curious and slightly apprehensive, I got up and opened it to see who it was. To my surprise, it was our aunt.

"Pickney, a weh oonuu momma d..?" she began, stopping short with her mouth agape. She quickly glanced over her shoulder, as if in fear of being followed, before she hurriedly stepped inside and made sure to close the door securely behind her.

I had never before witnessed her acting in such a frantic manner; she was typically the one full of laughter and lightheartedness, the sensible one. The exact contrast to her sister, Netty.

I snickered at the thought, realizing that the sight of us would trigger quite a surprising reaction in anyone.

Swofiyah looked at me with her fingers still stuck in her mouth, offering me a little smile, as if she knew exactly what was running through my mind. Did she actually? I found myself gazing at her intently.

"*Yes, Roboliac, I know exactly what you're thinking*," a commanding voice echoed in my head, reminiscent of how I used to communicate with my soul sisters. I shot a glance at her, silently trying to convey that this wasn't a laughing matter.

"Jesas Chrise! A how oonuu look suh?" My aunt asked in a panicked whisper, checking the closed door again, making sure it was securely sealed off.

I quickly turned to look at the two Nubian males, but to my surprise, they had mysteriously vanished into thin air. I sighed with overwhelming relief; their unearthly beauty and peculiar strangeness would have surely sent her spiraling into a complete coma. Humans really could be so strange and sensitive at times. A soft chuckle escaped from Swofiyah as she continue sucking her finger, completely unfazed by the chaos.

"Swofiyah's strangeness frightened the heck out of her; she decided that Bellevue Mental Hospital, across the way, was the absolute best place for her to be," I told my aunt, maintaining a serious expression, not so much as blinking.

I probably was the final straw that pushed her off the deep end, but in this moment, it was best that she remained blissfully unaware.

Swofiyah's burst of laughter was so delightful and infectious that it made me start laughing too, unable to contain my amusement. My aunt looked curiously at us, her expression shifting as she took out her phone. We watched her dial a number, then bringing the phone to her ear as she waited impatiently.

I glanced over at my little sister, raising my brows questioningly. She shrugged her shoulders in response, a silent gesture that said everything while saying nothing at all. We were two different kinds of strangeness, and I couldn't help but wonder what would happen to us in this increasingly bizarre situation.

"Chris, hurry and come ova Netty," she ordered abruptly before hanging up.

We watched as she replaced the phone in her pocket, scanning the one room for unseen details, her eyes darting around with a mixture of anxiety and determination.

"Oonuu hurry up, pack up oonuu things dem. We have to get oonuu out a here fast," she said, her voice sounding pretty urgent and laced with anxiety.

Since I was already packed and ready, I quickly rushed to help Swofiyah with her packing, attempting to keep the atmosphere as calm as possible. Just then, Chris walked in as his mother was frantically stuffing clothing into a small plastic bag, her movements quick and almost frantic.

"A wah a gwon?" he asked, glancing around for any possible danger, his voice filled with concern. His mother only ever used that tone when something was wrong or threatening. He relaxed slightly when he didn't see anything out of the ordinary—until, of course, his gaze landed on us.

"Look pon dem!" my aunt ordered him, but he was already staring at us, blinking hard in disbelief.

It was at that moment, I realized they both knew something significant that I didn't. Their reactions, although distinctly different from Netty's, were filled with a palpable mix of fear and unspoken secrets.

The small plastic bag struggled to hold all the clothing she was trying to cram into it. She even took a pillow from Netty's bed, her eyes darting around as if expecting more than just clothing to be an issue. We stood there, watching her as she pulled the pillowcase off and began hastily bundling all the clothes into it. I didn't bother to tell her that the clothes were far too small for her now; they simply wouldn't fit. Instead, I just watched, feeling a mix of helplessness as she struggled to force them into the case, determination etched on her face.

She grabbed the other pillowcase swiftly from its pillow, her movement filled with an urgent sense of purpose, coming to stand resolutely in front of Swofiyah, her intention unmistakably clear in that moment. However, Swofiyah, unfazed, simply took her fingers out of her mouth and raised her brows in an inquisitive manner at our aunt, it spoke volumes. Our aunt then turned her gaze toward me, her expression suggesting she was seeking some kind of reassurance or understanding. I quickly shook my head at her, trying to convey my concerns in a way that she would understand. She let out an exasperated sigh, her frustration evident, before she flung the pillowcase back onto Netty's bed with a hint of annoyance.

"Chris, guh bring the car come," she instructed him firmly, but he remained too entranced, still gazing at us with a mixture of wonderment and fear, completely oblivious to her call.

"Bwoy, me seh guh bring the car come!" she shouted at him in a loud whisper, her voice urgent and commanding. Startled by the suddenness of her tone, he finally turned and hurriedly left the room.

We continued to watch her as she dragged my suitcases outside, returning momentarily for my travel bag that was filled to the brim with my many cherished books. Swofiyah, seemingly unbothered, had resumed sucking her fingers, embodying a sense of relaxation as if she genuinely did not care about the fact that humans were seeing her in such an unusual state.

I, on the other hand, had learned from past experiences that humans typically harbored a deep-seated disdain for anything that could be categorized as otherworldly strangeness, making me feel more wary than ever.

She noticed the whirlwind of thoughts racing through my mind and promptly took her fingers out of her mouth. I observed as her golden hue became even more pronounced, as though it were a shimmering beacon of her essence; however, she did not undergo any further transformation. Just then, our aunt re-entered the room and halted abruptly at the sight, her eyes widening to the size of saucers, reflecting a mix of shock and disbelief. In that moment, I instinctively put my arm around Swofiyah, feeling her relax as the radiant hue around her beginning to tone down considerably.

"We don't need any of those things there," she firmly told our aunt, gesturing with her chin in the direction of the assorted luggages that crowded the space.

With a gentle but determined tug, she grabbed my hands and added, *"Roboliac, kindly tell your aunt thanks so we can be on our way."*

"Thank you, Aunty, for wanting to help us out. Thank you so much," I replied to her, trying my best to sound pleasantly professional and genuinely sincere in my tone.

"It's awright, oonuu a me niece, me have to take care a oonuu," she responded with warmth.

Before our aunt could say anything else, we were already on our way out the door.

9

THE COLD

I suddenly felt like I was being violently thrust from a plane at a ridiculously high altitude, the ground far below me becoming a distant memory. This kind of flight, this unnerving sensation, was something my soul had grown accustomed to, but I was human now, encased in this fragile vessel. My body, although growing, was still delicate and unfamiliar with this terrifying mode of travel. In that moment, I forgot how to breathe properly, as panic seeped into my every nerve. The sensation only lasted a fleeting minute, but to me, caught in this unfamiliar situation, it felt like an eternity.

Just as abruptly as it began, the sensation ceased, and we found ourselves engulfed in the most intense chill my vessel had ever experienced. It started shaking almost instantly, accompanied by my trembling lips and my pitifully chattering teeth. I tried desperately to appear composed, to mirror the coolness of my dazzling sister, who seemed entirely unaffected by the biting elements, but I was failing, dreadfully so.

Coming from the sultry heat of Jamaica to this harsh place enveloped by mountains of ice caps and relentless frigid cold seemed utterly absurd. I turned to gaze out at the vast, stark expanse of white, my two hands squeezed tightly together and wedged between my trembling thighs in a futile attempt to find warmth. My body hunched over in a defensive posture, shaking uncontrollably in the icy grip of the cold. The long sleeve T-shirt and jeans I had been wearing since yesterday clung tightly to my fast-growing slender body, now feeling short and achingly inadequate, providing me no protection from this unforgiving environment.

My long, thick hair was helping my back with warmth, providing a semblance of comfort in this biting chill. I tried to wiggle underneath it, wrapping it around myself like a cozy sweater. It helped a little, but, honestly, it was too freaking cold, and my hair was not enough to effectively combat the ruthless freeze settling inside me. I turned to look at Swofiyah, and I noticed she still appeared completely unaffected by the cold.

"Where are we?" I asked, struggling to get the words out; they tumbled from my lips with a tremor that was, admittedly, a bit shameful. The thick white fog gathered in front of my mouth, swirling gently, hardly disguising the brutal chill enveloping us.

She turned her head and looked directly at me, her expression softening as she realized I wasn't handling it too well. Without hesitation, she walked over, with grace and confidence radiating from every step, to my side. I made a mental note to practice that same walk of hers as soon as I was certain I wouldn't die of hyperthermia.

She put her slender arm around my shoulders, still intently focused on the vast expanse of whiteness that surrounded us. A thoughtful expression filled with both maturity and concern came over her face, which did much to ease my unease.

The warmth emanating from the arm she put around me, felt like being wrapped up snugly in a pile of warm blankets. I felt the cold slowly ebbing away, replaced by the enveloping warmth that traveled through my shivering extremities. I instinctively rested my head on her shoulder and let that comforting sensation wash over me completely. Soon, my body felt like it was floating gently, and I snuggled up closer to her, relishing the delightful feeling. The frigid cold was now completely gone, and I finally felt the most comfortable I had ever felt since arriving in the enigmatic Materealm.

The familiar distinctive sounds of the two ospreys, echoing in the air, greeted my ears, and seconds later, I saw them soaring towards us at an impressive high speed. Swofiyah, with that air of confidence, dropped her arm from around me and walked purposefully toward them. I felt a wave of stress wash over me, but to my amazement, the biting cold did not return, and instead, my body was still feeling wonderfully warm, almost as if wrapped in a protective cocoon.

Interesting!

The two birds flew straight at us with precision and landed just three feet away from her in their astonishing human form. It seemed like she was completely accustomed to their unique landing behavior. I, on the other hand, found myself bracing to duck out of their way, unaware of what might happen next.

They stood perfectly still in front of her, engaged in one of their mysterious silent conversations. Swofiyah pointed her hands in a few directions, and they nodded their heads in understanding before launching themselves back into the sky and disappearing.

She walked back towards me slowly, her movements almost ethereal, and I suddenly felt an overwhelming need to ask her, "Who are you?" My voice trembled slightly as I spoke.

She gave no indication that she had heard my question, but then, as if she were whispering directly into my mind, she sent her thoughts to me with clarity,

"*I Am Solstilert.*"

"Solstilert?" I asked, confusion evident in my tone.

"Yes, Earth. I AM EARTH," she replied, her voice echoing in my consciousness.

"Earth," I said, panic rising in my voice and shock playing across my face like a sudden storm. I knew exactly what that meant. Billions of years ago on the distant realm of Golealm, Golealm had taken shape in the form of a powerful, walking, talking being, and had annihilated almost all the inhabitants of that realm.

Those inhabitants had ruined Golealm so severely that it had catastrophic effects on the other planets within that solar system.

It had taken millions of years to re-establish the realm, but we persevered and emerged as a stronger, more powerful race as a result of those trials. The biggest lesson that ordeal had taught us was to never take the land for granted. We must treat it with the same respect and care that we showed our own bodies. We were intertwined with the land; we were the land, and the land was fundamentally a part of us.

Solstilert—Earth, confidently nodded her head at me, having caught the fleeting thoughts that swirled through my mind. She turned her back to me and began to gaze at the wide expanse of pristine whiteness that spread endlessly out in front of us, glistening like diamonds under the light sky and bright moon.

"We shall stay here," she proclaimed with a sense of authority that stirred something deep within me.

Her voice in my head had transformed; it no longer carried the familiar tones I was used to hearing. Instead, it now sounded like a soft yet firm amalgamation of human and alien qualities, an authoritative whisper that resonated with clarity, as if she had shouted at me from close range.

"Where are we?" I managed to ask, my curiosity getting the better of me.

"We are on the Continent of Antarctica," she replied, uttering the words with such unwavering finality that I immediately understood not to question her further—at least for the time being. I watched intently as she scrutinized the icy landscape and the elusive inhabitants that roamed this endless expanse. Raising her face to the sky above, she inhaled deeply, as if trying to absorb the very essence of this frozen world. Her vessel had matured into that of a fourteen-year-old, beautiful and slender, embodying an otherworldly grace that seemed to draw both admiration and wonder from the stark surroundings.

Her gorgeous long sisterlocks had become even more voluminous and dramatically longer, sweeping gracefully through the pristine snow. It looked extremely heavy, cascading down her shoulders like a waterfall of dark silk. The striking colors, a deep jet black and a shimmering platinum blond, created a stark contrast on each side of her face, glistening with a life of their own under the moonlight.

But even more astonishing than her hair was her face and skin, exposed to the frigid elements of the Antarctic night.

Her skin, much like her flowing locks, was radiant and shimmering, and I watched in awe as it changed with each passing second. Her naturally dark brown skin, imbued with a golden hue, shimmered and transformed to mimic the color of the surrounding white snow, allowing her to blend perfectly with the ethereal environment. Had it not been for the striking jet black side of her hair and the long, strapless white floral silk summer dress she wore, she would have effortlessly disappeared into the winter backdrop.

Her skin turned a translucent ivory, so delicate and soft that she resembled one of the enchanting inhabitants of the winged world in my galaxy. As she switched colors and forms that represented all the diverse ethnic groups of the world and beyond, she continued to gaze intently at the unfolding scene in the distance. Her face was a captivating picture of both serenity and impending destruction.

Here in Antarctica, it was night time, though the bright, reflective snow gave the landscape the magical essence of early evening. The birds and other native mammals of the land were already settling in to rest for the night, creating a soothing atmosphere of stillness.

The sound of the two majestic eagles returning from their flight drew my attention to the exquisite starry sky. From a considerable distance, I was able to make out the distinct shape of something unusual attached to their large, sharp talons, which glinted in the moonlight. It took them less than a few fleeting seconds to transform and appear in front of her in their striking human form. The two figures gracefully set down, in front of her, huge flags that represented the developed countries of the world. She looked at them intently, and in that moment, they ignited with an intense blaze. We watched, transfixed, as the fire roared to life and consumed the flags entirely, leaving behind nothing but ashes that floated off into the cool night air and gradually disappeared without a trace.

"We shall stay here," she repeated firmly, her lips not bothering to part as she communicated her intent.

One of the Nubians, with a fluid motion, opened a door that seemed to appear out of nowhere and stepped inside. She followed him without hesitation, then the other male entered, with me trailing closely behind them all, unsure of what awaited us on the other side.

~~~~~~~~~

The expansive space we entered made Jalaniac's underground grand palace appear like a mere chicken coop by comparison. Jalaniac's grand palace was not just a structure; it was a breathtaking replica of what we had once shared in Golealm. This remarkable palace was ten times the size of the exquisite Palace of Versailles in France and, without a doubt, much more beautiful in its intricate design and opulence.

The space I found myself in now was astoundingly one hundred times that and more, an awe-inspiring expanse that seemed to stretch beyond the limits of my imagination. Its sheer beauty and grandeur— echoing the might of the powerful being who was my sister—made me acutely aware of my own smallness, rendering everything I had known and everything I would come to know utterly insignificant in comparison. I looked around, admiring the surroundings in sheer awe. It was simply breathtaking. I had never encountered anything even remotely similar throughout my years traversing from planet to planet. I was utterly overwhelmed by the magnificence of it all.

As I continued to marvel at the magnificent palace, feeling like a microscopic particle lost in a vast universe, my belly suddenly growled loudly, a reminder of the fact that I hadn't consumed anything to eat since early that morning, or, rather, the entire day.

I turned to look at Solstilert, astonishingly beautiful with her shimmering locks and dark brown skin radiating a warm golden glow. I couldn't help but wonder if she, too, felt the gnawing hunger that I did.

Within the blink of an eye, they—all three of them —transformed into majestic Siberian tigers. Then one of them morphed into an even more magnificent-looking white lion, large and muscular, its mane thick and fluffy, as snowy white as freshly fallen snow.

"*Follow us*," she said, effortlessly sending me vivid mental images of a large dining table lavishly arrayed with food the likes of which I had never seen since my arrival on Earth. My ravenous belly roared in enthusiastic response to the enticing image presented before me.

10

THE TEACHER

At the age of forty-two, Marshane came to a stark realization that if she didn't make significant changes to the way she was currently living her life, she was destined to die a sad, lonely old woman surrounded by nine cats who, in a morbid twist of fate, would feast upon her lifeless body when there was nothing else left for them to eat. It was an unsettling outcome that filled her with dread, and not one she was looking forward to facing. She had developed a deep fondness for her imaginary cats, and the thought of such a grim fate for both herself and her beloved fictional companions was more than she could bear.

"The cat woman," they were sure to call her, a title that conjured images of a witchy, old hermit, forever mean and barren.

A wicked laugh escaped her lips at the thought, and she knew she needed to shed that negative image in her mind. Thus, she promptly went online to apply for jobs as an English teacher in Asia, feeling a spark of hope ignite within her. She had not anticipated receiving any responses on the very same day, so she was pleasantly surprised when she did. Without hesitation, she accepted a position in the vibrant city of Shenzhen, located in Guangdong Province.

Having spent the last fifteen years living in the United States, she felt that unless she get married to a man who would treat her with respect rather than as some kind of trophy merely to secure a green card, she would never make any real headway in her life.

Just two weeks later, she meticulously packed up her belongings and embarked on a journey to Mainland China, ready to begin her new adventure as a primary school teacher. This decision marked the beginning of a vital shift in her mental trajectory, and perhaps, while she was at it, she might even find herself a kind-hearted Chinese man who would appreciate her for who she truly was.

~~~~~~~~~

Dan, who firmly believed he was her twin flame, had keenly perceived the swirling thoughts racing through her mind and made a resolute decision: under absolutely no circumstances was he going to let her out of his sight. It became clear to him that wherever she was going, he was going to be there alongside her, no matter what. There was, without a doubt, no way he was going to allow her to "find a man" in the vast expanse of Mainland China. He was acutely aware of the people there; he had lived among them for longer than he could have ever imagined. Throughout his time, he had witnessed their cruelty, deep-seated aversion, and pronounced superiority complexes toward her kind.

It was unequivocally his duty to safeguard her, relentlessly, even if she remained oblivious to his existence or the peril she was about to place herself in.

He watched intently as she radiated with a captivating glow of inner excitement at the thrilling prospect of her new life adventure. Her infectious optimism was imbuing her with an added dose of confidence, evident as she handed the Asian woman at the Air China boarding gate her ticket, her face illuminated by a huge, beaming smile.

He couldn't help but smile in return, feeling a swell of pride. She had done her homework and thoroughly researched her destination. She knew precisely where she was headed and what to expect upon arrival. Aware that the flight was going to be an extensive one, she thoughtfully packed a book to read and gathered an assortment of snacks to savor along the journey.

As he observed her, he noted how she sighed with a mixture of relief and anticipation as she settled into her seat. She had chosen the window seat specifically to gaze out at the clouds, her favorite view. She had always possessed a rather unique fascination with clouds—perhaps it was their fleeting nature or their unending beauty. So, if she was going to be soaring high in the sky, she might as well enjoy the breathtaking sight of them up close and personal.

He chuckled softly at that whimsical thought, knowing the depth of her dreams.

She didn't even turn to look at the passengers who were going to be her immediate neighbours for the next fifteen to sixteen long hours. Instead, she was preoccupied with her swirling thoughts. She was wondering if she had truly made the right decision by locking up her apartment instead of putting it up for rent. After all, it would have earned her some much-needed passive income and significantly helped her with her savings at the end of the financial year.

The uncertainty loomed large in her mind; she wasn't sure if she was going to like the Mainland after a month or two, particularly in such unfamiliar surroundings. Caution filled her heart.

"Did I make the right choice?" she questioned silently, second-guessing herself endlessly.

"It's too late for second thoughts now," came a voice, surprisingly confident.

"I guess it is," she sighed in response, her mind unaware that she was actually conversing with a real entity.

She thought her male inner voice was simply a manifestation of her own thoughts.

"Don't worry too much; just enjoy the flight and embrace the new experience. If, for some reason, you find that you don't like it, you can always return home," he reassured her gently.

He watched as she nodded her head and sighed, intent on looking out the porthole of the airplane at the tarmac, deep in thought. He could see she was trying very hard to keep her composure amid the turbulence of emotions. Suddenly, she turned and looked directly at him, and for a brief moment, he thought she was going to say 'hi' to him, but instead, she merely turned back and resumed her gaze out the window, lost in her own world.

His disappointment was immense. He slowly took out a book from the briefcase he had been carrying and decided to pretend to read it, hoping to distract himself from the nagging feelings he had.

The moment she felt the airplane lift off the runway and ascend into the sky, he could sense her excitement and positivity gradually returning to her. *"This is going to be absolutely wonderful,"* she thought cheerfully.

"Yes, it is," he chuckled in response within her mind, feeling a flicker of hope for the journey ahead.

~~~~~~~~

She turned her head slightly and saw the very handsome looking Asian man sitting right beside her on the plane. He looked just like her favorite Korean actor, Lee Seo Jin, but appeared to be a younger version of him. The resemblance was striking and made her heart skip a beat. She almost said a casual "hi" to him, but then hesitated and decided against it.

Past experiences from her time at university had taught her that Asians were often not friendly towards her kind, a fact that had left her feeling somewhat alienated. She felt no obligation to be neighborly or initiate a conversation. However, her resolve began to waver when she glanced over at him again and noticed a very familiar looking book he was engrossed in reading. It was remarkably similar to the one she had brought along to read during the flight.

"I have the same book," she said impulsively before she could stop herself. With a mix of excitement and curiosity, she dug into her handbag resting on her lap and withdrew the book, proudly displaying it to him.

"Wow! I didn't know Asian males read these types of books," she exclaimed, genuinely surprised by her own words and the connection they seemed to share.

"That's a lot of assumption and stereotyping packed into that one sentence. Of course, some Asian males read intelligently written books that span a variety of genres."

"I'm truly sorry; I didn't mean for my words to be interpreted that way. I honestly didn't intend for it to sound like that at all."

She had consciously made the decision to mind her own business after that awkward exchange, returning her gaze to the view outside the window as the airport receded into the distance, growing smaller and smaller. She knew she would need to get used to interacting with Asian people without inadvertently causing offense. There were so many different things she could have said in that moment, yet, as was often the case, the wrong words had carelessly escaped her lips. She knew she would have to learn to be more mindful of what she said around them in the future. This was her first attempt at making friends with an Asian male, and somehow, she had managed to completely trip over her words. She let out a sigh of frustration.

"Don't sound so discouraged; I'm sure he was just pulling your leg," her inner voice gently consoled her in response.

"Maybe," she admitted, still feeling uneasy. Marshane suddenly realized just how exhausted she was, having hardly gotten any sleep over the past two weeks; thus, she leaned back in her seat and decided that a little nap before lunch was exactly what her weary body needed right now.

~~~~~~~~

Dan looked over at her with a warm smile on his face, a feeling of happiness washing over him. He kind of felt a twinge of guilt for teasing her, but he was far too elated that she had finally spoken to him after all these long years. After countless attempts he had made to strike up a conversation, she had finally broken the silence.

"You're such a schmuck," Starr, sitting in the aisle seat right beside him, said playfully in Korean, laughter dancing in her voice.

She, just like him, had assumed an Asian body, her features reflecting a vibrant sense of identity.

He chuckled elegantly at the memory, recalling how he had been wearing an African American body —average looking and undeniably shabby, a crackhead's visage etched across his face. He had overheard Marshane's friend, Suzzie, excitedly mentioning her plans to hook her up with her cousin. All she had to do was agree to pay him an upfront fee of two thousand dollars to initiate the process.

Dan had watched the palpable excitement blossom on her face at the thought of finally obtaining a green card, picturing the myriad of doors that would open for her life. But that bright promise was not meant to be...he stepped in to intervene.

When she was finally confronted with this dubious character, her friend's cousin, he looked like he was on the brink of desperation, clearly seeking his next fix. With a mixture of disappointment and relief, she sent him packing, realizing that her dreams were worth more than such a hollow promise.

Dan almost laughed out loud at the vivid memories that flooded back to him.

"A what yuh tek me for? A schmuck? You want me to pay you two thousand now, then next week yuh come back for another two thousand, and then, what? Another five thousand? Yuh look like yuh can hardly hold it together. Look here bwoy, you better go on home and guh sleep off yuh crackheadness."

She had slammed the door right in his face, then immediately went to the phone to blaze up her friend.

He sat there, watching her inconspicuously, wondering what she would think if she found him sitting there, quietly watching her sleep. It was something he had been doing for her past eighteen lifetimes, a habit he couldn't seem to shake.

"When is she going to snap out of this? Earth needs her," Starr wondered aloud, her voice tinged with concern.

"She will when she is ready," he responded firmly, trying to provide reassurance.

"Things are happening so fast. How did they get this way so rapidly?" she pressed, her anxiety palpable.

"Things never happened before its time, Starr. The Ancient One fixed all things at the appropriate moment."

The uncertainty etched on her face mirrored the same turmoil that resided in his heart, a heavy weight of worry and hope intertwined.

11

EARTH'S ANGEL

A meleki was born and raised in the quaint little farming village of Pipari, nestled in the heart of Khalasana, India. She lived there with her father and mother, who often worried that there was something inherently wrong with their only child. As their sole offspring, they were already grappling with the traditional expectations of finding her a proper suitor, which was a significant cultural obligation.

From a very young age, Ameleki had always felt a strange disconnection within herself. Despite being a girl, she was astonishingly stronger than anyone else in the village, and her beauty was unmatched, making her the most captivating female the villagers had ever laid eyes on. Unlike her peers, she was never interested in participating in what society deemed as 'girlie things.' Instead, she found joy and fulfillment working tirelessly on the family farm, where she dedicated herself to raising her beloved horses, cows, and chickens.

While the cows and chickens served as valuable cash crops, the thoroughbred horses were more than just livestock to her; they were her cherished pets and her beloved hobby.

Her parents had long since abandoned the idea of sending her off to a formal school setting. Although she was an exceptionally brilliant student, Ameleki had absolutely no interest in attending school and sitting down for countless hours engaging in tasks she believed she could accomplish on her own in just a fraction of the time.

For over a decade and a half, she had essentially been homeschooling herself, successfully receiving an array of invitations from colleges and universities across the nation. However, she showed no desire to pursue these opportunities. Her parents considered this decision to be one of the most abnormal things their teenage daughter had ever done.

The self-assured brilliance she began exhibiting from the tender age of one, along with her single-minded awareness of herself, was something they found both perplexing and frightening.

She simply cannot be told what to do, or when to do it. The essence of her independence is deeply woven into her character, showcasing a built-in system of thoughts and actions that her parents struggled to understand or effectively manage. She was their beloved daughter, cherished beyond measure and adored completely, yet the intensity of her capabilities frightened them too much.

From a remarkably early age, she had begun forming articulate words at just five months, and by seven months, she was confidently walking with the grace and coordination of a much older toddler. Concerned for her well-being, they took her to the hospital to ensure everything was alright, only to be informed that she exhibited a significantly higher level of awareness than most of the babies they had examined. The doctors assured them that their daughter was undeniably an above-average baby, destined to exhibit abnormal intelligence and behavior as she grew older.

As the years rolled by, they watched with both pride and bewilderment as she moved seamlessly from one brilliant creation to the next, her imagination seemingly boundless. Her latest obsession involved horses, and she had even taken to learning acrobatics with an enthusiasm that was both captivating and a bit concerning.

One afternoon, when she was just seven years old, her mother caught her in the act of thoroughly exploring herself. But instead of displaying any signs of embarrassment at being discovered in such a private moment, she bluntly informed her mother, in no uncertain terms, that she must knock next time and kindly requested that she leave and return later.

Shocked and bewildered, her mother left and walked to the barn where her husband was working. She was in such a profound state of shock that she felt torn between laughter and tears.

"What is she up to now?" her husband had asked, clearly curious about the latest development in their daughter's extraordinary life.

"She was in the midst of a period of self-discovery. She told me firmly that I should knock first before I entered the room next time and that I should come back only when she was finished with whatever she was doing."

"Yes, that's exactly what she told me last year when I stumbled upon her in the middle of it."

"What! You knew about this from last year and you never said a single word?" she confronted her husband, her shock evident in her voice.

"I honestly thought you were already aware of it and were simply keeping it hidden from me; after all, you are the mother. Mothers typically know about these things," he replied, trying to justify himself.

She let out a deep sigh then, one that carried the weight of her concerns. "What are we going to do? She's far too advanced for us to understand."

"Don't worry too much, my wife. We'll just allow her to be herself. I'm sure she will grow out of it eventually. She's only trying to understand and learn about her own anatomy," he reassured her.

"I truly hope you're right," she sighed once more, her mind still troubled.

But Ameleki never did grow out of it. It became the single most pleasurable experience in her life, and she sought to touch herself as often as she could whenever she was alone. It was as though something deep within her recognized the treasure she was given, compelling her to look at it and explore it as often as she possibly could.

When she turned twelve and began to sprout breasts, the very moment she noticed the changes, she stripped off her clothes and spent the entire day sitting in front of the mirror, engaging in a cycle of touching and examining. And touching and examining again. It was undeniably not normal.

Her parents had thought she was simply unwell. When they finally decided to check in on her, they were taken aback to find her sitting in front of the mirror, completely naked, gazing intently at herself as if she couldn't quite comprehend that the image reflected back at her was indeed her own. In a state of shock and concern, they hurriedly closed the door behind them, leaving her alone in her enthralling exploration.

As her body transformed and became more womanly, the entity within her grew increasingly fixated on her appearance; she couldn't resist touching and exploring herself with fascination. She loved her body to distraction, fully embracing her curves, and she simply didn't care who knew it.

At the age of sixteen, while exercising one of her many thoroughbred horses — an impressive stallion, a true giant among his kind — she suddenly became acutely aware of the way her breasts bounced rhythmically up and down as she rode. This newfound awareness ignited something within her, prompting her to bounce her bottom, purposefully and delightfully, up and down on the horse. The sensation was the most intense feeling she had ever experienced, and she let herself get completely lost in the moment, willingly giving the stallion full reign to move. In a powerful leap, he soared clean across the seventy-foot wide river that divided her land. As she screamed in sheer pleasure and exhilaration, it became clear to her that this was the single most surreal experience she had ever encountered; in that moment, she felt as though she was flying, her wingspan so vast that it seemed to cover nearly half the width of the river.

"You finally decided to show yourself, you freak of an earth angel," Dan chided with a bemused smirk, appearing right beside her as if he had materialized from thin air.

She was still reeling from the most amazing high she had ever experienced, feeling positively as if she was floating on an ethereal cloud of euphoria.

"Just like you to ruin my bliss. What in the world do you want?" she snapped, her annoyance barely masked by the remnants of her elation.

"Not even a little remorse, you unscrupulous addict. Earth needs you now more than ever," he replied, his voice imbued with a sense of urgency that pulled her from her reverie.

"Oh, she's actually here?" Ameleki asked Dan with a look of genuine surprise, momentarily snapping back to reality. "If she's really here, then something must be seriously wrong. What is wrong with her?"

"We're not sure yet, but we'll meet in another couple of hours, tree time," he explained, looking serious for the first time since he arrived. With that, he vanished almost as suddenly as he appeared, leaving her feeling bewildered and disoriented.

Ameleki turned back to her horse, who was grazing quietly, patiently awaiting her return. Too focused on the unsettling new information she had just received and the gravity of the situation unfolding, she allowed the stallion to lead the way, her mind racing with a myriad of anxious possibilities.

~~~~~~~~~

It was her last practice of the day. After rounding up the remaining horses and carefully settling them in for the night, she took a much-needed shower and changed into comfortable clothes.

That evening at dinner, feeling a mix of excitement and nerves, she told her parents, "I'm going to travel for a year."

The spoon fell clumsily from her mother's hand, suspended in mid-air halfway to her mouth, while her father's fork froze in place just as he was about to shovel the food into his awaiting mouth.

"I know, I know, I'm only a teenager, but it is precisely at this age that I need to explore all of my options," she continued, sensing their shock as they remained silent.

"What options do you want to explore?" Her mother, the first to regain her composure, asked slowly, picking up her spoon. She delicately put some food into her mouth and chewing the contents thoughtfully.

"I think it's time to see the world from my own perspective."

"So when are you planning on leaving?" Her father inquired gently, still trying to process the unexpected news.

"I was thinking of leaving tomorrow. There truly is no time like the present," she answered, determined not to look at them as she spoke.

The sound of the spoon clattering to the table as it fell from her mother's fingers once more was more than enough of a sign for her.

Her father cleared his throat and murmured, "I see."

"Who is going to help us take care of the farm?" Her mother expressed her deep concern, worried that neither of them knew enough about horses and other important aspects of farm management, which she felt her husband had not become involved with previously.

The farm had blossomed into a huge success, largely due to their daughter's relentless hard work, extensive knowledge, and brilliant decisions. They had miraculously acquired many thousand acres of fertile land, far exceeding anything they had ever dared to dream possible. With the chicken farm—recognized as the biggest in the entire region—thriving spectacularly well and with the numerous employees she had hired to assist both on the bustling chicken farm and in the expansive cow pasture, they felt confident and relieved, knowing they wouldn't have to worry about making any detrimental mistakes.

In addition, their farm was also the largest distributor of high-quality milk and prime beef. In total, they employed over three hundred workers, and she had recently hired another thirty dedicated individuals to specifically look after the horses.

Ameleki felt an immense sense of confidence that she could leave the farm safely in the capable hands of the nearly twenty skilled managers she had brought on board to oversee the daily operations of the business.

"The employees are there to take care of everything efficiently, so you really don't have to worry about anything. The twenty managers and Amir are all there to assist you diligently."

Amir was the head manager and her most trusted advisor.

"But can't we come with you?" Her mother wailed in a voice filled with both longing and desperation.

"You know we need a vacation too."

This unexpected plea surprised her. They had never once complained about wanting to take a vacation before, and it struck her as quite unusual.

"Alright, we have several properties in beautiful Bali, vibrant Oaxaca in Mexico, stunning Varadero in Cuba, and also in the bustling city of Hong Kong. I'll take care of all the flight arrangements so you both can leave at the end of this coming week. I'll meet you at each of these fantastic destinations, but I must be honest; I will not be able to stay with you for the entire duration of your trips. I will start my own journey first, as I leave tomorrow."

She managed to shock them once more with this announcement. They were looking at her with profound disbelief written all over their faces, and she simply smiled in response. It was a very rare display of emotion from her, and they seemed even more astonished than before. She was, indeed, the loveliest thing they had ever seen in their lives.

"Do you have any other questions," she asked kindly when they just sat there in stunned silence, watching her with wide eyes.

They knew she was truly brilliant. They should not have been so profoundly shocked at this knowledge, but somehow, they were.

When she had begun purchasing the neighboring properties after just two years of establishing her flourishing chicken farm, which began when she was around six years old on a generous piece of land they had allotted to her, they simply thought she was going to grow vegetables, much like the crops they were growing and selling themselves. But she had very different ideas.

They had enlisted helpers on the expansive plot of land they had used to cultivate a wide variety of vegetables intended for sale. The money they generated from these endeavors was diligently saved and put towards building their modest house, which had always been their primary goal before they thought about having children.

Ameleki was their only child, and they were very disappointed when they discovered they could not have any more children. They had really wanted a boy to pass on their legacy and family traditions. However, over time, that initial disappointment gradually transformed into something much more important when they realized that their remarkable female child was worth more than twenty sons combined. The small home they had purchased years prior had magnificently evolved into a stunning palatial retreat after Ameleki had finished her breathtaking work on it. She seamlessly took on the roles of architect, interior designer, and builder, creating a masterpiece that was a truly stunning sight to behold for the neighbors and anyone fortunate enough to pass by.

They had watched with a mix of curiosity and anticipation as development on the property adjacent to theirs began to unfold, and striking apartment complexes gradually took shape amidst the surrounding landscape. Over the course of a year and a half, an impressive number of apartments and houses—as many as a thousand—were constructed, transforming the area in ways no one had anticipated.

The architectural design of these modern buildings had drawn the attention of local reporters, prompting them to visit the site to take photos and inquire about the talented architects responsible for the impressive array of structures. Everyone, including her parents, was utterly shocked when they discovered that the mastermind behind the designs was their very own daughter. At the time, she was only ten years old, an age most would associate with childhood innocence rather than such remarkable accomplishments.

By the time she reached the age of twelve, her thriving chicken farm had become the largest success in the surrounding area, attracting attention and admiration from far and wide.

Many of the workers employed at the farm had transitioned into homeowners, purchasing their own apartments on the premises through manageable mortgage agreements with her. When their daughter eventually acquired additional land and invested in one hundred and fifty of the finest cows she had purchased from farmers all over the world, the need for more help arose. This led her to employ another fifty workers, who eagerly rented more apartments from her, solidifying her role as a key figure in the community.

It blossomed into a perfect community of hard-working individuals and friendly neighbors, creating a beautiful and restful place where everyone lived in an atmosphere of harmony and cooperation.

Given her strong character and proven tenacity, they really should not have been so surprised by her accomplishments. They knew her persistence and remarkable abilities, yet somehow, they managed to be shocked once again.

"I'll be in constant contact with the managers. And it's not like we don't have technology to keep us connected," she assured them.

"Don't worry; just enjoy your vacations, and I will meet you whenever I can." She reassured them, reading their worry that they would not get to see her during their travels.

She had purchased a plane ticket for a trip to Antigua, where she planned to inspect some properties she had acquired just a couple of months prior. After her time there, she intended to fly all the way to Antarctica, one of her old home, eager to reconnect with her roots and to investigate the problems.

12

THE DANCE

Marshane had been at Qingling Primary School, located in the bustling Longgang District of Shenzhen, for almost two full months now. She was already well settled into the cozy apartment provided for her by the school—a lovely one-bedroom flat situated in the apartment complex right on campus. Most of the other teachers lived there as well, creating a small community of educators. She had gotten used to being the only Nubian in this predominately Asian environment. It had taken her a few weeks to fully adjust to the cultural differences. Additionally, after her unfortunate and somewhat embarrassing mishap on the flight involving an Asian gentleman, she had been especially mindful of the words that came out of her mouth.

At school, classes had officially started two weeks ago. Although her teaching schedule wasn't overly hectic, each of her classes was packed to capacity with eager students. In every class, there were around sixty or so students eagerly waiting to learn. She had never taught such a large number of students before, which left her wondering how she was going to give each of them the attention and support they genuinely needed.

"Just reconstruct the way you focus. Instead of honing in on just one individual student, you can extend your attention to five or six at the same time."

Drawing in a deep breath and nodding her head thoughtfully at the suggestion, she took a moment to observe the many eyes of her students, all framed by expressionless faces, staring at her as she stood confidently in front of them. It was clear she was their first English teacher of the day, and with this being her very first class, it was crucial for her to set a positive tone for the subsequent English classes that would follow.

Fridays, she had discovered two weeks prior in this very classroom, turned out not to be the best day for teaching English effectively. Her previous experience had been nothing short of a disaster, and she silently prayed that this time would be vastly more successful.

She had equipped herself with a strategy and some ammunition for the task ahead—an unconventional form of positive reinforcement in the form of peppermint chewing gum, which happened to be her favorite. She was optimistic that perhaps this small bribe would encourage her students to participate more actively in the lesson.

The class was already arranged into four distinct groups, which conveniently made it easier for her to engage with individuals in each group without feeling overwhelmed. On the whiteboard, she wrote out the grading outline and clearly defined the expectations for the class. The overhead projector was already turned on, displaying her carefully prepared PowerPoint presentation on the screen.

"Good morning, class," she greeted enthusiastically, addressing the sixty or so students before her. One female student stood up abruptly and shouted something to the rest of the class. In response, they all got up as quietly as they could and greeted her in unison, "Good morning, Teacher Marshane."

"How are you?"

"I'm fine, thank you, and you?" They all responded in unison, their voices blending together harmoniously.

"I am great, thank you. Please be seated," she encouraged warmly, but to her surprise, they did not sit down as she had expected. She quickly noticed that they didn't quite understand her instructions.

Raising her right hand and pointing at one outstretched finger, she explained, "Please be seated," then pointed at her other finger and repeated, "Please have a seat." She brought the two fingers together and clarified, "Both phrases mean the same thing. 'Please be seated' and 'please have a seat' are the same."

As her explanation settled in, all the students started nodding their heads in understanding, while murmurs of "oh, oh." echoed among them.

She realized then that she needed to keep her communication simple and straightforward.

"Don't worry too much; you're doing great," her inner voice consoled her gently.

"I'm not so sure about that," she admitted quietly, still feeling a tinge of uncertainty about her teaching.

She had meticulously prepared some delightful English nursery rhymes specifically designed for the warm-up activities. She had purposefully allocated more time for this warm-up session because she had recently discovered that the children had numerous English classes throughout the day, yet they were still not engaging in conversation. Some students didn't consider English important, while others were simply too shy to speak up. She believed that if she could effectively help them condition their minds to eat, think about, and see English in a different light, they would be much more inclined to embrace speaking it. This particular class was the first opportunity she was going to get to test this hypothesis, and she had even brought along some peppermint chewing gum to enhance the experience.

She started with the familiar rhyme, "Humpty Dumpty Sat On A Wall," but before she delved into it, she presented the class with a colorful picture of Humpty Dumpty perched on the wall.

"Who is Humpty Dumpty?" she asked, eager to ignite their curiosity.

She was genuinely hoping that this engaging activity would successfully encourage the students to warm up and become more lively, rather than remaining shy and unresponsive.

Suddenly, a girl sitting in the back confidently held up her hand.

"Yes, go ahead," Marshane encouraged, her eyes sparkling with anticipation.

The student looked around nervously at her classmates before answering in a soft, shy voice, "he is an egg."

Marshane's face instantly broke out into a huge, radiant smile. "That's absolutely correct!" she exclaimed with enthusiasm.

She moved to the bag she had brought along to the class and took out a large pack of peppermint gums, eagerly opened it, and sent a gum to the girl as a reward. After that moment, it was full participation all around—the atmosphere in the room shifted completely. It made the conditioning process faster and more effective.

She recited the poem with vigor so the students could grasp the rhythm and intonation. After presenting the first line, she had the students repeating it after her, and they complied wholeheartedly. Then, she said it very loudly, and they followed suit without hesitation. Next, she said it very softly, almost like a soothing whisper, and they mimicked her gently. Then she screamed it excitedly, and they gave it their all as well. She continued this dynamic approach until the students had no need to look at the screen for the words; they were engaged and confident. She also had them learning "Jorgy Porgy Pudding and Pie," adding an extra layer of fun. Occasionally, she mixed the two poems together, cleverly guiding them to see and appreciate the differences in the words, the unique rhythm, and the varying intonations.

The students absolutely loved it. By the end of the class, most of the children were confidently speaking in simple sentences alongside her, their faces lighting up with newfound excitement and participation.

~~~~~~~~~

Dan was genuinely impressed with her remarkable skills. By the end of the class, he couldn't help but chuckle at her antics.

"You're such a cheat," he said with a playful tone, his eyes twinkling with mischief. *"But well done."*

"I knew I could do it," she replied with a hint of pride, puffing her chest out like a confident cat that had just devoured a canary.

He was trying hard to suppress his laughter, but her enormous, triumphant smile inevitably broke his resolve.

"White snow on sunny days, man, get a grip," Starr scolded him exasperatedly, materializing beside him with her familiar playful annoyance. "It's just some peppermints; what's the big deal?"

"Don't you have something important to do over at the palace? Maybe go check on Klam or something," Dan suggested, intentionally disappearing her.

He watched as Marshane walked confidently back to her office, unable to suppress the broad smile that formed on his lips. As he trailed behind her discreetly, a group of teachers caught sight of Marshane.

"Wow, can you imagine being so black? Look at her lips," one of them remarked mockingly.

They all erupted into laughter, their collective voices echoing in the otherwise quiet hallway.

As they drew nearer, Marshane greeted them with a radiant and very happy smile that lit up her face. "Good morning, dear co-workers, how are you all doing today?" She didn't wait for a response, as she continued cheerfully on her way.

Dan blinked his eyes lazily. He realized he would have to have a chat with them soon.

Her next class was scheduled for ten, but it was still only eight in the morning. He decided it would be a good idea to pay a visit to the principal — a person he knew very well.

"I see you have gotten all settled in and comfortable here," he remarked to Principal Xue, apppearing out of thin air.

Principal Xue nearly had a heart attack when he turned around and saw the unexpected apparition.

"I was wondering when you were finally going to show up," he managed to say, trying desperately not to let Dan see how terrified he truly was.

"I'm glad to see you were expecting me," Dan replied to the principal with a mischievous grin that hinted at hidden mischief, fully aware that his words weren't exactly reflective of his true intentions.

"What brings you to these parts today?" Principal Xue inquired, a slight tremor noticeable in his voice as apprehension crept in.

"I have a charge here. Just make sure she's taken care of," Dan said, his expression shifting to one of marked seriousness.

This unexpected gravity instantly captured the principal's attention. He knew all too well that Dan didn't take care of anyone; rather, Dan was notorious for getting rid of people. He personified destruction and ruination, all wrapped up in an ethereal, almost otherworldly body. The principal momentarily recalled how fortunate he was to have survived the catastrophic earthquake that had nearly obliterated the entire population of Hunan almost two hundred and fifty years ago. He quickly pushed that unsettling memory aside and asked, "Who's the person you want me to take care of?"

"The new teacher from the Caribbean."

"Oh," he responded, genuinely intrigued now, his curiosity piqued by the unfamiliar mention. "What's so interesting about this one?" he asked, hoping to draw out more information that might shed light on this enigmatic figure.

"You don't ask questions. You simply do what you're told," Dan told him calmly, his voice cloaked in an unsettling finality that hinted at deeper layers of meaning, and then, without a trace of hesitation, he vanished into thin air.

~~~~~~~~

The rest of Marshane's day had gone by beautifully, filled with moments of quiet reflection and joy. He watched her walk gracefully to her apartment, her steps light and filled with a sense of purpose, a sight he had not witnessed in a long time. She truly liked the school and her job, which ignited a passion within her. She was already contemplating innovative ways to enhance her teaching methods to better accommodate every single one of her students.

"You're doing very well. Continue with this same mode of teaching until you notice some boredom setting in; then you can thoughtfully make changes to your strategy," he advised.

"Yes, but it's still quite beneficial to plan ahead," she replied earnestly.

He watched her stifle a yawn as she opened her apartment door, knowing she was going to take a well-deserved nap, as he could see in her thoughts. Her weekend had officially begun, and after the refreshing nap, she intended to explore the expansive malls and perhaps enjoy a movie.

~~~~~~~

Marshane found herself walking towards the same beautiful garden she cherished, with its stunningly lush green grass and vibrant, colorful monarch butterflies gracefully kissing every delicate flower in view. The birds were chirping melodically, and she was feeling blissfully happy, as if nothing could dampen her spirits. The sun shone brilliantly in shades of gold, casting its warm glow down from a cloudless sky onto the vibrant green vegetation of the earth below.

The entire scenery looked like a beautiful, living painting, straight out of an artist's imagination. The trees stood tall and majestic, their expansive limbs reaching out in every direction. Covered in velvety green moss, their trunks gave off a mystical green aura that enveloped the area with a sense of enchantment. It felt truly magical.

This was the sacred place she always came to when she was feeling wonderful and content. She was dressed in a stylish two-piece green bathing suit that complemented her radiant aura, with a flowing green floral silk scarf artfully tied around her hips. The tone of her exposed skin perfectly matched the dark brown color of the tree trunks that protruded through the lush, green moss.

She was carrying her favorite green beach bag, which contained a captivating book and her keys. As she stepped onto the beach, she noticed the soft green grass spread out in front of her like a luxurious carpet until it met the shimmering edge of the water, gracefully tapering off into light beige sand. She walked over to a comfy green lounge chair that was flanked by small mahogany tables on each side. There were some inviting green towels neatly arranged on one of the tables and a refreshing glass of kiwi drink with a charming little green umbrella perched on top for representation, on the other table, beckoning her to relax and enjoy the moment.

She carefully spread the soft towel on the chair before gracefully settling herself onto it. Feeling incredibly comfortable and relaxed, she took a moment, breathing in a deep, refreshing breath of the warm, salty air. After a brief pause, she retrieved her favorite book from her bag and then reached for her drink, savoring a delightful sip that tantalized her taste buds. It was so delicious that she was absolutely certain she had never tasted anything quite like this exquisite beverage before. Gently placing her drink down on the table, she stretched languidly, feeling a satisfying release in her muscles, and then looked around, noticing that all the other people on the beach were also lounging and stretching in the radiant sun.

There were over a thousand of them, basking in their own little slices of paradise. The neatly arranged lounge chairs formed large circles around the wide, steaming, glossy green lake that glimmered under the sun's rays. Each lounge setting was precisely twelve feet away from the next, granting everyone a sense of personal space. She stood up and made her way toward the inviting water, intending to take a refreshing swim. However, instead of sinking into the cool depths, she was astonished to find herself walking effortlessly on the surface of the water. Soon, all the others joined her on the shimmering surface, too. As they came closer, she recalled that she hadn't seen them in quite a while. The truth was that she hadn't experienced true happiness for a long time, and they only seemed to appear during her blissful moments. Overjoyed, she felt an ecstatic rush at their reunion. She observed that they were all in fine health, and she could feel the vibrant energy radiating from each of them.

Marshane looked at herself from all the earth-like planets in the different solar systems and beyond. They were not all the same color; a magnificent array of hues surrounded her. Some appeared golden, others silver, with varying heights, some tall, some short, and hues ranging from white and blue to green, yellow, and many other striking colors. Their hairstyles differed dramatically as well—some sported short straight hair, while others had long, flowing locks, whether blond or beautifully nappy. A few even proudly displayed thick locks, fine sisterlocks, or bald heads of varying shades, while others had hair so long that it swept the floor. Yet, despite the differences, they were all uniquely her.

Every Marshane was blissfully happy, enveloped in an aura of joy that seemed to radiate from their very beings. They started dancing, engaging in a unique and enchanting form of movement that only they knew and cherished, a dance that flourished when they were together. They were all perfectly in sync, moving as one cohesive unit on the hardened water, resembling ethereal water sprites—beautiful, harmonious, and wonderfully aligned.

When their captivating dance finally came to an end, they returned to their lounge chairs, ready to indulge in a delightful lunch. After savoring their meal, they succumbed to a peaceful nap, where silence spoke volumes; they didn't need to utter a single word, for they already knew what each other was thinking. This was their cherished space, a sanctuary where they gathered to unwind and recalibrate—an escape from the overwhelming goings-on of their respective worlds.

She had been joining them for as long as she could remember. Only when experiencing such blissful contentment could she be in their company.

Soon, it became time for them to part ways and return to their lives. Deep down, she knew she would see them again, although the exact moment remained uncertain; she quietly promised that it would not be long at all. With anticipation bubbling within them, they all packed up their bags and exited the green beach, exchanging affectionate waves and smiles as they departed.

When she finally awoke from her serene nap, she felt an unparalleled sense of happiness coursing through her veins, one that she hadn't experienced in years. In that moment of clarity, she vowed aloud that she would never again allow the heavy burdens of the world to weigh her down, so much so that she chose to ignore them.

When they were finished they went back, each to their lounge chair, for lunch. After lunch they took a nap. They didn't need to speak, they already knew what the others were thinking. This was their space they all came together to relax and aligned themselves —away from the going ons of their worlds.

She had been meeting with them for as long as she could remember. Only when she was in that blissful state of happiness.

Soon it was time for them to return. She knew she would see them again. She wasn't sure when, but she promised it would not be long. They all packed up their bags and exited the green beach, waving at each other.

When she woke up, she was the happiest she had ever been in years and she promised out loud that she would never allow the weight of the world to bring her down, so much so, that she ignored them.

13

THE BALD EAGLE

I found myself soaring high up in the beautifully clear, cloudless noon sky, gliding effortlessly against the gentle, warm breeze and savoring the exhilarating feel of endless space surrounding me. I was an eagle, a magnificent bald eagle to be exact.

Deep down, I knew I was definitely in a dream, because I had never experienced being a bald eagle before in my life.

Since entering Materealm, I had never had a single dream, making this unexpected and vivid experience all the more astonishing and delightful. I allowed myself the moment to fully embrace the exhilarating freedom within this expansive and breathtaking landscape. As I gazed around, I realized that I had somehow returned to the vibrant sixteenth century. Suddenly, a panic surged through me; I couldn't breathe, and inexplicably, I had no wings. I was plummeting out of the sky, descending fast and hard towards the ground below. Desperately, I couldn't escape from the confines of the bird's body. It felt as if I was stuck, grappling with the chaotic rush of fear as I prepared my soul for a new beginning just moments before my inevitable impact with the earth.

Then, to my astonishment, I felt warm human hands swiftly catching me. It was Ysafari, the wise shaman whose body I had temporarily resided in, reaching out to save me.

My heart started beating again upon the sudden recognition that flooded my senses. I tried to speak, but only an odd squawking sound escaped my lips, a noise utterly foreign to me. My wings were still non-existent, a strange absence that I could not comprehend, and the lone feather on my body stood up defiantly as I attempted to converse with my rescuer.

"I know, I know. Don't bother yourself so," Ysafari reassured gently, stroking my feather-less head with a tenderness that calmed my racing pulse. He was walking home with me tucked securely in his arm, still tenderly stroking me, providing comfort amidst the chaos of my mind. I was utterly exhausted to the point of falling asleep—still grappling with the fact that my wings were missing.

I opened my eyes, just for an instant, only to find the shaman's mouth seemingly opening wide around my head in a surreal, nightmarish moment. Panic surged through me, and I squawked loudly in fear, desperately trying to break free of his tight hold, but his sharp teeth sank into my neck before I could pull away.

Suddenly, I woke up with a start, my heart beating fiercely against my ribcage, the rhythmic thumping echoing in my ears. I breathed heavily, clinging to the belief that it was only a fleeting dream.

As I looked around the spacious bedroom of the luxurious suite I was occupying, I felt a moment of relief. My king-sized bed, adorned with soft white satin sheets, was the most luxuriously comfortable bed I had ever slept in since arriving in this strange sphere. I reveled in its inviting comfort, stretching languidly as I kicked the nonsensical dream from my mind, determined to ground myself in reality.

Later, I will attempt to dissect it in greater detail, but for now, I was planning to engage in my usual morning meditation, take a refreshing shower, and then enjoy a nourishing breakfast. The mere thought of breakfast caused my belly to growl audibly, tempting me to consider bypassing my other carefully planned activities. I recognized that these cravings were merely my human desires manifesting from my ever-present human consciousness.

The more I merged with the essence of my vessel, the more my mind seemed to lose their discipline and control. I chuckled softly at the amusing thought, reveling in the feeling of intense love and appreciation I was experiencing for my own humanity.

Turning onto my other side for one final stretch before tackling task number one, I unexpectedly met the curious gaze of two ospreys perched on my shiny gold bedhead, observing me intently. I sat up, regarding them suspiciously, for they had become the most mischievous creatures I had ever encountered, their heads swiveling from my feet to my face as if they were performing some kind of delightful head dance. Instinctively, I shifted my eyes downward to my exposed feet, only to discover formidable talons instead. My body had been engaging in these strange transformations ever since I arrived here. Some mornings, I would awaken to find lion's paws and a goat body, or an alligator head coupled with chicken wings and a rabbit body. On other days, I would see an elephant's head atop my human silver body.

I used to believe that it was the two ospreys who were responsible for these bizarre changes, but I soon learned that their powers were reserved solely for Earth.

I was also beginning to understand that this peculiar earth…Materealm…was not what it appeared to be, and that reality could shift dramatically with the blink of an eye. It was a truly magical experience, so instead of panicking, I chose to embrace it.

As I looked up at the two birds, I was startled to see that in their place were two the stunning Nubian males, shirtless and adorned in flowing white silk baggy pants. They sat there, seemingly relaxed, observing me intently, as if I were their fascinating test subject.

They had been doing this peculiar thing from the very first night that Solstilert had situated me in this lavish suite of the palace, which was now three months ago. The very first time I awoke in the dead of night, I found them mysteriously hovering over me, their presence both mesmerizing and alarming. They swiftly flew off before I was fully conscious, leaving me with an unsettling mixture of curiosity and confusion. Two mornings later, I noticed they were simply perched there, silently watching me with an intensity that made my skin prickle. As I sat up in bed, they immediately took flight, disappearing as quickly as they had come. I had often wondered if I was taking up their precious space, especially when Solstilert informed me, through a telepathic connection, that I shouldn't mind their behavior. It was just their unique way of getting accustomed to me, considering I hailed from another planet and that this was all so new to them. Eventually, they ceased their flighty behavior and settled into a pattern of simply perching there, observing me intently.

I often wondered which option was worse— them flying away at the slightest motion or them scrutinizing me as if I were a specimen under a microscope.

They had only recently begun to transform into their alluring human shapes, and while I did find pleasure in admiring their masculine beauty, their constant stares felt unnerving and, quite frankly, annoying. I was well aware that they couldn't delve into my thoughts; only Solstilert possessed that particular ability, and I felt a rush of relief when she had informed me about that aspect of their powers.

"Don't you two have anything better to do with your time than to watch me so intently? I know I'm an intriguing subject, but seriously, you are really starting to get on my last nerve."

But nothing changed; they remained there, just staring at me in silence. "How exactly did you manage to get in here anyway? I thought I had... You know what! Never mind, don't answer that."

I was rambling, I know, but it was undeniably very difficult to insult them, despite my many attempts. They just sat there, radiating their undeniable beauty and enchanting magic, watching me with those captivating eyes.

Sensing their calmness, I decided to do the same thing and reached for my MP3 player resting nearby. I turned it on to Chopin's Nocturne, the soothing notes filling the air, and carefully inserted the earplugs into my ears. I crossed my legs comfortably and assumed my preferred meditation pose. I didn't close my eyes like I normally did; instead, I just intentionally watched them, my gaze unwavering, while allowing the music to wash over me. To my surprise, they moved a little closer, each positioning themselves on either side of me.

Hmm, that's certainly a first. They both emanated a delightful scent that reminded me of hot cocoa on a rainy morning—a smell that was decidedly not good for my hungry belly. To my astonishment, both took an earplug from my ear and placed it into theirs, sharing the experience with me. I observed them as they pulled the earplug from their ear, then, in an astonishing display, they materialized a solid diamond iPhone 17—an object that has yet to be seen or manifested in the real world.

One of them expertly turned the music on to what had just been playing on my MP3, and we sat peacefully like Apache Indians resting in the middle of my king-size bed. Eventually, I closed my eyes and surrendered to the music, allowing it to envelop my mind completely. I mentally left my physical vessel to explore the vast outer world. I visited different realms for half an hour before finally traveling back in time to the sixteenth century to see what Ysafari had been wanting to share with me.

"Thanks for visiting," he said with a relaxed demeanor, not looking a day over twenty-five years old.

"Did you really have to bite my neck?" I asked, giving him the intense look I had copied from

Solstilert and meticulously practiced until it had become distinctly mine.

"You've changed; you look good," he remarked. "And you, my friend, appear to look exactly the same."

"Your sister is going to change up the global landscape in ways we can hardly begin to imagine. Inform her that we don't want our landscape to be altered entirely; we simply desire more water on the lands that are currently dry and of no use to us. Additionally, we want the beings who wish to control us to be eradicated from our existence. Let her know that we are eagerly looking forward to all the positive things she will be doing to help us reach that lofty level."

Beep! Beep! Beep!

"That level?" I asked, but he disappeared at the sound of the timer going off. I slowly returned to the room with the two beautiful Nubian and Solstilert.

"You got that?" I asked my magnificently beautiful sister with the ever-changing colors, swirling around like a kaleidoscope.

She was now sixteen, still sucking her fingers in a way that reminded me of our childhood.

"*Yes. Roboliac. Thank you*," she replied, her voice soft yet full of confidence.

"*See you at breakfast*," she said, and then vanished from sight as if she were never there.

I looked at the two Nubians, raising my eyebrows in a silent question. They seemed to have understood its gravity. Seconds later, they shifted gracefully and flew out, each one leaving behind a delicate feather, light as a whisper on the wind. I carefully picked up both feathers and placed them in the growing, colorful pile nestled in a stunning golden bowl resting atop my Tiffany Range, which features a gracefully designed half-moon console that boasts its exquisite golden undertone. Feeling the comforting ambiance around me, I wandered into the spacious and well-designed bathroom that radiated tranquility. Everything within my luxurious suite brought me immense joy and contentment. In that moment, I felt transported back to my own home, on the familiar landscape of my own planet. A fleeting thought of Netty crossed my mind, and I couldn't help but hope she was safe and well.

I moved to brush my teeth with my new wooden toothbrush, accompanied by toothpaste uniquely crafted from mushroom and ash. Each morning, I eagerly anticipated using a fresh new toothbrush. Initially, I found myself worried that I might accidentally use someone else's toothbrush, but after a couple of days, I let those concerns fade and embraced the routine. I tied up my gorgeous hair, a glorious afro curl now completely silver with striking blue tips, which had stopped growing once it reached below my waist—the very same way I used to style it back in my realm. My eyes gleamed, a mesmerizing silver void devoid of pupils. I cherished the sight of every inch of my being, feeling a profound sense of appreciation for myself.

I finished brushing my teeth and slowly stripped out of my soft white satin pyjamas, relishing the sensation of the fabric sliding off my skin. With a sense of anticipation, I walked over to the ridiculously huge jacuzzi bathtub and gracefully sank into the comfortably warm, scented water, a moan of pleasure that escaped my lips.

This soothing ritual was truly my absolute favorite part of the morning. The intoxicating scent of earth after a refreshing rain, along with floral notes of sunflower and rose, mingled with the smells of freshly cut grass and rich sandalwood, all blending together seamlessly to assail my nostrils. I sank even further into the water, preparing to enjoy the next twenty minutes of delightful bliss.

Just as I was about to succumb to the dreamy embrace of sleep, Starr, my ever-dedicated trainer and one of Dan's reliable assistants, appeared in my bath. I was accustomed to her sudden appearances, and she very well knew not to disturb my serotonin and oxytocin high, so she kept quiet, surrendering herself to the inviting scent and the enveloping warmth of the water as well.

Thirty minutes later, we were finally dressed and making our way to breakfast, still blissfully under the influence of our natural chemical release that made everything feel vibrant and alive.

Suddenly, Dan appeared by our side, his expression unusually preoccupied and distant. I had never seen him in such a state of distraction.

"Your girlfriend shut you out?" Starr asked, breaking the awkward silence that had settled over us.

"Girlfriend?" Another being, a strikingly beautiful Indian female, interjected, gracefully tucking in her impressive giantess wings. "I didn't know you had a girlfriend," she remarked, her voice laced with intrigue as she regarded him with curiosity shining brightly in her captivating brown eyes. Her accent suggested she hailed from Central India.

Instead of engaging with us, Dan ignored our curious gazes and continued walking, lost in his own thoughts.

14

PURPLE QUEEN

It was a quiet Sunday, two weeks after she had ventured into unexplained territories, visiting with her intriguing selves from the myriads of earths that sprawled across the vast sky and beyond. Lately, her inner voice, which had once flourished with vibrant thoughts and ideas, had fallen silent, leaving her feeling uneasy and adrift. She worried incessantly that she might never hear it again, and the thought brought a chill to her heart. That voice was the only thing that had been keeping her going through life's complexities; without it, she couldn't fathom what she would do or who she would confide in.

Marshane was sitting on her plush sofa, utterly unable to focus on the movie that was streaming on the internet television, a modern convenience that had come with the apartment she now inhabited. It was far too early for dinner preparations, and so she found herself allowing her mind to be obsessed over the troubling absence of her inner voice. Finally, feeling overwhelmed by her thoughts, she decided to take a nap and was instantly asleep the moment her head made contact with the soft, welcoming cushions.

She found herself in a dense jungle of some sort, standing directly in front of an eye-catching purple RV affectionately named the Purple Queen. Wisps of smoke were billowing out from the front of the vehicle, creating an ominous atmosphere. A very familiar young dark-skinned woman was hunched over the RV's engine, dressed in an elegant long purple sheer dress that flowed around her like a gentle breeze. On her head sat a small silver crown adorned with striking purple stones that gleamed even in the minimal light filtering through the thick foliage. Her shoulder-length dreadlocks were perfectly held together by a bright purple scrunchy, adding a touch of flair to her appearance. Despite her attempt to maintain a calm façade, the weight of the political and racial tension hung heavily in the air; she was acutely aware that her kind was unwelcome and not safe in these parts. Taking a deep breath, she pulled out her android phone and dialed AAA, her fingers trembling slightly as she did so.

Closed the hood of the vehicle with a quiet thud, she walked slowly and deliberately toward the entrance of her RV, trying to keep her anxiety in check. Just as she reached for the bug screen door, four menacing figures emerged from the dense woods around her. They were all dressed in white, trailing billowy white sheet head coverings that concealed their faces except for two glaring holes for their eyes. Each of them held a rifle aimed directly at the young woman, and as they shouted menacingly, "Don't move nigger, where you think you're going?" her heart raced, a mixture of fear and defiance igniting within her.

Purple Queen stopped and looked at them serenely, her expression calm and composed despite the impending fate that awaited her. Preparing to meet death, she thanked the Great Mother for finally granting her the singular wish she had always dreamed of along with a multitude of other experiences she had only fleetingly imagined throughout her life. With a heart full of hope, she prayed that her next life would be even more spectacular and vibrant than this one and wished the Great Mother a truly wonderful day filled with blessings.

She stood there, patiently waiting for whatever would come next, but it never arrived in the form she had anticipated. Instead, out of nowhere, a magnificent huge white lion—boasting a snow-white mane—arrived alongside two ospreys and an Asian male, all appearing like specters summoned by divine intervention. In an astonishing display of power, they launched an attack on the four white-clad intruders. Suddenly, the rifles that had once been firmly clutched in the intruders' hands were no longer there, as the two ospreys—now transformed into formidable men—swiftly disarmed them, vanishing the weapons into thin air before they ever had a chance to pull the triggers.

She watched with wide saucer-like eyes, her heart racing as the Asian male opened his mouth wide, astonishingly managing to swallow all four men simultaneously. Purple Queen felt an overwhelming rush of confusion and disbelief; she had never witnessed anything like this—not even in the wildest scenarios depicted in movies or tales of fantasy. Panic began to bubble up within her, threatening to take over, but her mind was subtly trying to console her, whispering that it was okay, reassuring her that she was among friends and allies in this surreal situation.

Her gaze shifted towards the large white lion that was slowly prowling in her direction, its golden eyes locked onto her. It licked its lips, almost like a cat that had just caught the scent of something delicious, and then, in an enchanting twist, it transformed into the most astonishingly beautiful dark-skinned girl she had ever laid eyes upon.

"Look here, Purple Queen, dis is not a good place for yuh to be right now," she said, her voice smooth and melodic, carrying the rich accent and charming mannerisms of a Jamaican. "Yuh tribe over there suh, just a couple miles away from here, guh align yuhself with them."

As she spoke, Purple Queen felt a strange sense of urgency and empowerment.

All three males appeared by the girl's sides, standing protectively around her like loyal sentinels, their presence a comforting shield against any potential threats. Meanwhile, the Asian male walked purposefully away from the group, making his way toward the RV. To her astonishment, it roared to life the very moment he laid a firm hand on its surface, the engine producing a powerful sound as though it were brand new and more than ready for action.

Purple Queen had a profound realization; she knew she was not going crazy. The Great Mother had sent these extraordinary beings in perfect timing to save her.

"Thank you Ma'am. Thank y'all. Thank you," she expressed her gratitude to them all, giving them an elegant bow of her head before retreating into her purple house on wheels, where she promptly locked the doors behind her and drove off into the twilight.

Marshane woke suddenly from the vivid dream, her body slick with sweat and her mind racing. It was such a bizarre dream. She had thought they were gone, but it seemed they were returning. This particular dream was the most intense and vivid she had experienced in quite some time. She felt a sense of relief that the cute Purple Queen was saved, but she couldn't help but wonder, what did it all really mean?

"It's just a dream; it meant nothing. Hurry up and go get dinner."

"*Oh, you're back*," she said aloud when she heard the familiar sound. But she got no reply, leaving her with a sense of lingering uncertainty.

~~~~~~~~~

Marshane thought briefly about going to Pizza Hut, located in the Mall, which was not even ten minutes away from her cozy apartment. However, she ultimately decided against it. Recently, she had made a disheartening discovery: the people in that area had developed a rather disturbing and unsavory way of demonstrating their dislike for her.

She was particularly shocked when she first experienced this unwelcome treatment; she could hardly believe her eyes as she observed a group of strangers holding their noses at her during her initial visit to the Mall. This bizarre reaction had disturbed her so profoundly that the mere thought of heading there for dinner now completely turned her stomach. Instead, she resolved to prepare a comforting meal for herself, opting for a rich red peas stew simmered gently in creamy coconut milk, paired with flaky salmon, steamed white rice adorned with sweet corn, a refreshing salad of crisp cucumber and juicy tomatoes, and a delightful slice of moist potato pudding for dessert. To accompany her meal, she still had a jar of homemade sorrel beverage that she had crafted just a couple of days earlier, sitting in the fridge and waiting to be enjoyed.

With her enticing menu in mind, she found herself on her feet and bustling about in the kitchen, eager to whip up her amazing dinner. She chose red peas from a can, a particular brand she had recently discovered and had quickly grown to absolutely love. In less than an hour and a half, she had dinner for one elegantly arranged on the table, and just in case someone thought to drop by while she was eating, she made sure to set another place. This was a lovely habit she had developed since moving out on her own, embracing the idea of inviting connection even in solitude.

15

THE MORNING FEAST

S udan was finally living her long-awaited dream. This was not just any dream; it was one that had taken her more than two and a half arduous years to achieve. She was now confidently driving her unique seven-window school bus, which proudly featured a roof raised an impressive three feet higher than usual. The exterior of her beloved bus was painted a delightful milk coffee brown, adorned with playful pink and white ribbon-like stripes that gracefully wrapped all the way around it. With its glossy glaze finish, the bus looked as if it had rolled straight out of a factory, glimmering under the sun.

Inside, the interior of the bus resembled something out of an exquisite modern interior design catalogue, showcasing her meticulous taste and creativity. This intricate design was not only an obsession but also a necessary distraction that kept her inspired and motivated.

Every single day, she would wake up with a fresh design idea for her dream space. Initially, it was a cozy van with a high roof, but she later realized that if she was going to dream big, she might as well add a luxurious king bed to the mix. In the van, it was simply not feasible to incorporate a soundproof acoustic recording studio, which was essential for the days when she wanted to record her beloved audiobooks. This was yet another dream of hers, and one of the few ways she envisioned supporting herself while pursuing the ultimate nomadic lifestyle she had always longed for.

She had made a significant switch from a high top van to a spacious five-window school bus, but she thought to herself that adding two more windows wouldn't hurt the overall design.

She diligently researched the necessary measurements and then eagerly embarked on the intricate designing process, starting with a three-foot raised roof to enhance the bus's functionality. The color scheme was a creative aspect she had changed repeatedly, experimenting with various palettes until she found one that felt just right. To gain more inspiration and ideas, she binge-watched numerous YouTube videos, carefully noting what was too common, what was particularly effective, and what ideas simply did not resonate.

In addition to aesthetic choices, she began designing her very own innovative re-circulating water system for the shower, aiming to eliminate the worry of running out of water when it came to washing her hair, body, and even her clothes. She envisioned a properly sized dry bathroom that incorporated a composting toilet, one that should resemble what she would typically use in a regular house—a C-Head being her preferred choice. Furthermore, she meticulously planned for the pee-pipe and the waste water pipe from the kitchen to be effectively attached to the same grey water tank, ensuring efficient waste management. To manage the water effectively, she was going to install two grey water tanks, with the second tank designated specifically for the waste water from the shower, which she intended to re-circulate for sustainability.

She meticulously planned on having, at least, one hundred gallons of potable water on board, accompanied by a compact yet efficient portable washing machine. However, she found herself increasingly worried about the water she would require for essential cooking and drinking, particularly while spending extended periods immersed in the beauty of nature.

What would happen if she unexpectedly ran out of water while she was engrossed in getting familiar with the energy of the towering trees and the breathtaking, endless landscapes surrounding her? To prevent that potential crisis, she ingeniously designed another water collection system that would enable her to catch rainwater directly from the roof of her bus. This system included an advanced extra filtration mechanism to remove any microscopic particles that the rain might collect from the air as it fell. As she considered her energy needs, she realized that she would require at least four solar panels capable of emitting a total of eight hundred watts of energy. Additionally, she knew that a three-thousand-watt inverter and four lithium batteries, each one capable of storing around two hundred and fifty watts of electric power, were essential. Furthermore, she decided to include a portable gas generator for those days when the sun decided not to shine. A girl simply had to be prepared for every situation that could arise.

~~~~~~~

Before the manifestation of her long-held dreams, her everyday reality was quite tedious and overwhelmingly challenging. She found herself living with a boyfriend who was not only verbally abusive but also incredibly controlling, which made for a toxic situation that was difficult to endure. This was not a great combination for someone who was diligently working toward her baccalaureate degree at the University at Buffalo.

In addition to her studies, she was also juggling a part-time job on campus in one of the bustling food courts — a position for which she was exceedingly grateful, as it provided her with essential financial support. Without that job, she feared she would have starved time and time again. Although she desperately wanted to drop the boyfriend and find some peace, her part-time earnings simply weren't enough to cover the costs of renting a place on her own. She even contemplated leaving school, yet she understood that a BA degree was her vital ticket to securing a better job in the future. Moreover, the ever-present student loans she had taken out to finance her education served as an additional source of stress that she desperately tried not to dwell on. So she kept her head down, studied hard, suffered through the painful relationship, and frequently escaped into the comforting world of her dream bus whenever things became too unbearable to handle.

During the bustling holidays, she would diligently work three demanding jobs to begin the long-awaited repayments of her hefty student loans.

The years gradually passed by, and she finally achieved the remarkable milestone of graduating magna cum laude. The first real job she secured after her graduation provided her with the financial means to move into a cozy small studio flat. Most of the essential appliances and kitchen utensils she purchased were the very items she had originally intended to use in her future bus. Eager to progress, she started juggling two full-time jobs: one to diligently pay off her student loans and the other to cover her day-to-day bills while saving up for the purchase of her dream bus, complete with all the necessary upgrades it was going to take.

However, after receiving a substantial amount from an investment she had made, she discovered that she didn't have to work as hard anymore. Sudan made the brave decision to focus on just one job and later realized that she could work from home, she didn't even have to go into an office anymore. It turned out to be the best and most transformative opportunity she had ever experienced.

She bought the charming bus at a lively auction, it was almost brand new, making it a perfect fit for her adventurous spirit and her desire for freedom. After making the significant and life-changing decision to give up her cozy apartment, she embarked on a long and exciting drive all the way to sunny Florida, where she met her vibrant and eclectic tribe: Tusk, Barry, James, Sandy, John, Lukas, and Betty. Each of these remarkable individuals became an integral part of her transformative journey and were among the key reasons she could now proudly stand in front of her wonderfully designed bus, sporting a triumphant and radiant grin on her face, just five months after leaving her apartment behind.

In that heartfelt moment, she felt a profound wave of gratitude wash over her as she gave thanks to the God of her forefathers. The Ancient Of Days had shown immense patience and understanding in guiding her every step of the way. It was truly during this moment when she began to listen to SOURCE'S voice that real transformation, growth, and countless blessings began to unfold in her life.

~~~~~~~~

The day the entire crew gathered together to take her and her bus on their exhilarating maiden voyage, she was an absolute nervous wreck, filled with anticipation and excitement. She kept stealing glances at her beloved bus as if it might suddenly disappear in a whimsical puff of air, vanishing before her very eyes. The silly grin that plastered itself across her face made them all laugh heartily, a joyful reminder of the adventure they were embarking on together.

They drove a grueling twenty-four hours from the sunny state of Florida to the breathtaking landscapes of Maine, spanning the journey over five eventful days. The campground they were destined for was nestled deep within the enchanting Madawaska Jungle, which bordered the United States of America and New Brunswick, Canada. This drive to Maine represented the longest road trip she had ever undertaken — a fitting preview of the future she vividly imagined, where she would live on the open road and explore the wonders of the world.

Each day, they drove for a leisurely five hours, while the remaining hours were dedicated to touring the charming cities and quaint towns they encountered along the way. They took delight in capturing every unforgettable moment through pictures and videos, sharing their experiences on their lively YouTube channels, engaging blogs, and vibrant Instagram accounts.

Sudan's YouTube channel had remarkably gained her over a hundred and fifty thousand dedicated subscribers, with an impressive view count exceeding three hundred thousand enthusiastic viewers. Her channel had truly begun to flourish from the moment she released her first bus-built episode — an additional source of income she had never thought would be possible or achievable for her. She felt incredibly pleased and proud of herself for this unexpected accomplishment.

When they had finally driven into the campsite after a long journey, they were utterly exhausted yet exhilarated. They had exchanged heartfelt goodnights and turned in for the evening.

Tusk had taken the wheel of the bus during the first day, ensuring everything was functioning properly with the engine and confirming that no other critical components were falling apart. Once he was satisfied that all was well, he graciously handed the reins over to her and returned to his own bus, which was being driven by his supportive wife, Betty.

During the various stops they had made along the scenic route, Sudan had seized the opportunity to load up on essential goods and other items she needed for the final decorative touches of the bus. To show her deep appreciation to the cherished members of her tribe, she made elaborate plans to cook them a delightful feast of a breakfast on their first morning waking up in her beautiful van, nestled comfortably at their designated campsite.

She carefully prepped the succulent chicken, taking her time to ensure every piece was perfectly seasoned. She soaked the vibrant red beans in a fragrant mixture of garlic and water, letting them simmer gently on low heat for thirty minutes before finally turning off the stove. Meanwhile, she boiled a big pot of fresh sorrel infused with aromatic ginger and rosemary, allowing it to bubble and release its delightful flavors. After boiling it, she decided to leave it on the stove to marinate and deepen in taste. Later, she washed up thoroughly in her beautifully designed bathroom, appreciating the calming ambiance before turning in for the night.

Nestled on her spacious king-sized bed, she smiled hugely, expressing her heartfelt gratitude to God for the day's blessings. At precisely five-thirty, she awoke and eagerly dove into the exciting meal preparation. It had been years since she last embarked on an endeavor like this, and upon reflecting, she realized how much she had truly missed it.

Full of energy, she began singing and dancing, joyfully cooking up a storm in her very efficient kitchen while trying not to make the bus sway too much with her enthusiastic movements. By eight-thirty, the folding tables and chairs she had thoughtfully purchased and stored in the garage, at the back of the bus, were elegantly set up. She dressed up each table with charming tablecloths she had bought at Costco, adding a touch of sophistication to the setting. The tables were adorned with the exquisite china wares she lovingly brought with her from her old apartment. To top it all off, two scented bug lanterns were lit, filling the morning air with a delightful floral fragrance that complemented the cheerful atmosphere.

An electric coffee pot, a shiny electric tea kettle, and another charming small teapot filled with her favorite aromatic coffee brew were all expertly plugged into the side of the cozy bus and arranged neatly on the attached table. This table was something she had initially opposed to, resisting its placement, but after witnessing the numerous advantages it provided, she had come to agree and appreciate its presence.

As she gazed at the beautiful array of coffee pots and the charming teapot paired with delicate cups and saucers, she also admired a lovely bamboo container that housed an assortment of fragrant tea bags, not to mention the milk and sugar containers that sat alongside, complete with dainty little silver tea spoons.

This delightful setup had her smiling warmly to herself. Sudan felt a sense of satisfaction that everything was turning out fabulously. Who ever said that you couldn't live a glamorous life while fully embracing the nomadic lifestyle?

The inviting aroma of the coffee brewing wafted through the air, doing wonders to entice others nearby. A few curious heads poked out of their bus windows to investigate the source of the delightful smell that had captured their attention.

Just as Sudan was carefully placing the jugs of freshly squeezed orange juice and invigorating sorrel juice onto the table, she heard the unmistakable sound of a vehicle driving into their cheerful camping spot. It turned out to be a vibrant bright purple RV, emblazoned with the whimsical words "Purple Queen" written across its side. At this sight, most of the members of her group eagerly rushed out to see what all the commotion was about.

A young woman emerged from the RV, her long, sheer purple dress flowing gracefully around her. Atop her dreadlocks, she wore a silver crown adorned with sparkling purple stones, and her lips were painted a vibrant shade of purple that beautifully complemented her dark skin. The sound of her purple glass slippers clunking against the asphalt only added to the enchanting vision she presented in the morning light.

As the members of the tribe emerged from their buses, they stood in awe, captivated by the sight of this regal figure striding towards them.

"You won't believe me if I told you what just happened to me," she said breathlessly, "but one of my rescuers told me that my tribe was waiting for me a couple miles up the road. And seeing that y'all are the only ones within the direction she told me, I assumed you're my tribe."

Sandy, the blue-haired comedian, responded in a mock Maine accent, "Why yes, your royal purpleness, the morning feast will be served in a few. Please, grab a throne and be welcome into our oneness," giving the visitor a mocking bow.

The group erupted in laughter, but Sudan, rolling her eyes, approached the young woman and said, "Don't mind them, that's their way of saying welcome. If you want to freshen up, breakfast will be served in five minutes." She then turned to the others and repeated, "Breakfast will be served in five minutes."

While they were all busily getting ready, she busily finished bringing out the delicious food. What greeted them when they finally came back outside was something they had never seen in all their years of traveling in their trusty buses.

They all rushed back to their vehicle, eager to grab their cameras and capture the moment. For it was a breathtaking sight to behold, and not capturing it would surely be like missing the best opportunity they had ever had on their adventures.

The tables were elegantly placed on an oversized red and green oriental area rug that added charm, sitting squarely in the middle of a lush grassy patch. This setup was nestled comfortably under moon shade awnings, designed to protect the tables and the delicious food from falling leaves and pesky bird droppings. The pristine white linen cloth that covered the tables hung gracefully down to the rug, enhancing the overall picturesque scene.

The wooden stacking chairs and soft cushions perfectly matched the inviting color of the plush rug underneath. Each chair was thoughtfully placed with ample space between them, creating an illusion that the entire setting looked significantly bigger than it actually was.

The elegant green and white china breakfast set was meticulously arranged on the tables, accompanied by polished silverware that gleamed in the light.

On the tables, an array of food in vibrant, eye-catching colors was beautifully displayed, showcasing the artistry of the meal. There was ackee and salted fish, crispy bacon and fluffy scrambled eggs, and fresh slices of juicy tomatoes and crisp cucumbers. In addition, brown stew chicken, fragrant curry chicken, and a hearty vegan stew peas complemented the feast. Red peas stew was cooked in rich coconut milk, while a refreshing salad of leafy green vegetables and perfectly fried plantains added to the variety. Further enhancing the spread were delightful platters of French toast, freshly baked biscuits, and an exquisite assortment of decorated fruit platters, all strategically placed around the table for visual appeal.

It was a grand multicultural affair that made the mouth water with anticipation. Sudan knew she might have overdone it with the extensive menu, but her excitement to finally be cooking for her newfound family overwhelmed her, allowing her to indulge in the moment. She made sure to capture every detail, from the meticulous food prepping to the final laying of the table. Additionally, she set her camera for filming in a prime area—perfectly positioned right beside her chair—to document this special occasion.

She watched the frenzy in which they were enthusiastically taking pictures, and a thought crossed her mind about the delicious food that was getting cold. Luckily, she had placed the items meant to be enjoyed warm in 'keep warm' platters, ensuring they would still be at the perfect temperature.

"I really think we should dress for this special occasion," Betty said, momentarily halting her photo shoots to look down at her somewhat crushed T-shirt and frayed cut-off jeans. They all paused for a moment and exchanged knowing looks, nodding in agreement. With a burst of excitement, they rushed back to their buses to change into something more fitting.

Sudan was already elegantly dressed in her favorite long, flowing white summer dress that billowed gently around her legs, complemented by matching flat slippers. Her beautiful long locks were neatly caught up in a scrunchy, cascading down her back in soft waves.

Purple Queen emerged looking noticeably less stressed than before. Her mouth dropped open in surprise at the delightful sight that greeted her, and she felt a wave of happiness wash over her for having followed the guidance of the beautiful girl.

"Don't be shy, make yourself at home," Sudan encouraged her warmly. She made her way to the meticulously arranged tea table and poured herself a steaming cup of coffee, carefully adding just the right amount of sugar and cream. She closed her eyes in pure bliss as she swallowed the rich, tasty brew, savoring each delightful sip.

"Oh, this is undoubtedly the best coffee I have ever tasted in my life," she exclaimed to Sudan with genuine enthusiasm as she savored another rich sip.

"It's Jamaican Blue Mountain coffee, you know. Nothing but the very best for my beloved family," Sudan replied, her pride evident as she spoke shamelessly.

That comment earned a beaming smile from Purple Queen, who appreciated the gesture warmly.

The gang didn't take as long as they had initially anticipated to get ready. They all emerged, dressed beautifully in their summer best, radiating joy. It took them just a couple more minutes to adjust their cameras and set them to automatic recording mode. Once everything was in place, they took their seats around the table, laughing heartily, chatting animatedly, and expressing their gratitude while showering her with compliments on the wonderful surprise she planned.

Sudan felt a deep sense of happiness swell within her, knowing that she had done this for them. She had never witnessed them looking so blissfully happy before. It filled her heart with joy to see them enjoying themselves like this. And in that moment, she knew she had made the right choice.

16

THE OTHERWORLDLY GUESTS

A round the large and ornate table, Sudan sat at one end with Purple Queen gracefully positioned to her left and Sandy comfortably situated to her right. Beside Sandy, John was seated, glancing around the table with enthusiasm. On John's right side was Betty, who was eagerly listening to the conversation. At the very end of the table, on Betty's right, was Tusk, who commanded the attention of the group as he was at the head of the opposite end. Lucas took his place on the right side of Tusk, ready to engage in discussion. James was positioned on the right of Lucas, and Barry found his spot nestled in between Lucas and Purple Queen. "Before we proceed with our gathering, Purple Queen, why don't you share a little about yourself so we can officially embrace you as part of our family?" Tusk, the eldest of the group, said with a warm smile, looking directly at Purple. The others nodded their heads in agreement, eager to hear her introduction.

"I am Purple Queen, and I was born and raised in the vibrant streets of New York City. Six months ago, to be exact, I made the significant decision to move into my RV and embark on a journey toward Canada, passing through the beautiful landscapes of Maine. Unfortunately, during my travels, my vehicle broke down, putting me in a precarious situation where I nearly found myself in trouble. Thankfully, a kind group of people came to my rescue and encouraged me to come here, and I am genuinely grateful I decided to heed their advice."

"Welcome to our group," they each said warmly, taking turns to introduce themselves to her. "But how did you come by the unique name Purple Queen?" Sandy inquired, her curiosity piqued.

"I was born with strikingly purple hands and feet, so my father, who is a Rastafarian from Jamaica, decided to gift me with that meaningful name," she replied, smiling.

"Interesting," Lucas remarked, clearly captivated as his gaze remained fixed on the savory stew peas before them.

"Before we all dive into this delicious meal," Sudan interjected, "can we take a moment to say the prayer?"

"Since you provided us with this wonderful bounty of food to share, how about you lead us in the prayer, dear?" Betty suggested kindly. She held the role of the oldest female in the group and despite not being very religious, she was deeply spiritual and believed in the universe's greater wisdom.

~~~~~~~~

They all clasped hands tightly together as Sudan gracefully bowed her head, took a deep breath, and thoughtfully said, "Oh Ancient Of Days…" At that very same moment, in an entirely different timezone far away in China, Marshane, with her hands clasped just as firmly, reverently uttered, "Oh Ancient Of Days…"

Her thousand other selves, existing simultaneously, were perfectly aligned with her, performing the same sacred action on various spheres, across different planes, and on distant planets in a multitude of solar systems, all under the vast, endless sky that connected them.

Ysafari, in the very distant past, under that same expansive sky on this same significant day, echoed the same heartfelt prayer, saying, "Oh Ancient Of Days…"

Meanwhile, in the Rastafarian Village, nestled in the heart of Montego Bay, St. James, Jamaica, unbeknownst to them, a group of wise elders was sharing a quiet breakfast together at that very moment. The Overseer of the congregation, with genuine humility, lifted his head and earnestly said, "Oh Ancient Of Days…"

In the very freezing and crisp early morning of the Antarctic, gathered within the ethereal, invisible palace in the expansive dining room that seemed to stretch into eternity, every worthy otherworldly being, who had taken up residency on earth, was assembled, including the notable Jalaniac and Laliac. They all surrounded the grand, opulent breakfast table that was lavishly loaded with every conceivable kind of edible delicacies made specially for the esteemed members who were partakers of this momentous feast. Solstilert, magnificently beautiful and radiant, sat regally at the head of the table, while Klam, looking less silver and much more human than usual, occupied the seat to her left. On Solstilert's right sat Dan, and beside him were two strikingly handsome male beings, one positioned on Dan's left and the other on Klam's right.

Another Powerful, a formidable entity created especially to guard the earth, looked up at Solstilert, and she gracefully nodded her head in acknowledgment. Earth's vigilant guardian bowed his head reverently and closed his eyes in silent concentration. Following his lead, everyone else in the room mirrored his actions. He then opened his mouth to speak an ancient language that was incomprehensible to the majority present, except for Solstilert and a very select few, including Dan and the winged beings diligently working alongside him. After a full minute of rattling off an enigmatic string of words that filled the air with mystery, curiosity, and intrigue, he finally uttered, "Oh Ancient Of Days…"

As the past intertwines with the present, the future melds with the near and the far, the mighty harmonizes with the feeble, all voices resonated together in unison, urgently calling out on the same sacred name at precisely the same moment.

An immense and powerful ripple radiated through the globe, causing the very Earth itself to rise up, trembling and shaking in response to the collective outcry. Those souls across the vast expanse of the world who were spiritually connected to her began to cry out and scream in a cacophony of emotion, notable figures among them like Marshane, the illustrious Purple Queen; Sudan; Lucas; Klam; and Ysafari, the esteemed Overseer of the small group residing within the Rastafarian Village.

Along with them stood several others from indigenous villages, scattered far and wide around the world, all united in this pivotal moment. They stood together, moaning in a haunting chorus, as if they were collectively experiencing an excruciating pain that echoed deep within their very beings. A few indigenous individuals in various regions—spanning Africa, Europe, South America, North America, Asia, and other remote corners of the globe—who were also connected to her, though perhaps not as intensely, continued with their daily activities and sacred rituals. Some were peacefully sound asleep when they felt the unexpected ripple, accompanied by the overwhelming energy surging from the very core of the Earth itself. Those who were caught in the web of slumber awoke abruptly, startled, and rushed outside, their bodies trembling with confusion. They searched frantically for something elusive, something just beyond their grasp, something they couldn't quite see or comprehend. Meanwhile, those who had been actively engaged in their daily routines and rituals came to an abrupt halt when they sensed the disturbance. In a wave of sudden panic, they all dashed indoors, their voices rising in unison, shouting, "Go inside!!! Inside!!!"

In one united voice, the sayer of prayers collectively uttered the same heartfelt prayer, "Oh Ancient Of Days, we have gathered together in one voice and one soul, imploring you for your much-needed forgiveness. We have fallen prey to the insidious mechanisms of the other one, and now we find ourselves paying a steep price for it. Strengthen us as we prepare for the next critical phase. Open our eyes wide so that we may truly see the ones whom we are fighting against with clarity and understanding. Align us all so that we may come together in one shared consciousness, allowing us to ascend to the next level of understanding and being. We are almost there, but, regretfully, we are still too easily distracted to get any closer on our own. We urgently seek your guidance. Our bodies are weary and weak, so please let your divine spirit infuse the food that we are about to consume with strength and vitality. Grant us the nourishment we need to maintain our focus in this material world we are currently living in. Let us come to realize that without the earth, we will not be able to exist here together in harmony. We need the earth's support, and in turn, the earth needs us. Help us to restore her." The Overseer interjected, "Help us to restore her." Marshane, along with her many selves, resonated throughout the vast, limitless sky, "Help us to restore her."

Sudan pleaded, "Help us to restore her." Ysafari echoed, "Help us to restore her."

"Thank you!!!!!" A chorus of voices arose in unison. They all finished their prayers, and the profound silence that followed enveloped the globe like a thick, heavy blanket, an unprecedented stillness that no one had ever encountered before. Even the ancient trees, which often danced with the wind, dared not to stir from their rooted positions.

The partakers of the global feast gathered around the earth, every last one of them lifting their spoons in unison, dipping them deeply into the rich, vibrant red peas stew before bringing it to their lips at the same moment. They savored the moment before taking refreshing sips of the sorrel juice, which was thoughtfully poured into their drinking glasses. With a collective sigh of contentment, they all swallowed together, shattering the enchanting spell that had momentarily bound them.

17

THE TRIBE

Only three persons in the group felt the unsettling ripple that went through the earth beneath them. Purple Queen, Sudan, and Lucas sat together in a heavy silence, watching as the others eagerly delved into the food spread before them. Their expressions were solemn, filled with unspoken understanding. They knew what the ripple signified, even if they couldn't fully articulate it. A sense of foreboding hung in the air; they grasped that something significant was approaching, but they had no idea what it would entail or when it might arrive.

"Sudan, this is the best breakfast I have ever had," Tusk exclaimed from across the table, a grin lighting up his face. "My mouth feels like it's having a party!"

The others laughed their agreement, filling the room with cheerful chatter.

"I am very glad y'all liked it," Sudan responded warmly, taking her spoon and piling some fluffy scrambled eggs onto her plate. The other two, now more relaxed, followed suit and soon they too were delightfully lost in the exquisite taste of the sumptuous feast laid out before them.

The food, indeed, was the most delicious meal she had ever cooked in her life, and she felt an overwhelming sense of joy for having chosen this particular day to prepare such a feast for them. She generously shared some more of the rich red peas stew, lovingly cooked in creamy coconut milk, onto her plate and added a warm biscuit alongside two perfectly sliced pieces of golden fried plantains. As she soaked a piece of the biscuit into the aromatic stew and brought it to her mouth, a wave of flavor washed over her. It was in that moment that she truly understood what Tusk had meant when he enthusiastically exclaimed that his mouth felt like it was having a grand party. She had never experienced a taste so utterly delicious before.

Setting aside for the moment the burdens and turmoil that the world was about to face, she closed her eyes and genuinely began to savor her meal. Purple Queen was enjoying the feast in a similar manner, her plate stacked high with the flavorful stew, peas, and fluffy biscuits. A huge, contented smile spread across her face as she exclaimed, "I am really happy things ended up like this."

"I am very happy, too," Lucas said, with a warm and genuine smile that lit up his face.

It was over an hour later when they all eventually settled back into their chairs, each one of them holding their full bellies in a state of delightful contentment. The food had all been devoured, and they were utterly stuffed, basking in a profound sense of satisfaction after such a hearty meal.

Sudan thought she had perhaps cooked a bit too much, yet she was quite pleased to see it all cleared away, a clear sign that everyone had thoroughly enjoyed the meal and savored every bite. She was also cradling her belly, feeling immensely content to simply sit for the moment, listening to the cheerful songs of the birds chirping in the trees above and the gentle breeze that lazily drifted through the air, enhancing their sense of nomadic freedom and the overall joy of their gathering. This moment was truly a treasured experience that they would remember fondly and cherish for the rest of their lives.

They remained sedentary for another hour engaging in small talk and relishing the serene tranquility, when Lucas stood up and exclaimed with a note of urgency, "We have to hurry up and move out; it's not feeling safe anymore."

The group immediately sprang into action, each person quickly grabbing a couple of plates and various other utensils, determinedly taking them back to their buses, promising to wash them thoroughly and hand them over once it was safe to do so.

Sudan swiftly grabbed the colorful tablecloths, meticulously folded up the tables and chairs, and, with the assistance of their new member, returned them to her garage. They carefully collected all the coffee and tea pots that had been used during the gathering and placed them into the sink located in her bus. As for all the pots and pans that she had utilized and were now scattered about, Sudan diligently found suitable places to secure them down firmly to prevent any unnecessary movement.

Once everything was cleared away and in order, Purple Queen hurriedly ran over to her RV, while Sudan securely locked the door of her bus. She then started the engine and patiently waited for her new friend to carefully drive out before she began to follow closely behind.

Tusk was the last one to exit the campsite and felt a sense of deep relief that they had Lucas on their side. As he looked through his side mirror and utilized the back-up cameras, he was taken aback to see a group of ten individuals dressed entirely in white, with white sheets covering their heads, leaving only two small holes for their eyes visible. They ominously carried rifles, creating an unsettling atmosphere.

"One for Lucas," Betty whispered quietly, her voice barely breaking the tense silence.

"History is out in full view," he agreed, a sense of foreboding settling over them as they drove away.

18

NETTY

Netty was standing in her doorway, casually smoking a spliff and observing the relentless rain sheet falling steadily on her veranda when she suddenly felt a powerful ripple course through the earth beneath her feet. As she blew the smoke gently through the warm, damp air, a wave of dizziness and nausea unexpectedly assaulted her senses, forcing her to extinguish the spliff and swiftly tuck it behind her right ear with a slight grimace. With a sense of urgency, she headed inside to fetch a refreshing cup of cool water to drink, hoping it would help settle her stomach. As she swallowed the water in large gulps, she thought to herself, I really should stop smoking so much; it's clearly not helping.   However, the unsettling feeling only intensified, and she soon found herself violently vomiting the water back up on the floor, the taste bitter and unpleasant.

"Jesas, a wonda if mi a breed again?" she pondered loudly, feeling a knot of fear tightening in her stomach. But then she quickly recalled that she had tied up her tubes several years ago; there was no way she could possibly be pregnant, and yet the discomfort lingered, leaving her on edge.

The nausea surged through her again, a relentless wave that quickly became crippling; she collapsed onto her knees, heaving violently as she expelled more water and black, tar-like bile from her stomach. The room began to spin mercilessly around her, a dizzying blur of colors and shapes that made her feel completely disoriented. She felt utterly powerless, succumbing to the visceral urge to fall into the pool of her own vomit. The oppressive sensation intensified, clawing at her insides. In a desperate attempt to find some semblance of relief, she remembered the technique her mother had taught her in her childhood, trying to roll her chin into her chest.

Just as she was about to despair, believing she couldn't endure this horror any longer, the pain escalated to an unbearable level. This marked the second time in her life when she truly believed she might die. The first time had been while she was pregnant with Klam, when she feared she was losing the precious baby. This experience, however, felt exponentially worse. She tried to scream out for help, but no sound escaped her lips; only a series of desperate grunts emerged from her throat. Desperately, she squeezed her eyes shut, bracing herself as she tightened her muscles and kept her body stiff. She braced for whatever may come next, waiting for the torment to pass. Then, as suddenly as it had overwhelmed her, the torturous feelings vanished, leaving her sprawled helplessly in her own vomit, shocked and reeling from the unexpected absence of pain.

She laid there, fighting against the heavy thoughts of death and dying while feeling increasingly numbed to her reality. Memories flooded her mind as she revisited the moment she had received that devastating news about her mother and the baffling diagnosis they had given her when she suddenly fainted away, unable to be revived.

She couldn't shake the image of Klam, who seemed to be suffering from the same debilitating disease, and she couldn't help but wonder if it was finally catching up to her as well.

The truth was, she had not thought of her two children even once since returning from her friend's place, where she had just picked up some headache pills from her friend who worked at the Bellevue Mental Hospital.

Now, she felt a wave of guilt wash over her. She had tried her very best to keep them out of her mind, but now that death felt so imminent and close, she simply couldn't help herself.

She was still lying there on the cold, hard floor in her own vomit when she heard footsteps approaching. Someone had come up onto her veranda.

It was her sister, Norma, desperately seeking refuge from the rain that had just started, beneath a bright orange umbrella while being accompanied by two other mysterious beings that seemed to emanate an otherworldly aura.

In a moment of panic, Norma dropped the umbrella and rushed into the cramped one-room house when she caught sight of her sister lying on the floor in her own filth, her condition unmistakably dire.

"Jesas! A weh wrong wid yuh?" she exclaimed, kneeling down beside her with wide eyes filled with concern.

Netty couldn't find the strength to speak; instead, she was too captivated by the unsettling figures lingering by the orange umbrella, unable to enter the house. They looked eerily similar to the beings she had glimpsed that fateful night when she feared Klam was going to die within her.

"Mi a dead," she finally murmured to her sister, who was frantically trying to turn her over and out of the vomit that surrounded her, a grim reality settling in.

"Stop chat foolinish and help me get yuh up," Norma exclaimed, trying hard not to hiss her teeth in frustration. "Yuh fi stop di raasclaat smoking, dat's what yuh must duh. It a guh kill yuh one a dem raas day yah if you don't cut it out."

Netty could feel her energy slowly returning, and she allowed her sister to assist her in sitting up properly.

"Shut up yuh pussyclaat and guh bring mi some water inna di pan," she snapped back at her younger sister, pointing firmly under the table to where the pan was located. She was feeling a whole lot better now that she had her sister there for company, providing her a sense of comfort amid the chaos.

Norma carefully walked over to the specific spot she had just pointed out and retrieved the white pan from its resting place. She then poured some water from the white bucket into the pan with a deliberate motion. After ensuring the pan was sufficiently filled, she brought it back to her sister with purpose.

As she glanced around the room, Norma noticed some cleaning rags tucked away in a corner, under the table. She quickly gathered them up and set to work, wiping away the remnants of the black vomit that marred the floor.

"Dis a what come out a yuh when yuh don't tek care a yuhself," she said, her voice tinged with concern as she pointed at the soiled rags that had absorbed the mess.

Netty, sitting quietly in her own little world, didn't respond verbally; instead, she calmly continued wiping herself down with a clean white washcloth dipped in water mixed with some homemade soap, her expression steady and focused.

"Yuh feel the sensation coming out a di earth, earliyah?" Norma inquired, seeking connection with her sister amidst the chaos.

"Yea, it was after mi feel it, mi get sick," Netty replied, her brow furrowing slightly as she tried to understand.

"Sup'm a come, we must prepare for it," Norma lamented, her tone suggesting that they were on the brink of something significant and perhaps unsettling.

"How wi a guh prepare for something wi nuh know bout?" Netty asked, wiping down the back of her arm where some vomit was still clinging to her skin, a clear reminder of the unsettling events that had just transpired.

"Wi have to guh a Spanish Town tomorrow," Norma stated, her voice steady yet accompanied by a faraway look in her eyes, as if seeing something beyond their current reality.

"Yuh bring two ghost pon mi veranda. A good thing dem couldn't come in here, otherwise, things could have gone even worse."

"Me see dem," Netty replied, "Me nuh know weh dem a falla, falla me suh. Me notice dem the day yuh two children dem decide to disappear. It still botha mi when think about it."

Norma said with vexation, her tone laced with frustration. "Dem sey a bad luck when ghost start following yuh, but me naw sey not'n yet. Me and dem to bumboclaat."

Netty sighed heavily, trying not to let her thoughts linger on the disconcerting occurrences. She looked at the empty spots beside the umbrella where the two apparitions had lingered moments ago, their presence still echoing in her memory.

"Wi have to guh a Spanish Town first thing in a di mawning," she reiterated her sister's statement, trying to instill some positivity amidst the chaos.

Norma shook her head in agreement, deep in thought, as a heavy silence settled between them, both women grappling with their uncertain future.

She didn't leave her sister's side until she was completely certain that everything would be okay and that she had at least something substantial and nourishing in her belly.

Netty was losing weight far too quickly for anyone's comfort, which raised alarm bells in their minds. In her family, there were only two main reasons why someone experienced significant weight loss; either something was seriously wrong with the body or something was deeply troubling and distressing the mind. In any case, they were resolutely determined to uncover the truth tomorrow, no matter what it took or how challenging the journey might be.

19

THE NETTY'S IMPOSTER

Netty was up and about by three-thirty the next morning, fueled by an anticipation that she could hardly contain. She didn't bother to wash down the veranda, as was customary for her morning routine, feeling that it could wait for another day. Instead, she quickly showered and meticulously got ready for her rendezvous with her sister.

By four-fifteen, she was on the road, eagerly waiting for the familiar sight of her nephew. It didn't take long for Chris to pull up in front of her in his reliable Toyota Corolla. Without hesitation, she got into the back of the vehicle, and they drove off into the early morning. They traveled in comfortable silence to Spanish Town, where their eldest sister, a wise and intriguing voodoo priestess, resided.

An hour later, they were turning into the quaint lane that led to Priscilla's home. The sun was slowly creeping over the hills, gently basking everything in its path with its warm ambient lighting and soothing solar heat, creating a picturesque morning.

Priscilla's door was wide open when Chris turned into the spacious, beautifully designed driveway, which already had three cars parked, indicating that the morning was bustling with activity. They got out of the car, and all three walked up to the inviting porch, ready to embrace whatever awaited them inside.

Priscilla burst out of the house, her steps hurried as she rushed past the group, stopping abruptly in front of the two mysterious beings that the others had seemingly lost sight of.

"Oonuu, don't come any further, not until oonuu clearly tell me oonuu purpose for being here," she demanded with a fierce tone.

"Guarding, why oonuu guarding har?" they heard her ask, her curiosity piqued.

"Har majesty authorized oonuu to guard har? Who exactly is har majesty? And why did she choose to authorize oonuu to carry out this guard duty?"

Frustrated, she pressed on, "Not at liberty to say, huh? Oonuu better come outta me yawd and go wait fi har by the gate. Not at liberty to say? Who di raas oonuu think oonuu is?" She cursed vehemently, her words laced with indignation.

Her three visitors stood quietly, their eyes fixed on her as she approached the weathered porch, her expression betraying a clear sense of vexation.

"Oye, Norma, when yuh a come a me yawd, nuh bring yuh otherworldly beings dem come in yah," she said sharply, her tone leaving no room for argument.

"Otherworldly beings? I think dem was just ghost," Norma attempted to defend herself, her voice tinged with uncertainty.

"No, dem from a different planet, and they were instructed by her majesty to guard yuh," she replied, hoping to clarify the bizarre situation.

"Har majesty who? And guard har for what?" Netty interjected curiously before Norma could say another word, her brows furrowing in confusion.

"Dem kyaan say. Me nuh have nuh more information, suh nuh bother ask. Oonuu come inside mek me lock me door," she said, her voice rich with authority and impatience, sounding just like Netty.

Priscilla, looking much like her two beloved sisters but just a tad older, clearly inherited the intelligence and sharp wit from their mother. Her house stood tall as the largest and most beautiful in Spanish Town, specifically in Central Village, on the charming Big Lane.

"Business good for yuh, Aunty?" Chris inquired, his eyes scanning the tastefully decorated interior that reflected Priscilla's exquisite taste and flair for the aesthetics.

"In my line of work, business will always be good, my dear," she replied warmly, ushering them with a graceful wave of her hand toward the back of the house, where the inviting kitchen awaited.

She was fully expecting them, so she thoughtfully made them a delicious breakfast. As they approached the house, the nearer they got, the stronger the enticing smell of freshly brewed coffee wafted through the air. Inside the cozy, warm, and welcoming kitchen, the rich aroma of coffee permeated the space, making it feel even more inviting, and the dining table was set perfectly for five.

"Marshane come back from China?" Norma asked, her brows furrowing with concern.

"No, but I hope she come back before the disease break out, cause me nuh know why she tek herself gone suh far for," came the response, laced with worry.

"Disease? What kind a disease yuh a talk bout?" Chris inquired, his curiosity piqued.

"A disease a guh break out in a China and affect the entire world, but it will only be the beginning of something much larger. A lot of things will start happening after that, trust me. But mek we nuh talk bout that yet, mek we eat first," she concluded, trying to keep the mood light despite the gravity of her words.

They nodded in understanding and moved towards the kitchen sink, taking a moment to wash their hands thoroughly in preparation for the meal ahead. As they settled themselves comfortably around the dining table, Priscilla thoughtfully brought over a container filled with rich, red peas stew that had been lovingly cooked down in creamy coconut milk. Carefully, she served generous portions onto the plates of Norma and Chris before returning to the counter. There, she retrieved two large platters: one was filled with perfectly golden fried dumplings, while the other held vibrant, steamed callaloo, which she placed proudly on the table in front of her family.

"Suh, a weh my stew peas deh?" Netty inquired, her eyes widening as she looked expectantly at her older sister.

"No, yuh not getting any stew peas; yuh a get dis," Priscilla replied, lifting a green pot from the stove, steam wafting around her as it released an unsavory aroma. She dished out some of its contents onto Netty's plate and then took the rest back to the stove, where she carefully replaced the lid to keep it warm.

"A weh di raasclaat dis?" Netty exclaimed in disbelief, her gaze fixed on the green item that wiggled on her plate, small frogs seemingly jumping around atop the dish. "Yuh expect me fi nyam dis?" Her incredulity was evident as her face contorted in shock and confusion.

"Yuh betta hurry up and start nyam, cause if the frog dem jump off a yuh plate, a dead yuh dead," Priscilla warned in a tone they all knew far too well, a serious note laced with an unmistakable edge of urgency.

Netty, feeling the pressure of those words, grabbed a fork with determination and jabbed it into a frog that was precariously perched on the edge of her plate, her heart racing. Without giving it a second thought, she popped the slippery creature into her mouth and began to chew rapidly, barely allowing herself a moment to consider throwing her plate at her sister and storming off in dramatic fashion.

Desperate to keep the critters at bay, she skillfully maneuvered both her fork and her spoon to prevent any of them from attempting an escape. When the last frog was finally swallowed, she triumphantly picked up the plate and gulped down the gravy, savoring every drop as if it were a victory. Satisfied that she had managed to eat it all, she placed the spoon and the fork on the now-empty plate and leaned back in her chair, letting out a loud belch that echoed through the room like the rumbling of a herd of pigs.

The astonishing sound drew the attention of the others, who were watching her with a mixture of disbelief and fascination, so much so that they had completely forgotten to continue their own meals.

"Oonuu tek up oonuu plate and move. Now!!" Priscilla barked, her voice slicing through the moment like a knife.

They were a little slow to react, but just in time, they moved to see a large green snake, glistening in the light, unwinding itself with a sinuous grace from around Netty's neck to launch itself at Norma's carefully prepared red peas stew. Priscilla, sensing the urgency of the situation, rushed forward with determination and caught the snake in mid-air, where she hurriedly took it to the chopping board that was precariously placed over the kitchen sink. With swift movements, she grabbed the dangerously sharp-looking chopper and began chopping up the snake into two-inch increments, her focus unwavering despite the strange circumstances. When the entire body was completely chopped up into manageable pieces, she used the chopper to scrape the pieces into a large, shiny pot that gleamed under the kitchen lights. Taking a moment to gather her thoughts, she lit a small piece of green paper, muttered an incantation under her breath, and then threw the lit piece of paper into the shiny pot with a flick of her wrist. In an instant, the contents exploded dramatically, sending the rich scent of cinnamon and Irish moss wafting through the air, filling the kitchen with an aromatic haze.

"Me know da smell deh," Netty said with an air of certainty. "Dat bloodclaat ee see mo…"

Suddenly, another green snake, larger and more menacing than the one before, came rushing out of her mouth, abruptly cutting off the flow of her words. Priscilla sprang into action, launching herself toward the snake as it threw itself hungrily at the red peas stewed in rich, fragrant coconut milk. With quick reflexes, she caught the snake firmly by its tail, but it retaliated by turning its upper body and charging at her with startling speed. However, she was prepared. Its head landed with a thud on the extra plate, while its long body continued to wriggle furiously in her relentless grip. Remaining composed, she executed the same swift motion as before, and once again, there was a tremendous explosion, this time even louder than the last.

"Don't move, there's another one," Priscilla warned urgently, just as Netty was about to get up from her chair.

She quickly sat back down, a bit startled, as the last snake made its unsettling appearance. It uncoiled its long, sinuous body from the crown of her head, looking like the biggest of them all with its vibrant scales. The snake slowly slithered down the side of her face and then traveled down her back. It appeared to be more interested in the red peas stewed in rich coconut milk, but seemed to possess no hurry in its movements. After a moment, it decided to go back up and wrap itself snugly around Netty's upper shoulders, its tongue flicking in and out of its mouth curiously.

"Jesas Chrise, duh sup'm," Netty whispered loudly to Priscilla, her voice tremulous with both fear and disbelief.

"Shhh!" Priscilla urgently whispered as she pulled Norma closer to her.

Netty understood immediately that she should not utter another sound.

"A who send yuh?" Priscilla inquired, her eyes widening as she gestured toward the large green and brown creature that was tightly wrapped around her sister's shoulders.

"We want the body; it belongs to us," the creature declared, its voice sounding eerily alien and otherworldly.

"What body?" Netty asked, her mind racing with confusion.

"The first child's body belongs to us, and they stole it away from us," the thing moaned, its voice tinged with both anger and deep regret.

"What first child?" Priscilla continued to press, still baffled by the entire situation.

"Klam's body belongs to us," the creature insisted, its tone now resolute and demanding.

While Priscilla engaged it in lively conversation, trying to distract it with her words, Norma stealthily moved closer to it, holding the enticing red peas stew simmering in rich coconut milk. The snake, seemingly unable to resist the delicious aroma wafting through the air, slowly began unwinding itself from Netty's shoulders, inching closer to the tempting plate. Its slithering body moved with a deliberate slow grace, almost as if savoring each moment.

Finally, Priscilla seized an opportunity and swiftly threw the large chopper with precision. It caught the formidable snake, slicing it cleanly in two. Without wasting a second, she hurriedly grabbed the half with the head, while deftly picking up the other wiggling half and raced over to the sink, where she stuffed the head half securely under a kitchen bucket. The tail section she began to chop on the wooden chopping board, using a smaller chopper that proved to be less effective than desired.

"Somebody, hand me the big choppa," she ordered firmly, noticing the smaller chopper was simply too dull for the task at hand.

Norma, the swiftest and most agile out of the group, quickly reached for it and promptly brought it to her, ready to assist in this unexpected kitchen crisis.

Because this one was so big and monstrous, Priscilla began carefully chopping it up into manageable one-inch increments, meticulously scraping the pieces off into the gleaming shiny pot beneath the cutting board. She then lifted the heavy bucket to reach for the other half, but to her surprise, it was preparing for her unexpected move. It hoisted itself into the air with an unnatural ease and launched directly for her, its bottom half already regenerating with alarming speed.

Chris, sensing the imminent danger, drew his gun, and before Priscilla could scream out a warning or say "No," he was already firing at it. Each shot he fired resulted in a limb sprouting forth, grotesquely resembling Netty's features, as if mocking their horror.

"Chris, nuh shoot it," Norma urgently warned from the sidelines, but he was already locking onto his target and blazing it with more bullets than necessary. None of those rounds seemed to have any actual effect on the beast's chaotic form. Instead, more misshapen limbs continued to grow, each one weirder than the last, defying logic with their unsettling appearance.

"Bloodclaat Norma, you better tek you pickney out yah before him fire nuh more shot," Priscilla shouted urgently at her sister, her voice rising with panic.

Norma swiftly grabbed her son by the neck, pulling him out of the chaotic kitchen, desperately trying to prevent him from shooting. She returned just a minute later, swiftly locking the door behind her with a sigh of relief.

Turning her attention to Netty, she found her sister slumped in her chair, utterly exhausted to even lift a hand. Meanwhile, Priscilla was wrestling with the terrifying creature, fierce determination in her eyes.

"Weh yuh want me fi duh," Norma asked loudly above the cacophony of noise that the creature was making, almost drowning out her own voice.

"There's a silva box in a di cabinet ova yuh head, tek it out," Priscilla instructed urgently, her eyes locked on the chaotic scene unfolding before them.

Norma went into the cabinet, carefully took out the ornate silver box, and turned to hand it to Priscilla, but she was still in a desperate battle against the chopped-up pieces of snake that were now violently launching themselves, like missiles, at the misshapen creature before her. Sweat poured off her brow, dripping down her face, as she realized that all the incantations she was furiously muttering had no discernible effect on the grotesque being. The creature was growing rapidly, taking on the shape and size of Netty's body with every additional piece of severed snake parts. Minutes later, a terrifying replica of Netty, complete with a huge green and brown snake head, was standing ominously in front of them, a grotesque mockery of Netty.

20

THE PRIESTESS

I n all the years of practicing Voodoo-ism, Priscilla had never before encountered anything even remotely akin to this bizarre manifestation. The eerie Netty replica, complete with a grotesque snake head that seemed to shimmer in the dim light, was standing brazen and bold right in the center of her kitchen, looking as if it truly belonged there.

"Mi nuh mad a bloodclaat," it said defiantly, its voice cutting through the thick silence with a chilling clarity, while its tongue darted in and out of its mouth in a disturbingly snake-like manner that sent shivers racing down Priscilla's spine.

"Pass me di pussyclaat stew peas." The creature was mimicking the way Netty flashed her hands with exaggerated flair during her animated conversations, and it sounded hauntingly identical to her, to the point that a cold chill ran down Priscilla's spine. Meanwhile, Netty remained slumped in her chair, utterly unable to move, shock and disbelief clearly written all over her pale, drawn face.

"A weh yuh come from?" Priscilla asked the creature, her mind racing as she desperately tried to devise a plan to get rid of it before it could cause any harm.

Norma, standing nearby with wide eyes, was diligently trying her best not to look completely freaked out while carefully passing the plate of stew peas to the strange, unsettling creature.

"A weh me come from," it repeated disdainfully, taking the plate with a quick, jerky motion before turning to face Priscilla with an unsettling intensity that made her heart race in both fear and confusion.

It dipped its Netty-like fingers tentatively into the stew, savoring the rich aroma before bringing the morsel to its mouth. As it closed its eyes in sheer delight, a soft moan escaped its lips.

"Hmmm, earth food nice," it declared with genuine appreciation. Slowly opening its slitted, snake-like eyes, it shifted its gaze to Priscilla, a glimmer of curiosity evident in its expression. "Weh di sorrel deh?"

Priscilla instinctively glanced over the thing's shoulder and nodded toward Norma, who was standing right in front of the refrigerator with an expectant look. Without hesitation, Norma opened the fridge, retrieving a jug of vibrant red sorrel and poured some into a clear drinking glass. She then handed it to the creature, who drank thirstily, the refreshing liquid cascading down its snakelike jaw.

"A weh mi come from," it repeated, almost breathlessly, passing the empty glass back to Norma. "Put some more in a it," the creature ordered nonchalantly, barely acknowledging her presence. "I come from the planet of snakes and skins, not very far away from this earth."

"Then what yuh doing here?" Norma asked, momentarily forgetting that she was supposed to pour more sorrel into the glass in front of her. The creature turned and looked directly at her, its snake-like head bending slightly to the side as it suddenly found her utterly fascinating. It moved closer to her with an almost predatory grace, as if it couldn't help itself.

"What mi a duh yah? Death needs mi. A nuff things a guh tek place on this earth. Death a guh need us and more fi help with the attaclapse."

It took another step closer to Norma, trance-like expression painted across its unusual face.

"Yuh, a know yuh," it said, its voice a mix of hypnotized awe and utter confusion.

The creature held its hand out, eagerly requesting the sorrel refill, still maintaining its unwavering gaze upon her. With a swift movement, it lifted the glass toward its head, but abruptly slammed it down on the counter before the vibrant liquid could touch its tongue.

"Cho bumboclaat, a weh mi know yuh from?" The thing asked, its tone noticeably agitated and tinged with a hint of desperation.

Norma was deeply disappointed, for she had carelessly thrown some of the precious content from the silver box into the swirling drink. She stood there, transfixed, as she watched the creature turn and react.

In the brief minutes of distraction it afforded them, Netty had managed to gather some unexpected strength and was now standing defiantly in front of the beast, the chopper firmly gripped in her raised hand. With fierce determination, she swung the weapon with all the strength she could muster, and to everyone's shock, the snake's head fell off, landing with a sickening thud on the ground.

"Norma, quick, throw the powder on it!" Priscilla shouted urgently.

Norma, fully aware of the gravity of the situation, already had the powder clutched tightly in her hand, prepared for action. She had witnessed Netty struggle to rise and had quietly seized the opportunity to grab the chopper herself.

As Netty continued to chop at the creature with a fervor that seemed almost like she was still possessed, Norma swiftly threw the remaining contents from the antique silver box onto the grotesque creature, desperately hoping to end the nightmare once and for all.

Green liquid spewed violently out of it, splattering onto everything in the kitchen, creating a chaotic and surreal scene. The dismembered creature's torso writhed and shook uncontrollably when Priscilla, with determination, threw three pieces of the green-lit paper onto it. In mere seconds, the body was engulfed in flames that danced and flickered wildly, and then it exploded outward with a ferocious force. The deafening noise coming from the creature sounded like the rapid firing of grenades, a cacophony so unbearably loud that they each instinctively had to cover their ears.

The Netty imposter was melting and burning simultaneously, filling the kitchen with an overpowering and bizarrely nostalgic scent of cinnamon combined with Irish moss. Amidst this chaos, Priscilla remained focused, still muttering the incantation fervently, while the other two continued to clasp their hands over their ears in a futile attempt to block out the horrific sound. They stood in awe, their eyes glued to the blazing figure, watching as it slowly burned and vanished into nothingness, leaving behind an eerie silence that was almost palpable.

~~~~~~~~

Priscilla stepped into the cabinet where Norma had previously tucked away the silver box. With a sense of urgency, she reached inside and retrieved a small white vial, cautiously handing it over to Netty.

"Before yuh duh anything, tek off all a yuh clothes. There's a composting toilet positioned just behind that piece of cloth there suh. Once you settled down, chug this down yuh throat and wait for ten full minutes. Don't yuh dare move until yuh shit," she instructed, her voice firm and unwavering.

Netty lifted the cloth as instructed and followed her sister's guidance precisely. They both watched intently as she gulped down the liquid from the white vial with determination. One minute ticked by and, surprisingly, nothing happened. Three minutes passed, and still, nothing occurred. By the seventh minute, however, panic set in as she began screaming bloody murder, her voice echoing through the air at Priscilla. The torment was overwhelming as all the frogs she had hastily chewed and swallowed earlier were now forcefully making their exit, causing her immense pain.

"Dutty gal, look how me a guh fuck yuh up," she spat out angrily, glaring at Priscilla and threatening her with a temper that was boiling over.

Ten minutes passed, and in what felt like a whirlwind, it was all over. A powerful wave of relief washed over Netty, a sensation unlike any she had ever experienced before, and she slumped back against the wall, trying to catch her breath.

"Yuh can tank mi later. Hurry up and guh wash yuh shitty bottom. I've got clean clothes waiting for you in a the bathroom," Priscilla urged her, her voice firm but caring. "Yuh tuh," she then turned to Norma, her expression grim as she surveyed the mess the creature had made.

It was a full forty-five minutes later when the two re-emerged, looking fresh, clean, and surprisingly vibrant. The short curly wigs they wore only added to their newfound energy, bouncing with each step they took.

The kitchen was immaculate, every surface gleaming brightly, and the real meal was beautifully arranged on the table, just waiting for them to arrive. Chris was already there, seated comfortably, alongside Priscilla, who had also taken the time to shower and change into fresh clothes, both of them now poised and ready for the real breakfast.

"But Aunty Priscilla," Chris remarked thoughtfully, curiosity evident in his voice. "With all the ruckus that was happening here earlier, how come none of your neighbors came over to see what was going on?"

Priscilla responded gently, "The people dem used to it now me dear, and dem afraid a me too; they're simply not going to come out," she informed him, a frown etched across her face.

They still couldn't quite believe what had just transpired; the shock of it all lingered heavily in the air. They were still reeling from the events—except for Netty. She was lost in a spiral of thoughts about her children and the way she had treated them over the years. Deep down, she had wanted so desperately to stop herself from the hurtful behavior, yet she found she couldn't. Now, in this moment of reflection, she finally understood why that was. Overwhelmed by the weight of her remorse, she began to cry, her head sinking into her palms as painful memories flooded back, memories of the ways she had hurt and abused them throughout their lives.

"Me treat me pickney dem bad. Me can't believe me treat dem suh bad," she lamented, her voice heavy with sorrow. Her body shook violently with grief as the painful memories flooded back to her, making it hard to breathe.

"It wasn't yuh, Netty. It was the thing in a yuh. Hurry up and eat something before yuh get overcome again," Priscilla said, her tone gentle and encouraging, as she watched her sister struggle to regain a sense of calm.

~~~~~~~

Dan, Ameleki, and Starr were gathered in Priscilla's kitchen, intently observing everything that was unfolding around them with a sense of urgency and anticipation.

"Why didn't you help them?" Starr asked Dan, her voice a mix of genuine curiosity and deep concern.

"They had to learn how to take care of themselves in this challenging world. You heard what the creature said, didn't you?" He replied, his tone firm yet reflective, conveying his belief in their independence.

He looked over at Priscilla and gave her a reassuring nod of his head, a silent agreement passing between them that spoke volumes. She, in turn, offered him a slight nod of hers and watched with a heavy heart as all three of them turned and quietly disappeared from sight, leaving a palpable tension in the air.

Earth was in grave danger, teetering on the brink of disaster. We have to learn how to come together as a united front and fight as one if we genuinely want to survive against the looming threat that threatens our very existence. With a deep sigh that echoed her worries, she glanced at her crying sibling, feeling the immense weight of the situation bearing down on her, and sent up a heartfelt prayer to the heavens above, hoping for guidance and strength in these tumultuous and uncertain times.

21

THE VILLAGE

In the vibrant Rastafarian Village, where the wise elders had gathered for an important meeting, the rhythmic sounds of beating drums resonated through the air, accompanied by passionate chanting and the unmistakable scent of marijuana smoke that surrounded the gathering. The deep, resonant secrets that the drums were revealing were enveloping all those who had ears to hear, plunging them into a profound sense of hopelessness.

There were twelve individuals present in total: eight males and four females, each with their own stories and experiences. As one powerful chant concluded, another seamlessly began, creating a continuous flow of sound that spread throughout the surrounding communities, reaching the curious ears of the residents. They were alert and attentive, acutely aware that something was different about the way the words were intricately weaving themselves between the strong beats of the drums. The emotions stirred by these unique combinations were thick with a sense of hopelessness and impending doom.

A few of the villagers found themselves moving their bodies in rhythm to the beat, unable to resist the captivating call of the music, while others observed in trepidation, their expressions reflecting the unsettling intensity of the moment.

They knew something significant was coming, an undeniable change looming on the horizon. They understood all too well that they were living in what many believed to be the end times, yet the precise moment of when this culmination would occur remained a mystery to them.

The Rastafarian Villagers were proud descendants of those who had survived the devastating remnants of a distant past, a lineage that had been diligently observing and adhering to the first set of sacred instructions given to humankind. These time-honored instructions had been lovingly passed down through countless generations, rooted firmly in the very beginning of time itself. The trials of slavery and the myriad other tribulations of history had not been able to strip these enduring principles from their souls. They were simple, yet profound instructions: to care for the domestic animals of the earth, to cherish the flying creatures that soared through the sky, and to ensure that everyone thrived by living off the abundant vegetation provided by the earth.

Due to their diligent observation of these deeply rooted instructions, they were able to live in harmonious coexistence with the many souls who walked on four legs. Respect was unfailingly given to all forms of life, both seen and unseen, as they honored the interconnectedness of existence. They consumed the nourishing food they carefully planted in the rich soil of the land their forefathers bravely fought to protect, a legacy earned through sacrifice, blood, sweat, and tears.

They understood that the land was not merely a backdrop to their lives, but a vibrant, living entity that deserved to be treasured and treated with utmost respect and reverence. They held a firm belief that the salt that nourished their bodies should come exclusively from the wholesome food the land graciously provided. As a result, the villagers, alongside the few others around the world who faithfully observed these cherished instructions, were regarded as some of the healthiest individuals, enjoying a profound spiritual connection to the land. However, despite this harmonious existence, things were changing in ways that had not been seen before. Unlike previous times of balance and tranquility, something was markedly different, as the Elders keenly noted with growing concern.

The rulers of the earth, along with their vast global conglomerates, were steadily encroaching upon the peaceful realm. The vibrant energy radiating directly from the Rastafarian Village was shooting up into the stratosphere, creating a spectacular display that was impossible to ignore. It was drawing the attention of those who possessed the necessary advanced technology to detect such phenomena.

Their insatiable curiosity and greed was compelling them to journey to the island. Disguised in an air of altruism, they arrived with ulterior motives, intent on conquering and controlling.

It felt as if the sixteenth century was repeating itself, albeit with a modern twist in the strategies and preparations of the European colonizers. Meanwhile, on the island, those in positions of government had succumbed to a deep slumber of forgetfulness. In their negligence, the land was being surrendered to the dragons of the East, who promised development in exchange. This inattentive government had failed to uncover the hidden agenda of these forces. The dragons were determined to ensure that every last inhabitant was eradicated, treated as mere pests. However, before executing their nefarious plans, they were sending in their global developers—individuals who held no respect for anyone or anything, except for the Almighty dollar, the acquisition of knowledge, and the consolidation of power for their own nation.

Meanwhile, the majestic trees and the diverse wildlife, which had long protected the island from countless elements, both seen and unseen, were ruthlessly being destroyed, leaving the land vulnerable and exposed.

They built extensive infrastructures in exchange for the island's most valuable resources. They lent substantial sums of money to the government, fully aware of their glaring inability to repay such debts. Sending in their own people to work and reap the economic benefits, they ensured that the earnings would be swiftly forwarded back to their home country.

It was a meticulously crafted, well-thought-out plan conceived by the dragon clan. Tragically, our complacent and sleeping leaders did not possess the foresight or strategic thinking necessary to thwart such insidious plans. The capital that was supposedly lent to the government never truly existed. However, the government officials were far too gullible and severely lacked the critical thinking skills needed to comprehend the true nature of what was really transpiring around them. The dragon people went even further to secure the trust of the locals by distributing free phones and electronic notepads— items that the people genuinely needed. Unbeknownst to them, the intruders were collecting invaluable information and utilizing it to their own advantage. They carefully learned which individuals had parcels of land but lacked the means to develop them. Then, under the pretense of benevolence, they rushed in like saints to the rescue, presenting those individuals with the necessary means to build and develop their properties.

The foreigners did not lend any money to the locals; instead, they brought in their sub-par materials and employed their own men, unjustly claiming that these men were prisoners working for far less than minimum wage. Then, they proceeded to build houses on the lands that rightfully belonged to these people, all while promising that the locals would simply pay them a monthly mortgage for these structures. However, unbeknownst to the locals, the dragon people quietly eavesdropped on the conversations that the locals were having with their local banks, conversations facilitated by the phones that were ceremoniously given to them. Taking advantage of their technological prowess, they managed to hack into the banks' main systems to ensure that whatever loans the banks were poised to offer to the locals would never materialize. By the seventh month of living in these hastily constructed houses, the angry and disheartened locals were forced to hand over the entire lot. As a result, the locals were left homeless, hopeless, and filled with despair.

There was nothing that anyone could do to reverse this unfortunate outcome. An agreement was an agreement, it seemed. It didn't matter that this so-called agreement was made with cunningness or ulterior motives in mind.

The dragon people were slowly and insidiously taking over, while the sleeping locals, much like the times of long ago, were failing to see the end plot unfolding right before their very eyes.

Every corner of every street on the vibrant island was adorned with shops owned by the powerful dragons, who cleverly sold their goods at significantly lower prices, fully aware that the local people would flock to their bustling businesses. The money they made was never reinvested back into the struggling local economies; instead, it was siphoned back to their own distant country to build up their thriving economy, while the locals grew increasingly unable to support themselves. It seemed that no one truly understood the underlying issues, as the insidious practices continued unchecked.

The dragon people poured toxic poison into the ground whenever it rained, contaminating the land. They mixed harmful foreign substances into products designed for hair, skin, and body, only to sell them to the unsuspecting locals. Additionally, they used engineered synthetic materials to create products that imitated staple foods, luring the people into purchasing them to feed their hungry children.

A significant portion of the population was tragically dying from cancer and various other diseases related to poison exposure, leaving them with no clear understanding of the underlying reasons for this alarming situation. Meanwhile, the dragons of the East harbored their ultimate ambition: to bring about the destruction of the formidable Blue Mountain Peak, which stood as a stalwart guardian, protecting the land and its inhabitants from harsh elements as well as persistent invaders. To achieve their nefarious goals, they sought after the precious treasures that the mountain concealed within its ancient confines.

Under the cover of darkness, they stealthily emerged from their hidden submarines, carefully planting bombs beneath the mountain's foundation, which lay submerged beneath the deep, dark waters. When those explosives detonated, the startled inhabitants of the nation believed they were merely experiencing a series of minor earthquakes. It never even occurred to them that their once-trusted business alliance from the East was covertly attempting to destabilize their protective sentinel mountain.

The people of the land were regrettably not vigilant as they had been warned to be by the wise elders. When the next powerful earthquake resonated ominously from the towering Blue Mountain, a wave of fear engulfed them all like a dark cloud. The thought that if the formidable Blue Mountain could be made to topple, then their entire land could be brought to destruction filled their minds with dread. As they shook with terror and uncertainty, the dragon people were mockingly laughing in their faces, reveling in their panic.

These dragon-like creatures, with their sinister appearances and malevolent intentions, were scattered all over the world, digging deep into the earth and sowing their seeds of wickedness while openly mocking the faces of the innocent and frightened. They had become the earth's new predators, causing chaos wherever they went. But like all predators of the past, present, and future, the resilient earth knew how to take care of them. It was only a matter of time before nature would reclaim balance.

~~~~~~~

The few clairvoyant individuals who truly understood the gravity of the situation were desperately shouting out their warnings, but unfortunately, their impassioned voices were falling on deaf ears, and they were soon vanished into thin air.

A couple of members from the Rastafarian Village had mysteriously disappeared, leaving the remaining villagers increasingly concerned about their safety and wellbeing. The land on which the village was situated was prime real estate, highly coveted and in high demand, but the occupants were fiercely protective of their home, as they had no intention of ever selling. For the moment, they felt secure, or at least that's what they repeatedly told themselves in an attempt to quell their rising fear.

That fateful morning, as the unsettling ripple passed through the earth, those deeply connected to the land felt it surge beneath them, prompting them to hold their heads in deep lamentation. Something ominous was approaching, they sensed that much, but they were left in the dark about when it would arrive, or what it would entail.

The overseer had felt it too, an unsettling sensation that gnawed at the edges of his conscience, but he was one of the many who had consciously chosen to ignore their spiritual inclinations in favor of pursuing an endless array of selfish desires. He allowed overwhelming greed to cloud his judgment and obstruct essential matters, and as a consequence, he now found himself standing on the wrong side of the impending attaclapse.

He didn't care in the slightest; he was far too absorbed in accumulating wealth and devising strategic plans alongside the dragons disguised in the skin of people, all the while pretending to embody holiness in the eyes of his own people. Little did he realize that time was swiftly running out for him. On the following night, after the strange ripple had occurred, the dragons infiltrated the village, donning expertly crafted black skins that bore an uncanny resemblance to the individuals from the community. They were armed to the teeth with guns, tear gas, gas balls, and various other forms of deadly ammunition. Their grim mission was one of death and destruction.

They moved cautiously into the tranquil village just as the final echoes of the beating drums faded into a profound silence, and the acrid scent of marijuana smoke was replaced by the sweet, earthy aroma of cerasee flowers that were growing wild and freely along the fences and walls, dancing gently in the breeze. A small but determined army of them entered, quietly and stealthily, into the sleeping village, their footsteps barely making a sound on the ground. Two by two, they paused at each modest hut, their movements synchronized as they patiently awaited the covert signal. They held little expectation of encountering anyone outside, save for the overseer, who was presumably directing them toward the homes of the decision-makers in the village.

When the long-anticipated signal finally came, they swiftly aimed the gas balls at each door and fired, but to their bewilderment, nothing happened. In a state of confusion, they launched the tear gases at every window they could find, yet still, there was no reaction. Ultimately, they leveled their weapons at the houses where the innocents lay in peaceful slumber. Suddenly, as if summoned by some unseen force, three ethereal beings appeared: two female angels with magnificent wings that spanned wide and an Asian-looking male, radiating an aura of power. Within mere seconds, these celestial beings began rounding up all the soldiers, who were disguised as builders in their skillfully crafted black skins, along with the overseer, leaving the soldiers utterly bewildered. The ammunition that they had meticulously brought with them had inexplicably vanished without a trace.

The Asian-looking being opened his mouth wide, and an inky darkness shot out, engulfing all fifty-one men in a suffocating shroud. Except for the overseer, there was no trace of the men anywhere to be found after the mysterious Asian being closed his mouth.

The overseer lay helplessly on his back in the lush green grass, a sight both unsettling and tragic. No hands or legs could be discovered; he was reduced to just a torso with a head.

Dan approached him calmly and said with a hint of irony, "Choose your companies wisely next time." In an instant, all three beings vanished without a trace.

The following day, when the villagers woke up and stumbled upon their overseer lying on the grass, utterly defenseless and missing his arms and legs, they couldn't shake the belief that he had been viciously attacked. However, he eventually stirred and confessed to the dark deeds he had perpetrated. The other elders gathered, engaging in heated arguments over the fate of their overseer. They debated fiercely, convinced that for his treacherous actions he deserved to be put down, but surprisingly, the majority of the elders interceded on his behalf, advocating for mercy instead of vengeance.

"It's not our job to judge and do justice; it's the job of the Great Mother. She had left him breathing for a purpose."

With that profound understanding resonating in their hearts, they carefully transported him to the hospital, where the shocked doctors swiftly began to work on him, expertly repairing his broken body with advanced prosthetic arms and legs that promised to offer him a new chance at life.

After enduring a couple of long, challenging months spent undergoing extensive recovery and rehabilitation, the hospital finally discharged him. He was meant to live, but more importantly, he was meant to serve as a powerful warning to others who found themselves on a similar path.

The overseer, now fully aware of this heavy responsibility weighing on his soul, realized the importance of his role. Consumed by his thoughts, he fasted, wept, and prayed fervently for days following his departure from the hospital, desperately begging the Great Mother for forgiveness while seeking clear guidance for the uncertain path that lay ahead_

22

THE DEMON

M arshane woke up feeling very stressed, yet simultaneously relieved. The dream she experienced was incredibly vivid, filled with swirling colors and chaotic imagery that lingered in her mind. As she reflected on it, she couldn't help but worry about the people who appeared in her dream until she began conversing with herself for reassurance.

"*I really should avoid eating so much before bed; it's probably why these troublesome dreams keep coming back,*" she mused thoughtfully.

"*They are just nonsensical dreams, you shouldn't place too much thought on them,*" her inner voice gently counselled.

"*You're absolutely right,*" she conceded with a heavy sigh, feeling her thoughts gradually shift to the students she had for the first period. "*The children are changing,*" she confided to her inner voice. "*I really don't know how to handle them. There are three classes in particular that are exceptionally challenging, and I have the worst of the worst this morning."*

"Well, when you get into the classroom, if they are acting up, just use your imagination and see what would happen."

"Okay, I will try," she promised, getting ready for work with a heavy heart, reflecting on the challenges that lay ahead.

Marshane hated conflict and confrontation. She deeply valued peace and quiet in her life. That was one significant reason she had ultimately decided to leave behind Spanish Town, St. Catherine, Jamaica, and make the bold leap to Rochester, New York. Attending school and living quietly was all she ever wanted, a dream that felt increasingly elusive. But when the school fee ran out and she lacked the motivation to borrow more just so she could stay in school, it became too much to bear as she imagined all the complicated problems that could arise from her inability to repay.

Coming here to teach English had seemed like such a promising and exciting idea at the time, filled with hopes for a fresh start. She had been taken in by the innocent, demure, sweet faces of obedient kids depicted in the media, enchanted by their potential. However, the reality she faced was far from that ideal as she grappled with the indiscipline and spoiled bratty behaviors she was currently experiencing in the classroom.

They had seemed so angelic during the first couple of weeks, their innocent smiles and charming demeanor making everything feel blissful, until they gradually began to reveal their true colors.

"*You can always go home, you know*," her inner voice suggested quietly, offering a hint of an escape.

"*You're not helping me right now*," she replied to it, unkindly, feeling a surge of frustration welling up inside.

~~~~~~~~

Dan chuckled heartily at her sarcastic retort as he strolled leisurely beside her on their way to class. He could distinctly feel the rapid beating of her heart, a rhythm that seemed to resonate with his own. The overwhelming desire to reveal himself and offer her the consolation she needed was immense, but he knew he couldn't just yet. She had to see him, truly feel him, and remember the connection they once shared before he could take any steps toward comforting her in a tangible way.

He understood that she was surrounded by a pretentious group of individuals who sought to be perceived as virtuous and harmless, rather than the devourers that they genuinely were at their cores. However, he noticed that she was beginning to perceive their true colors, which would undoubtedly trouble her. That realization was precisely why he had encouraged her to tap into her imagination. He felt a keen curiosity about what visions and ideas would spring forth in her mind. With that thought, he chuckled once more, and then turned to her with a playful gaze.

"What's so funny?"

"You heard that?" he asked, his eyes widening in surprise as he looked at her intently.

"Yes, why are you so curious to see what I am going to imagine? I'm quite sure those chaotic fragments were not my thoughts at all. You know what, don't answer that; I'm already feeling like I'm losing my grip on reality."

Dan suddenly stopped short, his heart beating furiously in his chest, an intense sensation he had not experienced in centuries. He held onto it tightly, convinced it might just fly out of him at any moment.

Marshane, on the other hand, suddenly clutched her chest and doubled over, gasping for breath. "Happy thoughts, happy thoughts," she was muttering repeatedly, like a desperate mantra, seeking solace in her own words.

Dan stepped forward to stand directly in front of her, his magnificent raven-black wings fully exposed, casting a shadow over them both. She instinctively looked up at him, and in a surge of panic, quickly closed her eyes, squeezing them tightly shut.

"Oh Goddess, I can see demons. This is too much for me, oh no. Focus on happy thoughts, happy thoughts, happy thoughts...," she repeated in her mind, her thoughts racing in a frantic whirl. Just then, David, one of her brightest and most well-behaved students, came running towards her, his face lighting up with a big, infectious smile.

"Teacher Marshane, how are you today?" he asked, his enthusiasm palpable.

"I'm okay, David. Thank you for asking. Now, run along and don't be late for your next class," she replied warmly, hoping to regain her composure.

"Okay, Teacher Marshane!" he exclaimed cheerfully, bouncing away eagerly.

She watched him dash to his class with the kind of enthusiasm one might reserve for a marathon run, his small figure moving swiftly through the crowded hallway.

The little distraction helped clear her mind and alleviated the strange heaviness that had settled in her chest. When she looked up again, she realized the ominous thing that had been hovering nearby was completely gone. Breathing deeply, she took a moment to center herself, counting slowly to one hundred while reflecting on the many other versions of herselves.

"Happy thoughts, happy thoughts, happy thoughts," she chanted softly, encouraging herself to embrace positivity as she walked purposefully toward her own class.

~~~~~~~~~

Dan was watching her intently, every detail of her movement capturing his full attention. She had seen him, that much he knew. He did not dare show himself to her, yet the fact that she had perceived his presence filled him with an inexplicable joy. He was so elated, he felt like shooting up into the endless sky and soaring back down in sheer exhilaration, but he carefully contained himself while putting on an extra layer of shrouding. He chose to stay with her, not wanting to leave her side for even a moment. In truth, he knew he couldn't leave, even if he tried. They were finally making headway together, albeit small, but it was undeniably a start that held promise. He was feeling remarkably hopeful. He watched as she entered the classroom, her expression one of deep distraction, muttering softly to herself. She still carried the vision of his angelic blackness in her mind, mistaking it for something demonic. He chuckled softly to himself again, amused by her misconceptions.

~~~~~~~

In the classroom, the students were shouting noisily and throwing crumpled papers at each other, creating quite a mess while completely ignoring her presence. She took a deep breath and dedicated a few moments to writing down some important points on the whiteboard, calming herself in the process and hoping that they would be ready to pay attention once she was finished. A few of the rowdy students impulsively approached her desk and began tampering with her personal belongings, carelessly rifling through her things.

"Please put that down, and go to your seats," she firmly ordered them, trying to maintain her composure.

They tossed her belongings down onto the table with a sneer and laughed mockingly, then walked casually towards the door and out of the classroom.

Since the bell hadn't rung to signal the start of class yet, she chose to take their disruptive behavior in stride as best as she could. When the bell finally rang, she felt a sense of relief, having organized everything in a neat manner. The overhead projector was on, displaying the details of the day's lesson plan prominently on the screen, and remarkably, her frightened nerves were finally under control.

"Good morning class," she said loudly, trying her best to capture their attention amid the overwhelming chattering.

Most of the students completely ignored the ringing of the bell and were still carelessly throwing crumpled papers, screaming at one another, and running around the classroom, creating sheer chaos. A few of the students who were sitting in the front row tried to stand up and responded with half-hearted greetings. However, the loud noise echoing throughout the classroom drowned out their attempts, forcing them to reluctantly sit back down in disappointment and frustration.

She had previously complained to the head of the English department about this particularly unruly class, but when that didn't yield any positive results, she resorted to putting the disruptive students out of the classroom in a bid to regain control. Unfortunately, her supervisor soon brought them all back and sternly told her that she should not take such actions. He insisted that if the students were not interested in being taught, she should simply maintain her silence and endure the bedlam.

That revelation had truly shocked her to her core. It was at that moment she realized she was not actually there to impart knowledge or provide guidance. Instead, she was merely a figurehead for the school, a tool for the administration to secure additional funding from the government. The disappointment at that unflattering suggestion made her want to take a strap to all their little bottoms, including the bottoms of the head of the English department and her own supervisor.

She watched the students as they thoroughly ignored her, engrossed in their own conversations and distractions. Resolved to regain their attention, she decided to put on *Boss Baby*, a movie that was a definite favorite among the kids. They hurriedly took their seats and quieted down as the familiar opening scenes began to play. However, just five minutes into the movie, she turned it off abruptly.

"Good morning class," she said with a faint smile, attempting to reclaim her authority.

"Good morning, Teacher Marshane," they all responded in unison, standing up eagerly.

"How are you today?"

"I am fine, thank you, and you?"

"I'm fine, thank you very much. Please, go ahead and take your seats."

Everybody settled down with high expectations buzzing in the air, but she quickly turned the screen to reveal the lesson plan and began the class without delay.

"Teacher Marshane, where is Baby Boss?" a very innocent-looking boy—who was, in reality, the head mischief maker in the class—asked with a curious expression.

She gave him a no-nonsense look, signaling that she meant business. "The movie is not intended for you, Mark. It's specifically meant for the students who are truly good and deserving of it. So, are you being good in your actions today?" she asked him slowly and deliberately, fully aware that his English was more than sufficiently good to understand her words without any confusion.

"You beach!" another innocent-looking boy shouted at her, his voice rising in pitch with indignation, filled with a mix of surprise and anger.

"Not beach, bitch," a female student sharply corrected him in a loud whisper, trying her best to maintain some semblance of order.

"You bitch," the boy reiterated, his frustration palpable and overflowing in his tone as he struggled to express his emotions.

Marshane looked at all the students in the bustling classroom and saw firsthand what privileges could do to a person's character and perspective on life. She thought deeply about the underprivileged kids in schools such as St. Michael's Primary on Tower Street in Kingston and in other impoverished parts of Jamaica, who would do absolutely anything just to be able to learn in conditions like this. In her heart, she wished that she could somehow switch places with them, giving them the opportunity they so desperately desired.

23

THE SWITCH

S he looked intently at the little monsters, cleverly disguised in innocent children's bodies, and imagined with all her might that she could somehow switch them around. During each school session, she fervently wished for the students of St. Michael's to have the invaluable opportunity to learn everything that these privileged, spoiled beings were indulging in, and then at the end of the day, they would return to their lives of normalcy. She carefully observed as the group in front of her resorted to their mischievous behavior when they didn't receive what they desired, sparking her vivid imagination of teaching the eager students from St. Michael's Primary School, now dressed up in these bodies, right in this very classroom. The mere thought of it filled her with uncontainable joy, making her heart start to sing with delight.

"You know that if they are here learning, it will be nighttime, and this group of students would be sleeping peacefully?"

"Even better, they won't have the opportunity to misbehave or get into any trouble," she snapped firmly.

~~~~~~~~

Switching the kids around, Dan thought to himself. It was a brilliant idea that had struck him unexpectedly. Not even he had anticipated such a clever solution.

With determination, he went to work fulfilling her deepest desires and wishes. Returning to the old school she had attended many decades ago brought forth a flood of nostalgic memories that danced vividly in his mind. It was well after dusk. The empty hallways of the school were alive with the lingering essence of all the students who had ever walked its corridors since it was first constructed so many years ago. Yet amidst all this, he focused solely on the present-day students. They were all safely tucked away in their homes, nestled in their beds and on the verge of drifting off to sleep, he noted quietly. Standing in the very center of the playground, he slowly turned around, taking in the various buildings that surrounded him. He could feel all the unwanted essences he had sent filtering slowly into the empty structures, mixing intricately with the haunting memories of the past.

Focusing intently on essences that were the same ages as the students in the three classes she was teaching, he meticulously ensured that the numbers all added up perfectly. When he was absolutely sure he had gathered the correct ages and had determined the correct number of essences, he carefully transplanted them at Qingling Primary School, all the while taking the essences of the unsuspecting students from the three classes and placing them securely at St. Michael's Primary School.

The entire process was a highly technical one. It was very delicate and required utmost precision. He had to be entirely certain that the two groups were harmoniously on the same physical plane.

While the students in Jamaica were nestled in their warm beds, on the brink of falling into a deep slumber, the students in Qingling were engaged in a similar routine. They were quietly seated in their classrooms, heads resting gently on their desks—a tranquil mid-morning ritual that the entire school participated in every single day. A familiar piece of classical music floated softly through the air, creating a serene atmosphere that helped them to unwind and relax.

They were indeed very tired after waking up so early in the morning to start the school day. Soon, one by one, they began nodding off as the soothing melodies enveloped them. It was at that crucial moment, just as they were teetering on the edge of sleep, that he made the pivotal switch, finalizing the intricate process he had been working on. He had undertaken this process before, but never with such a diverse array of essences. He felt a swell of satisfaction wash over him, proud of himself for successfully accomplishing this challenging task that she had set before him.

~~~~~~~~

Finished with his task, Dan, feeling a mix of determination and frustration, proceeded to give Principal Xue an unexpected visit.

"You did not honor my words," Dan said quietly, materializing right in front of the principal.

The principal had been anticipating this confrontation. Despite his efforts to persuade the other teachers to show respect to the new English teacher, they could hardly tolerate the sight of her blackness. Their deep-seated prejudices made it clear they wanted the children to stop living in fear of heiren—the negro people. Unfortunately, he couldn't stop them from using her as a target of their disdainful practices.

"Is that so?" Dan asked, his voice low and deliberate, slowly blinking his eyes as he processed the tumultuous thoughts swirling through the principal's mind. "You of all people should know that what's on the outside doesn't truly matter."

"I'm really sorry, I will try harder," the principal begged, desperation creeping into his tone.

"Too late," Dan replied with a cold finality, opening his mouth wide as he summoned the darkness, enveloping the principal completely in a shroud of blackness and making him disappear from view. It was an action he realized he should have taken a long time ago, and in that moment, he felt a strange sense of relief.

~~~~~~~

Marshane felt a wave of relief wash over her when the bell rang, signaling the start of their mid-morning rest ritual. She let out a sigh as she observed her students placing their heads down on their desks, lulled by the soothing strains of classical music that began to fill the air around them. For a brief moment, she simply watched them, shaking her head in quiet defeat as uncertainty gnawed at her insides. It was evident that she truly struggled to know how to effectively manage this particular group of students. She had not been trained, nor had she received any thorough briefing on strategies to handle challenging behavior like what she was currently encountering. For now, however, their unexpected silence felt like a welcome reprieve. While they indulged in their much-needed rest, she took the opportunity to clean off the whiteboard and meticulously pack up her belongings, preparing herself to make an exit the instant the music came to a stop.

The entire mid-morning ritual lasted a mere fifteen minutes, but she mentally braced herself for a resurgence of their troublesome antics as soon as they opened their eyes. To her surprise, when the time came, their behavior remained calm and far more composed than she had anticipated.

However, as soon as the second bell rang, signaling the end of the class, she made her swift escape, slipping out of the door like a shadow.

Dan returned to the classroom and was met by a group of bewildered-looking kids, their faces reflecting the confusion of those who believed they were still caught in a dream. Meanwhile, he caught sight of Marshane hurrying out of the classroom in a flurry. In the ten precious minutes before the next class began, Dan worked diligently to calm all the switched souls, successfully quieting their uncertain murmurs and helping them to focus. He granted each of them the remarkable ability to both speak and understand Mandarin, opening up new avenues of communication and understanding among them.

~~~~~~~~~

Marshane entered her second most difficult class of the day and was shocked to see all the students sitting quietly, waiting for her.

She meticulously readied the whiteboard for the day's lesson, ensuring everything was in perfect order, and then turned on the overhead projector with a sense of determination. Bringing up the PowerPoint presentation she had diligently prepared for the students, she paused momentarily, taking a deep breath before turning to face the class the instant the second bell rang, signaling the beginning of a new learning adventure.

All eyes were fixed on her, waiting patiently and attentively, instead of engaging in the usual chaos of students fighting with each other, throwing papers, or recklessly shifting around the furniture while being excessively noisy.

"Good morning class," she said, projecting her voice loudly to command their attention.

"Gud mawning teacha," they all responded in unison, their greetings delivered with a familiar drawl, entirely unbothered by the expectation to rise from their seats.

She stood just a bit straighter, a hint of confusion creeping in, not quite sure what she should make of the response she had just received.

"How are you?" she inquired, genuinely curious about their well-being.

"We fine," they all drawled in that slow Kingstonian accent she knew all too well from her years of teaching. But despite their casual responses, she still wasn't entirely sure she was hearing what she thought she was hearing. So she pressed on, determined to maintain control of the classroom.

Banana, the absolute worst behaving student who seemed to thrive on chaos and despised everything about English—so much so that he consistently refused to learn anything in the class—raised his hand with an exaggerated flourish.

"Yes, Banana," she said, hoping he would continue his brief streak of compliance and be good for once.

"Teacha, wha yuh name? How comes yuh not tell we yuh name?" he asked, his hands moving animatedly as they normally did in Jamaica, drawing attention to himself like a classic showman.

"Oh Jesas, a wha dis?" She felt her heart race and almost fainted at the unexpected turn of events.

"Banana, I didn't know you could speak so much English?" she asked in a tone that carried both surprise and curiosity.

"Me nuh name Banana, Teacha. Me name Christopher. A so me name, Teacha," he replied confidently.

Marshane's heart started beating rapidly in her chest, a flurry of emotions swirling inside her. She felt as though she was about to faint from the overwhelming realization that the boy before her was indeed speaking in authentic Jamaican patois, a language that carried rich implications and a deep cultural heritage.

"Christopher, where on earth did you learn to speak like that?" she asked, genuinely curious and wanting to make absolutely sure she wasn't jumping to conclusions too quickly.

"A so me talk all de time, Teacha. Me learn fi talk in a school, a St. Michael Primary School," he replied, his voice filled with a mixture of pride and innocence.

She was freaking out increasingly. No! This couldn't be happening. She was going mad. But just to be absolutely certain about the situation at hand, she decided to call on another particularly disruptive student who often liked to sit right in front of her table during class sessions.

"Cindy, how are you doing today? Can you please tell the class what you had for breakfast this morning?" she asked with a hopeful and encouraging tone.

"Teacha, me nuh name Cindy, me name Jacqueline," the student replied confidently, turning to face the class with an assertive and proud expression. "Me eat callaloo and rice fi brekfuss dis mawning," she announced with a gleeful smile, as the other students listened with a mix of curiosity and interest, eager to hear more about her breakfast choices.

Marshane was absolutely certain she was losing her grip on reality as she watched the student quietly take her seat at the front of the classroom. She held on tightly to her clasped hands, desperately trying to prevent herself from coming apart at the seams with sheer fright.

As she smiled calmly at the students, projecting an image of serene composure, when what she really yearned to do was turn and run from the classroom, letting out a scream of panic.

"Thank you, Jacqueline," she said to the student, her heart rate escalating with each passing moment.

"Isn't this what you wished for?" her inner voice questioned, filled with doubt.

She firmly ignored that nagging thought and focused intently on the children, trying very hard to maintain a mask of calmness on her face despite the turmoil swirling within her.

Marshane didn't know which was scarier—the sight of Chinese faces that spoke with a distinctly Kingstonian accent, or the undeniable fact that what she had fervently wished for had suddenly manifested itself—and in such an incredibly short span of time. She really wanted to completely freak out in a bad way, but recognizing the tremendous opportunity they both had in front of them, she took a deep breath and steeled herself to get to work. She knew she had to scrap the lesson plan she had initially prepared and instead reinvent the day's lesson to better accommodate the new students who had unexpectedly entered her classroom.

With a sense of determination, she wrote down a few key words on the pristine whiteboard. Using her ruler as a pointer, she gestured to the words and instructed, "Repeat after me ... Teacher." With each word they pronounced in the Jamaican way, she guided them to articulate them with the proper pronunciation, putting an extra emphasis on the syllables that they tended to mispronounce, ensuring that they understood the nuances of her language.

By the end of the long day, she was walking home with a distinct pep to her step, already enthusiastically preparing her new lesson plans and feeling genuinely excited about seeing her students in the very next class.

"You're happy," her inner voice remarked playfully.

"You have no idea just how happy I am. I don't know why I didn't wish for this wonderful feeling sooner. If I had known that these kinds of wishes could actually come true, I would have definitely wished a little sooner and embraced this joy much earlier."

24

THE CHILDREN

T he next morning, when Marshane arrived at school, she was immediately met with a cacophony of strange whispers and peculiar behaviors exhibited by her teachers.

"What is going on?" she curiously inquired of one of the teachers from her department, a hint of concern in her voice.

"The principal is missing, and the students are acting very strange," the teacher replied, glancing around warily as if afraid of being overheard.

"Wow, that's really crazy," Marshane exclaimed, making a conscious effort not to appear guilty or anxious. Shifting her focus back to the unsettling situation regarding the absent principal, she probed,

"He's not at his house?" But before she could get a clearer answer, the teacher had already turned and walked away, leaving Marshane with a growing sense of unease.

Seconds later, a group of her switched students ran up to her excitedly, their voices blending into a delightful cacophony as they began talking all at once.

"Teacha, a wat is yuh name?!!!" Some eagerly asked.

"Teacha, we 'ave a new dance, yuh want to see't?!!!" Others chimed in enthusiastically.

"Teacha, a wha kine a place dis?" A third exclaimed, eyes wide with curiosity.

Marshane looked around nervously, scanning the area for any of the other teachers who might be observing this lively exchange, and felt a wave of relief wash over her when she realized she didn't see anyone nearby.

"I will answer all your questions when we are in class, but for now, it's time to go get ready for your other classes," she said firmly yet kindly.

"Awright teacha, buh-bye!!!" they all shouted enthusiastically before they dashed off to their individual classes.

She felt a wave of relief wash over her, grateful that nobody had witnessed their amusing display of camaraderie. Especially, their ability to communicate effortlessly in an unfamiliar language that she also understood quite well. As she reminisced, her thoughts drifted toward the missing principal, and she couldn't help but wonder what had really happened to him. He was never someone she had truly gotten to know on a personal level. During their brief exchanges, she often got the sense that he just wanted her gone, which left her feeling somewhat unsettled. It was his lukewarm behavior that she had used to form her judgments about the entire English department faculty.

She genuinely wished he was a little nicer; perhaps if he had been, maybe the others would have felt encouraged to be nicer as well. Unfortunately, they had continued to be mean and distant, so she learned to accept their behavior, recognizing it as a part of their cultural norms.

Her first class of the morning was the third grade, which happened to be one of her better classes. They were all seated quietly and ready for their lessons when she entered the room with a smile. It took her only five minutes to go through her regular routine, establishing a comfortable atmosphere. By the time the overhead projector was turned on and the day's lesson plan was displayed on the screen, she could feel their sadness permeating the air around her.

She turned around to make her greetings to those gathered nearby. A few faint sniffles reached her ears, slicing through the otherwise hushed atmosphere.

"What's the matter?" she asked with genuine concern, already knowing deep down what the answer might be.

"Our principal is missing, and many of the students think he won't return," the head girl of the class informed her, her voice trembling slightly with emotion.

"Why do they believe that?" she inquired, her heart sinking heavily at the troubling thought of such disheartening news.

"Because there's another teacher missing at the very beginning of the school term..." John started to explain, but Sandy abruptly cut him off, jumping in to finish his sentence.

"And nobody has even found him."

"He has not been found, yet?" Marshane asked, genuinely surprised by the situation.

"No, Teacher Marshane, nobody has found him, yet," Mary, a timid and shy girl, replied softly.

"Is there anyone actually looking for him?"

"Yes, Teacher Marshane," they all stated in unison, various expressions of concern etched across their young faces.

"Who's looking for him?" She pressed on, wanting to clarify.

"The school!!!"

"The police!!!"

"His wife and family!!!" They listed off eagerly, their voices overlapping with urgency.

"He was a bad teacher," Apple, another shy girl, interjected quietly.

"Bad? Why do you say that?" Marshane asked, her brow furrowing in curiosity.

Aware that she was getting full participation from her students, she made a concerted effort to avoid correcting them too much. She didn't want any of them to become overly self-conscious and shut down, which was a common reaction when they felt they were being closely observed. Instead, her goal was to encourage them to build confidence in their ability to speak English freely and authentically. However, it was still an English class, so she would tactfully repeat some of their statements in question form, using the correct sentence structure to guide them. Some of the students grasped what she was doing and were able to pick up on the subtle corrections without feeling too embarrassed or discouraged.

"He used to touch the girls and the boys when they went to his office," Tony was saying with earnest conviction.

"Really?" she asked, trying her best to mask her shock and maintain a composed demeanor.

"Yes, Teacher," they all replied in unison, their faces expectant and earnest.

"You mean he was a child molester?"

The revelation hung in the air, heavy with implications they had never confronted before. A few students, confused and curious, hesitantly asked what the term meant.

"A child molester is an adult who touches a child in places they absolutely shouldn't," she explained, emphasizing the seriousness of the matter.

As she spoke, she diligently wrote the definition on the whiteboard for clarity. She had learned through experience that many of the older students responded better to visual aids when it came to grasping the complexities of the English language. They often found they could read and comprehend information more effectively than they could simply listen and understand; this approach was essential for their learning.

She tried her best to encourage more attentive listening, recognizing that this area truly needed significant improvement, but today it seemed as though everyone was talking at once and not paying attention to their shyness. She certainly wasn't about to rock the boat or create any discomfort by making any potential suggestions for change.

"Yes, Teacher Marshane, he was indeed a child molester, which is why we didn't like him at all," another very shy boy stated, his voice barely rising above the chatter.

"But we really do like Principal Xue," the head girl asserted confidently.

"Our school is getting better and better because of him," added Sandy enthusiastically, eager to contribute to the conversation.

"But your Principal Xue cannot be considered a good leader if he allowed the teacher to remain here, fully aware that he was molesting the children," Marshane suggested thoughtfully.

That statement gave them something substantial to think about, stirring the stirrings of contemplation. She could see the wheels turning in their heads, processing the weight of her words.

"That's exactly what my mother said," the head girl agreed, looking around at a few classmates who were shaking their heads in disbelief.

Just then, the bell rang, signaling that there were only five more minutes left of class time.

"Please write down all the new words we covered today and create sentences using them. In our next class, we will practice using those sentences," she instructed the class with clarity and authority.

Marshane watched intently as all the students quickly rummaged through their bags in a frantic search for their writing tools, pencils, and notebooks, before they finally began writing. She was feeling rather optimistic and confident about today's class atmosphere. When a few of the students paused to put down their pens, she cheerfully said, "I do hope they find your Principal Xue soon, but if they don't, I'm sure they will discover another principal whom you will all love even more and connect with just as deeply."

The second bell rang loudly and resonantly throughout the room just as she finished her thoughts. All the students stood up in unison. "Thank you, Teacher Marshane," they all sang in bright voices.

"You are all very welcome, and please, have a wonderful day filled with joy and creativity!"

"Thank you, and you too!!!!!"

"Thank you class. You are dismissed."

She enthusiastically packed up her belongings and carefully ejected the thumb drive from the computer with a sense of accomplishment. James was diligently erasing the evidence of their lessons from off the large whiteboard, ensuring that everything was tidy for the next group. She smiled warmly at him and expressed her gratitude for his assistance.

Her next class was scheduled for two in the afternoon, which gave her a few precious hours to digest and reflect on the morning's lesson thoroughly. Walking back to her cozy apartment, she began brainstorming ideas for a lesson plan that would encourage a lively discussion in her upcoming class. She wanted to incorporate engaging topics that would naturally motivate her students to participate more actively. Her main objective was to help them understand how learning English as a second language could be incredibly beneficial in their lives.

As she approached the stairs leading to her apartment, some of her exuberant switched students spotted her and called out, "Teacha, teacha, look, me waan show yuh a new move."

Without waiting for a response, the enthusiastic student quickly tucked her uniform into her bloomers and burst into an energetic dance, showcasing the latest Jamaican dance moves to an imaginary beat, filling the hallway with laughter and joy.

Marshane was still getting used to listening to them speak in Jamaican Patois without getting freaked out, but this particular display was over the top. It was simply too much for her to process in that moment. They were going to be the death of her, she thought with a mix of amusement and trepidation.

A couple of other switched students joined in, and before she knew it, they were surrounded by an ever-growing number of curious students, all watching in wide-eyed wonder. It was so unusual to see the Asian bodies moving so freely in contrast to the Jamaican black bodies, which seemed to flow effortlessly to the silent beat of the music. This stark contrast made their display such a huge anomaly within the confines of the school. She could completely understand why the teachers were so concerned after observing this kind of behavior from students; they simply were not accustomed to such a display of freeness of spirit and movement of bodies coming from their own kind.

But she had to remind herself to allow them to be themselves and express their individuality. It was not abnormal for her to witness her own kind acting like this, as it was just another part of their cultural expression that felt completely normal to her.

"Wow, that was lovely," she praised them, her heart swelling with nostalgia as she remembered when she was their age and had also passionately loved dancing.

But this was certainly not Jamaica, and they were certainly not supposed to be behaving like Jamaicans. This kind of exuberant behavior was definitely not the norm in their context. Others around them were beginning to see them as though they were possessed by some spirited force.

"You must teach me to dance like that someday! Now, go to your next class, all of you," she ordered sternly, cutting off their attempts to speak any further.

She watched as they ran off enthusiastically toward their various classes. The girl, who had unfortunately tucked her uniform skirt into her bloomers, continued to gyrate to her imaginary music, blissfully making her way toward her classroom. The non-switched students observing this lively display were utterly in shock. The few teachers who were present and witnessed the unusual dancing looked even more flabbergasted. They stood frozen, still watching the switched girl as she rhythmically moved her waistline and her hips, gliding seamlessly toward her classroom without missing a single step.

Marshane walked away, smiling inside at the look on their faces.

"*You're happy?*" It was more of a statement than a question rather than an inquiry.

"*You have no idea. I feel like I'm going crazy sometimes, but at the same time, these switched kids are giving me such a rush of excitement. It genuinely feels like I'm no longer alone in this crazy journey."*

He watched her as she tried hard not to skip with joy to her apartment. She was glowing with such infectious happiness; it made him smile as he observed her enthusiasm. He was thinking about adjusting the students' behaviors to fit a certain mold, but he ultimately decided against it. Their spirited attitude was precisely what this school desperately needed to foster a vibrant learning environment.

25

THE EDEN-LIKE GARDEN

It was seven days after that eventful and unforgettable morning. Klam vividly remembered how Solstilert appeared to be in excruciating agony, sitting at the head of the grand table, surrounded by the energy of immensely powerful beings from all over the vast universe. Though she had skillfully concealed her suffering from the others present, I was her sister—of a sort—so I was acutely aware of the subtle ways she held herself when she was not feeling well. In that moment, she appeared even more beautiful than usual, glowing with an inner light that seemed to threaten to explode outward from her very core.

Most of the guests had only glimpsed a single captivating feature, but those of us who she allowed to come close to her were privy to the remarkable and transformative changes taking place within her.

We all had felt the palpable ripple that morning, an almost electric sensation that seemed to hang in the air. But for her, it permeated through every single living cell of her being, a deep unsettling presence that left her visibly affected. Although she had managed to keep herself upright throughout the long and solemn prayer, her young body was fidgeting, betraying the storm of emotions within. I watched every subtle move she made, each twitch of her fingers and flicker of her eyes a testament to her inner turmoil. Every single drop of sweat that ran down her forehead—the way it did when she was younger and more human—was a reminder of her struggles. Every breath she was unable to take had me on constant guard, leaving me to wonder if the human body she inhabited was the true source of her distress.

Occasionally, I would divert my attention to the large, vibrant gathering down the endless table. I had never seen so many diverse beings from different planets across the vast expanse of the universe coming together like this—except for those on my own home planet. I was utterly fascinated. I had always known that Materealm held its mysteries, some of which I had personal experience with, living in the revered body of the shaman and others. But this gathering was beyond anything I could have ever imagined. It ignited a deep curiosity within me and left me equally fascinated and bewildered by the enchanting scene unfolding before my eyes.

I looked around and caught the curious eyes of my two beloved sisters. They were gazing at me with a mixture of wonderment and intrigue in their expressions. I could sense that they were contemplating the striking similarities between me and my natural Golealm self. I didn't even need our mental bond to understand what they were feeling; the questions that swirled in their minds were clearly written all over their faces. A strong desire surged within me to go over to them and engage in light-hearted conversation for a while, but Solstilert was persistently flooding my mind with vivid images of Swofiyah, who appeared to be on the brink of tears. I understood she was urgently asking me for help, and deep down, I realized how much she truly needed me. Having me seated by her side seemed to have a soothing and calming effect on her. So, I reluctantly ignored my yearning to connect with my soul sisters and chose to remain beside my biological sister, Solstilert, offering her my silent support instead.

Everything had gone smoothly and without any significant issues. We watched the guests as they enthusiastically enjoyed each other's company and warmly greeted beings they had not seen in a long while. However, having so many high energy and powerful entities around her was clearly taking a toll on Solstilert; she simply vanished into thin air, leaving us to fully enjoy the gathering at our leisure. By that time, my sisters had moved on to engaging in socializing with other beings from our own planet, as well as those from various other planets in our expansive solar system.

The delightful breakfast ultimately ended with me heading off to training alongside the two other winged creatures, ready to embrace the next challenge.

~~~~~~~~

A week later, we found ourselves gathered for breakfast once more. While it was undoubtedly a meal, it wasn't nearly as extravagant or elaborate as the last one we had attended with Solstilert. It seemed that she was deliberately avoiding large gatherings filled with beings radiating high energy. Instead, our breakfast with her turned out to be a small, intimate affair, with just a handful of us in attendance. However, there were still more participants than the usual tight-knit group, and Solstilert once again held her usual place at the head of the table. This was the very first time we had seen her since the ripple event, and I couldn't help but notice that she did not appear to be her usual, vibrant self. A wave of concern washed over me, deepening my worry about whether her human body was indeed the source of her distress.

"Are you okay?" I asked her, silently, hoping for a reassuring response.

I initially thought she might remain silent, but to my surprise, she sent me a series of poignant images depicting Swofiyah crying. My heart ached as I gazed at those images, and I felt my eyes welling up with tears. As she stood up, I instinctively followed suit, standing beside her. I placed my arm around her waist in a comforting gesture, reminiscent of the times we shared when we were younger and smaller.

A few beings had their eyes on us, observing our interaction curiously, but Dan immediately sensed the need to shield us from their scrutiny. He quickly shifted their attention back to the breakfast, ensuring that our moment remained private.

The moment we were gently pulled out of focus, Solstilert tenderly placed her head against mine, and together we slowly made our way to her room. I carefully opened her door, allowing her to walk in first. However, before I could fully close the door behind us, she suddenly dissolved into an enormous, sprawling pile of mud that spread out across the floor. To my astonishment, the two ospreys, which seemed to have appeared from nowhere, were already there, eagerly digging into the rich, dark soil with their sharp beaks and fierce talons.

I took a moment to look around her expansive suite, admiring its vastness and grandeur. It was truly the size of a large community. Yet, instead of typical furniture and conventional human possessions, there were piles of earth strewn everywhere. The majority of these mounds were adorned with all kinds of trees, including an impressive array of fruit trees and curious bushes that sprouted with vibrant, unfamiliar colors and illuminating lights. The lively sounds of birds echoed all around us, creating a natural symphony. The suite was embraced by glass walls, allowing the brilliant sunlight to pour in, bathing everything in its warm, radiant glow. In that moment, I felt as if I had stepped into the enchanting image I had always imagined the beautiful Garden of Eden to be.

I watched intently as the two majestic eagles pecked and sifted through the thick, dark mud in a frenzy, all the while fertilizing the rich soil with their waste. I have witnessed a myriad of extraordinary events during my countless hundreds of thousands of years, but nothing quite like this. My gaze was locked onto them in rapt fascination, each movement drawing me deeper into their wild ritual. One of the eagles suddenly soared toward a door at the farthest end of the spacious room and vanished through it, only to return moments later, clutching a large snake that was wriggling frantically in its sharp talons. With great precision, it dropped the snake right in the middle of the mud, and the two eagles set upon it with fierce determination, tearing it apart and burying the severed parts along with the blood in the ever-growing pile of mud. When they finished their gruesome task, the snake was completely torn into finite pieces, leaving no trace of its existence behind. It was then that I realized, with a rush of understanding, that they were feeding the mud with essential nutrients. I continued to watch in astonishment as they each settled on opposite sides of the muddy terrain, closed their eyes, and entered a state of expectant waiting.

Making absolutely certain I wasn't anywhere near the dirt mounds, I carefully slid down to the ground, which was covered in the greenest, softest grass I had ever felt beneath me, enveloping me in its gentle embrace, and there I lingered, watching them in silent awe. A strange, hypnotic sound was emanating from the two sleeping birds, filling the air with an enchanting melody that was lulling me into a tranquil sleep, but I thought of Ysafari to prevent myself from succumbing to its soothing effects.

I sat on the ground for countless hours, utterly absorbed in the scene, watching the birds and the mysterious mound, wondering when she was going to assemble back to her old self the way she had that first time this encounter took place. I found myself questioning; was something wrong? Was it truly supposed to be like this? Or, perhaps, was it simply because she had grown so incredibly fast? Did her remarkable growth have anything to do with this strange situation?

I took stock of my own body, conscious of the same peculiar predicament I was in. Only, my body didn't transform into a pile of dirt. It, too, had evolved into a full-fledged teenager in the short span of just two months. Even though I felt perfectly normal, I was increasingly concerned that there would be some sort of aftereffect—something unpredictable that I would have no control over and would need to face alone.

I thought deeply about the remarkable growth spurt of my people. Truly, there was no real comparison to be made. Time was measured in a uniquely different way for us. We had an infinite amount of time that seemed to stretch and pass by at a wonderfully slow pace. In less than a mere span of two days, a young Golealm child could be magically transformed into a fully grown adult. However, we were not officially considered adults until we had completed a full Golealm year after our birth, which added an interesting layer to our maturation process. Interestingly, some of us continued to be treated like children even by the time we reached fifteen Golealm years, while others among us felt ready for re-procreation at that same young age. Nonetheless, many of us chose to remain single for hundreds of years, favoring the freedom to spread our wings and explore not only our vast galaxy but also realms that lay beyond.

I didn't dwell too much on the subtle half-changes my body was undergoing as it transformed into other life forms. In my own realm, we too possessed the remarkable ability to change forms, but I had not anticipated this unexpected capability emerging after my final merging. I was observing it all unfold before my eyes.

I looked over at the two majestic eagles sleeping gracefully and thought of the unforgettable moments when I, too, was an eagle, soaring through the expansive sky of the fifteenth century. A subtle envy overcame me as vivid memories of a time when I had the freedom to fly anywhere I desired, whenever I pleased, came rushing back to me. I curled into myself, wrapping my arms tightly around my knees and resting my chin gently on them.

I remained in that contemplative position for what felt like hours, pondering the strange and palpable energy that seemed to envelop our guests after the ripple had passed. What did it truly mean? Was something significant and potentially troubling on the horizon? In Golealm, we were taught not to dwell excessively on the future or linger too long in the past; we must remain grounded in the present moment. This practice made for a much simpler, more peaceful life. When we consciously focused on the present, we effectively prevented ourselves from cultivating a multitude of negative emotions that could dangerously shift our thoughts from 'what had happened' to 'what's going to happen?' Life was undeniably much more straightforward and fulfilling when we embraced the clarity of present consciousness.

The animals here on Materealm possessed that kind of present consciousness, too, which fundamentally made many aspects of my existence a lot easier for me. I clearly remembered my very first culture shock, which occurred shortly after I entered Ysafari's body. It was not just his physical form that left me awe-struck; it was the way he thought and processed reality. His mind had the past, present, and future intricately wrapped up and intertwined in one seamless experience. He spent far more time living in the past and contemplating the future than he did in the present moment, which was quite enlightening for me. As I learned to navigate my own existence in human form, I discovered that emotions can often become confused and that unrealistic ideations have the unsettling potential to turn into fallacies, easily misconstrued as the absolute truth. This profound kind of mindfulness seemed to be a distinctive mental construct of humanity. It made me wonder deep down if humans were able to think in the simplest terms — in the present, in the now — would life ultimately be better and more fulfilling for them?

As I gradually adjusted to the complexities of humanity, I also found myself contemplating life in the distinct manner that humans typically thought. It was a particularly tedious way of thinking, and it had, unfortunately, given me some of the most excruciating headaches I ever experienced in my second human body.

With this newly acquired body, I discovered that I didn't necessarily have to think using the normal mental constructs that defined the thought processes of other humans. Klam, for instance, didn't possess this particular way of thinking. It was something I would have to deliberately condition into her brain, carefully allowing it to form a kind of chemical reaction. This reaction would then attach itself to the area of the amygdala responsible for learning and memory, thereby facilitating these essential thought processes to take place. While memory and imagination are inherently natural functions of the mind, they can certainly be guided and taught to think more simply.

I didn't have to teach Klam to think simply, as she was already a very straightforward, simple-minded person who focused solely on the present moment. As a result, it became effortless for me to sit still, to fully embrace being in the present, and to forget about both the haunting past and the uncertain future. This kind of deliberate thinking prevented me from glossing over the myriad things that were not within my control, allowing for a clearer lens through which to view my experiences.

I watched in awe as the magnificent ospreys lifted up their heads and gracefully stretched their expansive wings, then extended their sharp talons. Seconds later, two beautiful males appeared, captivating my attention completely. They were shirtless, showcasing their toned physiques, and donned loose, white baggy pants that reached down to their knees. I lifted my head slightly and observed them as they steadily walked towards the vibrant fruit trees, some varieties of which I had never encountered in my lifetime on Earth. They continued their journey a little further to a very unusual tree, perfectly aligned with the sun's rays, and picked two of its strikingly vivid fruits. They were the most delicious-looking things I had ever seen, glistening temptingly in the sunlight. My mouth watered immediately at the enticing sight of them, and I felt an overwhelming desire to taste their sweetness.

It was a warm and tranquil evening, and I found myself feeling quite weak as I had hardly eaten any breakfast and had completely missed lunch. My stomach growled, reminding me just how hungry I was becoming. I watched with keen interest as they picked a few more vibrant fruits from the various trees, their laughter mingling with the sounds of nature. When their arms became too full to pick any more of the luscious offerings, they turned and walked back towards the makeshift pile of mud. I observed them as they carefully placed some of the mouth-watering fruits—alongside the two special fruits that I couldn't seem to take my eyes off—from their arms onto the beautiful, soft grass surrounding the mound, and then brought the remainder over to me. My gaze returned to the two exquisite fruits, and

I noticed unsettling movements in the grass as things began to emerge, seemingly intent on attacking them. I had unwrapped my body from its previous position and was now sitting cross-legged on the grass, feeling the cool blades beneath me. With cautious hands, I collected the fruits and placed them securely in my lap. After witnessing what had unfolded with the fruits they had carelessly set upon the grass around the mud mound, I was no longer convinced I could trust the ground or the grass with my precious bounty.

I reached for one of the strange-looking fruits, its colors unlike anything I had ever encountered on this planet, or even back on my home world. With great care, I delicately wiped the fruit against my clothing, wiping away any potential dirt, then cautiously bit into it, eager to discover its flavor.

Nothing I had ever tasted here, or even on Golealm, had ever prepared me for the incredible flavor that flooded my mouth. I closed my eyes and let out a soft moan, reveling in the delightful taste that attacked my senses with an intensity I had never experienced before. With every bite I took, I felt as if I was splintered, overwhelmed in the most delicious way imaginable. "Hmmmm!" I moaned loudly, utterly unable to control myself at that moment. The sweet juice of the fruit began to run down my chin, creating a sticky sensation that only added to the pleasure of the experience.

My body was feeling exquisite, overwhelmingly strong and dangerously electrifying, all at the same time. I felt the intoxicating power of the fruit coursing through my blood, igniting my bones, and saturating my very flesh. I wanted to shoot up into the air like a rocket taking off into the cosmos, breaking free from earthly confines. I longed to lift the entire earth off its axis, defying gravity and the laws of nature. I envisioned ripping my clothes off in a frantic fit and sprinting to the North Pole, feeling the chill of freedom in my veins. I couldn't take it any longer. I was going utterly crazy with the tumult brewing inside me. I wanted to pull my hair out in sheer desperation. The urge to claw at the grass beneath me was overpowering. I wanted to throw myself at the two stunning males who stood nearby, consumed by an uncontainable desire. The impulse to rip my heart out of my chest felt almost sweet. I wanted to scream bloody murder, letting my anguish echo through the night air. I wanted to stand up and leap as if I were a proud Zulu warrior, filled with fierce spirit. And yet, I also craved the peace of sitting down, finding solace even in my turmoil. I wanted to toss all the fruits away from me, rejecting their influence, and yet, at the same time, I yearned to chug every last one of them down my throat, desperate for the rush. I was lost, unsure of what I truly desired to do. I felt an overwhelming urge to travel back into my past and confront all those who had wronged me—murdering those who had abused me and taken my family from me without remorse. I felt compelled to return to Bower Bank and rip Netty's heart open, exposing the darkness within. I wanted to seize that grotesque thing that haunted me under the bed, that creature of nightmares, and tear it into shreds, finding some sense of resolution.

The intense feeling of anger and rage penetrated my every cell, bewildering me to a degree I had never before experienced. All the control I had meticulously maintained over my emotions for so many thousands of years began to crumble, wanting to explode from my body like a dam that had finally burst open under too much pressure.

The piercing scream that erupted from my throat was filled with an anger and violence so severe that it sent shivers down the spines of every living creature nearby, causing the trees in the vicinity to shake with palpable fright. Some of them even curled in on themselves, succumbing to despair and dying on the spot. The violent scream, fueled by overwhelming rage, seemed to stretch on endlessly, and I found myself unable to stop it. In a desperate frenzy, I began to yank at huge patches of my own hair, each tug amplifying the madness that coursed through every pore of my being.

The two Nubians materialized suddenly in front of me. One of them swiftly snatched away all the fruits, his grip unyielding, while he simultaneously grabbed hold of my hands, rendering me incapacitated. The other Nubian callously thrust his finger deep down my throat—so far down, in fact, that I began to retch uncontrollably. I watched in a daze as the grass seemed to recoil in horror at the moment my vomit splattered on its blades.

Yet, I could not stop the torrent of raging madness that surged within me. Before I fully realized what I was doing, I hurled myself at the Nubian who still had his finger lodged firmly in my throat, filled with a murderous vengeance that surged through me with an intensity I had never experienced before. The buildup of all the anger I had stifled since my arrival on this earth exploded into a primal urge to tear him apart like an enraged savage beast. I wanted to roar at him with the ferocity of a crazed lioness, my primal instincts spiraling out of control. I longed to rake my nails across his smooth belly, driven by a dark and lustful craving. But just as suddenly as those savage feelings ignited, they vanished, leaving me to crumble into the grass below, gasping for breath and reeling from the whirlwind of emotions. I found myself seeing stars, my vision blurred as reality slipped away.

"Oh Goddess, what was in that fruit?"

I found myself utterly spent. I laid back against the soft grass, gazing up at the two Nubians who were looking at me with the most bewildering, incomprehensible expressions on their faces. Did they somehow predict that I was going to react so dramatically to the fruit? My mind felt too heavy, too tired to ponder such questions in the moment. Later, I would definitely seek answers to this mystery. For now, I allowed myself to float gently off into a deep sleep, making a solemn promise to myself never to eat anything again from this wonderfully strange yet beautifully chaotic garden.

26

THE FRUIT OF RAGE

I woke up the next morning to the gentle songs of birds singing sweetly in the trees surrounding me. I had this exhilarating feeling of floating on air, though I was still splayed out where I had fallen the night before, quite unceremoniously. I stretched my body like a cat, flexing my limbs and arching my back, and felt incredibly good in that moment. Then, as if they were the tide, memories came floating back to me, and I sat up immediately, alarmed by their sudden influx. The two Nubians were sitting around the mound, observing me with keen, intent gazes. They got up slowly, sensing that I was about to approach them, but to my surprise, they suddenly transformed into ospreys and started scratching and pecking at the mound, their movements frantic and relentless.

I stopped to see why this strange occurrence was unfolding before my eyes. The mound was shimmering with an ethereal light, sifting itself as if it had a life of its own. The eagles—magnificent creatures—were carefully taking the small lumps out of the way, their sharp eyes scanning the area. Slowly, almost majestically, the mound began to rise higher and higher. Suddenly, the two Nubians appeared, each standing proudly on opposite sides of the now rising, glowing mound. Solstilert's stunning black and white sisterlocks, styled artfully, emerged first, followed by the formation of her exquisite face—if it was even conceivable, she looked even more beautiful than before. Then came her slender neck and graceful shoulders, seamlessly completing her appearance. Soon, she was fully present, standing completely naked between the two strikingly beautiful males. Young, vibrant, and as radiant as the sun itself, she looked like an otherworldly goddess descended from the heavens. Her dark brown skin glowed, radiating beauty, youthful vigor, and impeccable health. Suddenly, a white tailored shirt dress materialized on her body, cinched with a three-inch broad belt that accentuated her very small waistline beautifully. Delicate white sandals appeared on her feet, with intricate ribbons skillfully tied all the way up to her knees, and she adorned a couple of shimmering diamond bangles on each of her dainty hands, completing her breathtaking transformation.

I had never seen anything that looked quite like her, neither here nor in my own realm. The overwhelming urge to fall onto my knees and bow submissively to her authority almost seized me, but I fought against it and defiantly stuck out my chin, maintaining a sense of pride. She, however, wasn't paying me any attention; instead, her focus was directed entirely at the two remarkably beautiful males beside her, and I could sense that they were communicating with one another silently, sharing thoughts that transcended spoken words.

"*You ate the fruit of rage*," she stated quietly in my mind, finally turning her gaze to meet mine. "*I'm really sorry. Are you feeling okay?*"

I paused for a moment, reflecting on the chaos of emotions within me, before I responded, "Now, I'm feeling a lot better. I thought your boys might have fed me that fruit on purpose."

"*No, they would never do something like that. They truly didn't know what they were doing.*"

I looked at them and saw deep worry shining ominously from their concerned faces. I pursed my lips thoughtfully and nodded my head slightly at them, releasing a lengthy sigh of resignation. I supposed it was not entirely their fault that all that pent-up rage had suddenly erupted from deep within me. They had been there, bottled and stored inside, ready to burst forth like a volcano spewing molten lava.

She looked around her beautiful garden, filled with vibrant colors and fragrant blooms, and walked gracefully towards the trees that were affected by the crazy screaming I had in my fit of anger. I watched her as she gently placed her dainty hands on each of them in a soothing manner as she passed by. To my amazement, the trees stood to attention, coming back to life under her tender touch.

"*I will put a red tag on all the trees bearing fruits that are more palatable and gentle on the senses, just for you*," she declared with a warm smile.

"Okay," I nodded, momentarily losing interest in the alluring, delectable-looking fruits that hung from the branches. "But how about you? Are you feeling any better now?" I asked, genuinely concerned for her well-being.

"*Yes, I just needed to loosen up a bit, as you can see*," she replied with a reassuring smile.

I rolled my eyes at her bad pun and watched as a slight, almost mischievous smile creased her lips.

"Well, since you're finally feeling better, I think it's high time I go pamper myself," I told her, glancing down at my crushed, soiled clothing which was a remnant of all the chaos from earlier.

"*Thank you, Roboliac, for keeping me company during this ordeal*."

"You are most welcome," I replied with a small nod, exiting her suite.

I was now quite familiar with the extensive and opulent layout of the palace. On my way to my own suite, I made a brief stop in the grand kitchen to grab a 'to go' platter filled with delectable treats.

The workers had become accustomed to my spontaneous visits, no longer surprised by my unexpected appearances. They meticulously loaded me up, placing the delicious food in a very expensive-looking food carrier designed to keep everything piping hot. I expressed my gratitude with a heartfelt thank you and almost trotted eagerly to my room, excitement bubbling within me.

Hunger was tearing at my stomach like a relentless beast, and I simply couldn't wait to reach my suite. By the time I finally arrived there, a grueling twenty-five minutes later, my body was shaking from starvation, each tremor a reminder of my appetite. I carefully took the bag to the large dining table in the expansive dining room and sat down right in front of it. I felt an overwhelming urge to devour the bag and everything inside it in one go, but I was consciously trying to teach myself the virtue of self-control. Sometimes this effort worked beautifully, and other times—like in moments such as this—the lessons I had learned became nothing more than fleeting thoughts lingering in my mind.

The bag was carefully opened, and the very first container of food I took out was a delectable serving of salted fish, perfectly cooked down in rich, flavorful callaloo. Accompanying it were some freshly boiled dumplins and ripe boiled bananas. I didn't care that it was steaming hot; my hunger took over, and I dug through it with the fervor of a starving animal. Soon

enough, I had all the containers opened, and I was
eating as if I had not had anything to eat in years,
savoring every bite. When I finally finished my feast,
I realized I couldn't move a muscle. I sank back into
my plush chair, completely content, and basked in my
overwhelming fullness. I remained in that blissful
state for nearly forty-five minutes, allowing the
warmth of satisfaction to envelop me, before I finally
decided to venture back into the bag to see if there
was anything sweet to indulge in. To my delight, I
found a small Jamaican-style potato pudding, baked
to perfection with coconut. It was still warm to the
touch. The outside of it gleamed golden brown and
had a little crispy texture, just the way I liked it.
Without hesitation, I devoured it enthusiastically and
followed it up with the bottle of milk that was also
nestled in the bag. Now fully satisfied, I settled back
into the comfortable position I had just vacated and
savored the moment, relishing the afterglow of my
delightful meal.

I was lingering in a delightful sleep-wake mode
when the majestic sight of two eagles suddenly flew
into my line of vision. I decided to pretend to be
completely oblivious to their unexpected presence,
continuing to indulge in the warm, comforting feeling
of contentment that enveloped me. The thought of
moving, even just a little, felt utterly exhausting. I
was still recovering from the last night's ordeal, and
all I really craved was to simply sit back, relax, and

fully savor the sensation of fullness that settled deep within me.

Twenty minutes later, curiosity got the better of me, and I cautiously opened one eye to gauge the whereabouts of the two birds. To my surprise, I found them perched gracefully on either side of me, both gazing intently at my still figure.

"Are you ready to acknowledge us?" asked the eagle on my right, its voice cutting through the tranquil atmosphere. My heart skipped a beat, a strange sensation coursing through me; I wondered why my pulse quickened at the sound of its voice.

"No, I'm trying to pretend you're not here," I replied, struggling to maintain my facade.

"I'm sorry you're angry with us," the eagle continued, its tone now softer and more understanding. "You have every right to feel that way. We genuinely had no idea you would react to the fruit in such an unexpected manner. We had enjoyed that particular fruit before, finding it to be incredibly delicious, and we genuinely thought you would derive the same enjoyment from it."

This was the longest sentence they had ever spoken to me, and it lingered in the air like a captivating melody. Their voices sent delightful tingles spiraling down my spine, igniting a warmth within me that I couldn't ignore. I sat up a bit straighter in my chair, shifting my gaze from one to the other, unable to take my eyes off their astonishing beauty. My heart raced even faster, thumping loudly like a drum in my chest. I really couldn't tell them apart, as they both seemed to shine with an ethereal glow. I looked at their naked chests, finding no signs of scars or imperfections anywhere.

"It's okay; I didn't even realize I had all of that bottled up inside me. Sorry I went a bit jungle on you," I admitted with a half-hearted smile, hoping to lighten the mood.

"We will try to be extra careful next time," they replied in a perfectly synchronized manner.

"Okay." I was desperately trying to ignore the overwhelming sensation of liquid warmth flooding my body at the sight and sound of them.

It was merely the aftereffect of the fruit I had consumed, nothing more. This feeling, I assured myself, would eventually fade. However, as I sat there, I couldn't bring myself to meet their eyes; I was feeling too mushy and overwhelmed by their intense presence. Ultimately, I decided to get up. It was time for me to take my shower anyway.

"Don't worry about it too much; it's all in the past and gone now," I said, trying to reassure all of us.

I did learn that, much to my surprise, I had not truly gotten rid of all my anger. Instead, I had only managed to bottle them up tightly and store them away in the dark recesses of my mind. So, in reality, I'm really only angry with myself, which is a bitter pill to swallow. I should work on getting rid of those negative emotions entirely, rather than just storing them away until some supposedly opportune moment when they might bubble over. What's more shocking is that I didn't even realize I was engaging in this unhealthy behavior. I sighed to myself in resignation, whispering, "Just ignore the whole ridiculous display, or forget it even happened." With that thought, I turned my back on them and walked toward the bathroom, determined to leave behind the feelings and the sight of them, letting it all fade into nothingness at the thought of a long, soothing soak in the bath.

As I readied myself for my bath, a fleeting picture of them in the tub with me suddenly flashed in my mind, causing me to grimace in annoyance. I quickly shook that image out of my head. "Focus," I muttered to myself, steeling my resolve as I stepped into the warm embrace of the tub.

The scent of my favorite bath gel enveloped my senses as it assailed my nostrils with its invigorating sweetness. I slowly sank deeper into the medium hot water, letting myself submerge completely and staying under for a full five minutes, allowing the warmth to cradle me. I was desperately trying to push them out of my mind, but with each passing second, it became increasingly clear that it was no use. When I finally surfaced, I found them standing over the edge of my massive bathtub, their eyes transfixed on me, witnessing the water cascading down from my hair, glistening as it trickled over my ample breasts and splashed delicately back into the water.

I leaned back into the tub, gazing at them with a sense of indifference, not particularly concerned whether they chose to join me in this moment or not. There was more than enough space to comfortably accommodate a dozen people in this luxurious tub. Despite my efforts to suppress the awoken feelings stirring within me towards them, I soon realized that they refused to be ignored any longer. So, I decided to embrace those feelings fully, allowing them to take reign over my senses. Let's see what exciting developments might unfold in this tantalizing scenario.

I closed my eyes and felt the two Nubians effortlessly climb into the tub beside me. As I did, the overwhelming fruit of rage not only brought to the surface all my stored anger and frustration, but it also unbridled the strongest sexual urges I've ever experienced in my life. These sensations were magnified by my indisciplined teenage body and the full spectrum of my humanity. In previous incarnations and bodies, I had managed to maintain control over my impulses and desires. I found myself wondering if being merged with them had something to do with the intensity of these tangled feelings. Or perhaps, I was simply using my humanity, the intoxicating fruit of rage, and the surging teenage hormones as a way to excuse the undeniable attraction I had felt for the two handsome males since the very first moment I laid eyes upon them. As I looked over at the two very masculine figures, I nearly became undone by the sheer magnetism between us. The feelings they were evoking within me were tantalizing my senses in ways I had not anticipated. However, despite the overwhelming urge to give in, I did not allow myself to take advantage of this explosive moment.

I sat there, feeling the sensations wash over me, soaking it all in and comparing it to my Golealmness. I must say, this experience was even more intense and overwhelming. My teenage body was feeling absolutely wonderful, yet I was not some naive, innocent teenager. Regardless of what my body was saying and how much joy it seemed to derive from this moment, I was aware of the complexity of my situation.

I watched them as they watched me with keen interest. Soon, they were no longer merely humans in the room, but rather transformed into fierce lions, and the two of them prowled towards me with the grace and intent of predators on the hunt. I sat there in my tub, entranced, as I watched them come at me, my heart beating like thunder in my chest, each thump echoing in my ears. One of them jumped at me with incredible force, and I found myself inexplicably turning into a lioness — big, strong, and powerful. I stood tall and roared at the two approaching figures, then pounced on them with a confidence that surprised me. I guessed that the ability to change into something else somehow took my attention away from the once intense feeling, guiding me toward a sense of jubilation. We played like the young cub I was, revitalized and carefree, completely forgetting that I was no longer in the deep jungle of Tanzania. We frolicked roughly in the tub for an exhilarating hour before finally being brought back to reality.

~~~~~~~

"Hmm, what have we here?" Starr remarked with a playful glint in her eyes, leaning elegantly against the wall opposite the lavishly large Jacuzzi bathtub as she observed us shamelessly. I was the first one to transform back into my human self, followed closely by the two Nubian figures. I still found myself chuckling with unrestrained delight at the exhilarating fact that I could switch forms at will. It filled me with a sense of ecstasy. Starr lifted her right eyebrow at me, an expression that hinted she was holding onto some tantalizing secret.

"What?" I queried, adopting a look that said I was unbothered. We watched in awe as the two Nubians seamlessly transitioned into majestic eagles and soared gracefully out of the window.

"If I had known you were having a threesome, I would have eagerly joined you to make things even more exciting and thrilling," she quipped, a mischievous smile playing on her lips as her eyes sparkled with intrigue.

"Threesome? Who's having a threesome?" Ameleki, appearing seemingly out of nowhere, asked, her voice filled with curiosity.

"Little Miss Luminaire here," she said, pointing her chin at me with a teasing grin, still leaning casually against the wall with folded arms, exuding confidence.

I watched as Ameleki walked up to me, her gaze intensely studying my breasts with a discerning eye. She looked from one to the other, clearly impressed.

"Beautiful," she murmured appreciatively as if savoring every detail.

"Turn around." I obediently turned around for her careful appraisal, feeling a mix of anticipation and nerves as I heard her murmur once more, "Beautiful, very beautiful."

"I'm truly glad you like what you see," I replied, having grown accustomed to Starr offering compliments like this on numerous occasions.

I walked over to the closet and grabbed a soft, luxurious robe, draping it over my body and shield myself from their prying eyes, which felt a little overwhelming.

"What are we doing today?" I asked Starr, my curiosity piqued and eagerness bubbling within me. She was in charge of training me on how to fully maneuver my body and enhance my skills, and I was excited to see where the day would take us.

~~~~~~~

In Golealm, every single citizen had to diligently learn how to effectively defend the entire realm. For the first twelve thousand years of our youth, we tirelessly trained every single day, whether rain or shine. This rigorous training was an essential part of our way of life and our upbringing. However, upon coming to Materealm, I found myself unable to effectively utilize earth's material to its fullest potential because of its overwhelming mass. I discovered that I couldn't defend myself much within this new environment, so I had reluctantly learned to run away instead of actively fighting back. In this new body, however, I was assimilating remarkably well. I had grown accustomed to it. It genuinely felt like me. But I still needed to be fully present and engaged within it. Starr, having had a similar experience in the past, was delegated the significant task of training me, both mentally and physically, to truly embody this new form.

At first, I was quite resistant to the idea, but Solstilert had quietly informed me that I would soon find myself in need of these skills in the very near future. I didn't dare ask any questions, because I knew if she said it was necessary, then it was undoubtedly true.

27

THE STRANGE GAME

It was half past twelve in the afternoon, the sun shone brightly through the window, casting warm rays across the room. Marshane decided, with a determined mindset, to return to her office to tackle the task of grading papers, knowing that it would require her full attention. As she walked, she couldn't help but think about the children she had whimsically wished into switched lives, a smile creeping onto her face as she recalled the delightful fun she was having while getting to know them better. Was she truly a bad person for this? Deep down, she didn't believe so. How could she have possibly known that her innocent wish would manifest into reality? She had never encountered anything remotely similar to this phenomenon before. Although she tried her utmost not to blame herself too much, it proved to be a rather challenging endeavor.

Sometimes, the overwhelming guilt she felt for her role in the strange and unusual behavior of the children kept her awake through countless sleepless nights. But, as difficult as it was to admit, she had to concede that they, in their own quirky ways, deserved what was happening to them.

What about the other children? How were they managing through this situation? Were they actually learning anything meaningful? What were they doing while these particular children were engaged in their learning process? Should she even concern herself about them at all?

"Why should you concern yourself about them? You did them a favor by wishing for the switch. Stop worrying so much. Whatever they are doing right now, that's precisely what they're supposed to be doing."

She sighed long and hard, fully aware that her inner voice was probably right in her reasoning.

"Can't I wish them back?" she pondered, filled with doubt.

"Do you truly want to?" was the answer that echoed back to her.

She didn't answer. It would have been the right thing to do, but as her inner voice pointed out not too long ago, the school truly needed a little shaking up to disrupt the monotonous routine that had settled in. She was also very weary about the teachers' behaviors toward the recently switched students, who were now receiving unwarranted scrutiny. Others were questioning their mentality and the new, peculiar weirdness they were exhibiting. The students were not behaving in a culturally expected manner. The things they kept doing were clearly out of their established cultural norms. They were exhibiting such fiery enthusiasm, showing too much activity, and appearing too feisty compared to what was typically seen. They were excelling significantly in sports rather than placing their focus on academic achievements.

"They can't be normal!" or "Something strange is going on!" The teachers would blurted out in disbelief. But despite their strong suspicions, they couldn't do anything about it, as they were unable to provide valid reasons to substantiate their unfounded concerns.

~~~~~~~~~

Marshane decided to grab a steaming cup of coffee from the cafeteria on her way to the office, but as she got closer, she noticed a large gathering of excited students and teachers surrounding the basketball court, which was situated opposite the cafeteria. A lively atmosphere filled the air, with some students enthusiastically clapping while several teachers were busy capturing the moment on their phones, recording every detail of the unfolding scene.

Curious, she approached the crowd to see what was going on and quickly discovered that fourteen of the students had creatively switched up their outfits to play an energetic game of netball. Some of the players had tied knots in their T-shirts, while others sported similar knots in their skirts, creating a playful team distinction.   In the midst of the action was another student, who was officiating the game with a whistle held firmly between her lips.

"What is the name of that game they're playing?" someone near her asked, genuinely puzzled.

"I don't know," the person standing closest to Marshane replied, shrugging their shoulders in confusion.

"It's netball. A commonwealth game, very famous in the West," Marshane responded, her voice tinged with automatic enthusiasm.

"How do they know how to play it? Nobody here knows how to play this game," one of the PE teachers, who was also standing nearby and observing the scene, stated in disbelief.

Marshane, recalling her glory days, used to be an avid netball player back in high school. It had been her absolute favorite sport, yet she had not had a chance to indulge in it for over twenty-five long years. Lost in her memories, she wasn't thinking clearly when she walked over to the student who was refereeing the game and took the whistle directly from her hand. Without hesitation, she blew the whistle long and hard, determined to indicate that she wanted their full attention. When the students caught sight of their favorite teacher brandishing the whistle, they all ran up to her with eager expressions.

"We are going to start a brand-new game, and I want each of you to play your very best. Okay?" she declared confidently, already formulating an exciting new idea in her mind. Would it actually work? The thought made her pulse race with exhilaration.

They all shook their heads in enthusiastic agreement and quickly moved to take their respective positions on the court, passing the ball to her for the all-important toss-up. With youthful vigor, she made her way to the center spot, standing between the two opposing teams ready to toss the ball high into the air. In a moment of excitement, the team wearing the tied skirts successfully caught it. Marshane sprinted to the side of the court, brimming with anticipation as she prepared to lead the game.

Just a short while ago, the kids had been simply enjoying themselves, but now, with an adult supervising the game from the sidelines, the atmosphere had shifted to one of seriousness and fierce competitiveness. They felt a strong motivation to impress their favorite teacher, inspiring each team to resolve to give it their absolute best. With a sharp blast of her whistle, Marshane signaled the start of the game.

So focused were they on the unfolding match that they did not notice the new principal, who had recently taken over after the mysterious disappearance of Principal Xue, quietly observing them from a distance.

The spectators had also grown significant in numbers. Other students, who were initially supposed to be napping or diligently focusing on their homework assignments, found themselves caught up in the excitement and were there enthusiastically cheering from the sidelines. The game had escalated to a volume that was both loud and intensely serious. In the heat of the moment, the students completely forgot they were meant to be communicating in Mandarin; instead, they were fervently shouting at each other in Jamaican patois. Some of the observing teachers couldn't help but notice how remarkably similar the students sounded to their English teacher, but they didn't question this phenomenon. It seemed perfectly natural for English learners to adopt the accent of their English teachers. However, the most astounding aspect of the entire scene was that all students were speaking this peculiar version of English rather than their native tongues.

Many of the other students who were observing the game also found it somewhat questionable that so many students in the second grade were learning to speak English so rapidly. Even though they couldn't fully understand some of the things that were being said around them, they remained intrigued by the whole scene.

"Pass me di bawl nuh gal," shouted the wing attack from the tied skirt team at their center.

The center quickly threw the ball to the Goal Attack, who then skillfully tossed it to the Goal Shooter. The Goal Shooter focused intently, aimed carefully at the basketball net, and confidently shot the ball. To the delight of the spectators, who were enthusiastically cheering for the tied skirt team, the ball swooshed into the net, and the crowd erupted in joyous roars of excitement.

The game continued in an exhilarating manner like that for half an hour, with the tied T-shirt team surprisingly leading the other group ten to seven.

Marshane, who was thoroughly enjoying herself immensely, decided that it was finally time to draw the game to a close, so that the kids could have a full hour of much-needed rest before the afternoon class session begins. With a firm grip, she blew the whistle forcefully, signaling the definite end of the game. All the players rushed up to her, faces flushed, sweating profusely, and breathing hard.

"Teacher, why yuh blow di wissle?" asked the goal defense for the tied T-shirt team, a look of confusion on his face.

"Well, as much as we were having so much fun, you still need to rest up and cool off to prepare for the upcoming afternoon class session."

"But we not tiyad yet, Teacher," another eager player complained, their enthusiasm clearly unquenched.

"I know, but you will definitely be. Don't worry, I'm going to ask the principal if we can officially start a team with real netballs and a proper netball court."

All the players jumped up in excitement and shouted, "Yeah!!!" Marshane laughed heartily as she watched their joyful and enthusiastic faces light up with hope.

"Run along now, my little athletes. Make sure to wash your hands and faces thoroughly, and don't forget to grab something refreshing to drink before heading off for your afternoon naps."

"Okay, Teacher!!!" they all shouted in unison, running off the field with glee towards the students' bathroom, conveniently located near the cafeteria.

"*Are you sure you really want to start a netball team?*"

"*I know I have a lot to do, but I can definitely find the time to squeeze it in. The kids absolutely loved it. Did you see them? They were simply incredible,*" she replied, her voice bubbling with excitement as she headed towards the bustling cafeteria for the coffee she didn't really need right now. She was already buzzing with energy, riding the wave of a serotonin overload from the joyful moments she had just experienced.

~~~~~~~

The principal and a few other teachers were watching her intently as she confidently walked into the bustling cafeteria.

"Do you think she could teach us how to play that game?" the head of the PE department inquired with a curious expression.

"What do you mean exactly?" Principal Huang asked, raising an eyebrow in interest.

"Did you see the way those kids played? They really seemed to know what they were doing, and we have two enthusiastic teams of them ready to go."

"So, what you're suggesting is that you want to start an official netball team?" the principal clarified, looking intrigued by the idea.

"Yes, and they can also be trained to play basketball as well," the teacher elaborated, emphasizing the potential of the students.

The other teachers in the room listened attentively, nodding their heads in agreement at the promising suggestion.

"Okay, we'll see what she says about it," Principal Huang promised with a reassuring tone, clearly intrigued by the idea.

Meanwhile, Marshane was tucked away in her cubicle in the English teachers' office, diligently grading papers when Principal Huang walked in unexpectedly. As she had not yet met him, she failed to recognize who he was at that moment.

"Hello, how are you?" he asked, his voice friendly as he glanced around the office.

She glanced up, a smile breaking across her face, momentarily unsure if she was the person being addressed before responding. "Hi, I'm great, thank you! What about yourself?"

She went back to her paper grading without waiting for a response, her mind already filled with the tasks still ahead. She had a few more papers to go through, with only ten precious minutes to spare before the next class began. She was undeniably pressed for time.

"When you're finished with your classes today, can you please make your way over to the Principal's Office for a few minutes?"

Marshane's heart skipped a beat at the unexpected request. She looked up at the person speaking, trying to place him in her memory, though she couldn't quite remember where she had seen him before. "Okay, did he want to see me at a specific time after class?" She asked with a slight edge of concern in her voice.

"No, the time will be completely at your convenience," he replied, leaving her with lingering questions.

"*A wonda weh him a go talk to me bout?*" she asked curiously.

"You'll find out when you see him, in the meantime, don't worry so," came the reassuring reply.

"Cho, dis is all me a go think bout now," Marshane sighed, her eyes following the man as he walked out of the office.

She only had one class at two-thirty, and the anticipation was making her anxious. She really hoped it wasn't anything too serious or troubling that he wanted to discuss with her.

~~~~~~~

Many were increasingly noticing her unusual closeness with the switched grade twos, and a few curious individuals were starting to question the nature of that relationship. She shook her head vigorously to rid herself of those nagging assumptions, firmly knowing that they wouldn't get her anywhere meaningful in her current situation.

It was nearly two-fifteen when she finally mustered the courage to knock gently on the Principal's door.

"Enter," a commanding voice ordered from within.

As she stepped inside, she appeared very calm and composed, but deep down, she was consumed by worry that threatened to overwhelm her.

"What are you worrying about so much?"

"I don't know, I'm just worrying too much."

"*You know I tend to be a bit of a worrier,*" she admitted softly, a hint of vulnerability in her voice.

"*Well, don't let it consume you too much; whatever comes your way, just remember that you will eventually overcome.*"

"*Sound advice. Thank you,*" she replied, appreciating the reassurance.

Dan watched her closely as she breathed a deep sigh of relief, attempting to suppress the urge to chuckle at her sudden change in demeanor. The Principal stepped around his desk to warmly greet her.

"Hi, I'm Principal Huang, and I'm really glad you could see me at such short notice."

Marshane looked up at the man who had been in her office earlier that day and took his hand, shaking it firmly. "I'm really sorry; I didn't recognize who you were earlier today. It's truly nice to meet you now."

"You looked very busy, that's why I didn't introduce myself to you at that moment. Please don't worry too much about it; it was entirely my fault. Now, please have a seat, Ms. Campbell."

"Thank you." She sat down in the chair opposite his desk, making an effort to appear confident despite her nerves.

"Would you like a cup of coffee? Or perhaps a bottle of water?"

"Thank you. A bottled water would be nice," she

replied politely.

He stood up and walked over to fetch her a bottled water from the small refrigerator that he had tucked away under a counter behind him, then handed it to her with a friendly smile.

"Have we met before?" she asked him, taking the water from the table and glancing at him with a mix of curiosity and suspicion.

"No, I don't think so. Well, not before today. Maybe you saw me around the compound at some point."

Seo Jeo Lee! He looked so much like the young Seo Jeo Lee she vividly remembered from the plane coming here. Shit, how could she have possibly missed that connection before? "You looked like the passenger I sat beside on the flight to here," she blurted out, her eyes widening with realization.

"Oh, and you remembered him?" he replied, a hint of surprise in his voice.

"I remembered him because he looked strikingly like a younger version of my favorite Korean movie star. You even sound just like him," she continued, a smile creeping onto her face.

"Like the Korean movie star?" Principal Huang asked, raising his right eyebrow in intrigue.

"No, like the guy who sat next to me on my flight," she clarified, her cheeks flushing slightly with embarrassment.

"I'm going to take that as a sincere compliment. The children are absolutely raving about you," he said, skillfully changing the subject to something more uplifting.

"I'm genuinely very happy to see how joyful they are having you around."

"They are awesome kids. I love them dearly," she said, smiling hugely and her eyes twinkling with excitement.

"I'm very glad to hear that, because I have a rather important request. The PE teachers would really like for you to teach them how to play the game you were passionately coaching today. You will be compensated with additional pay for this important endeavor."

"Will you be forming a netball team here, at this school? The game is not widely known in this country, but places like Hong Kong, Singapore, Malaysia, and other surrounding nations proudly have teams that compete every year in tournament events held in Hong Kong," she informed him enthusiastically.

He looked at her, clearly very impressed by what he had just learned.

"I did some research," she responded with a warm, infectious laugh.

"I didn't know that at all! How did you learn this game?" He asked, taking a thoughtful sip of his coffee while maintaining an intense gaze on her.

"In Jamaica," she replied with a hint of nostalgia. "I used to play it quite often. I was very good at it, actually. It's a sport primarily enjoyed by women, even though guys participate as well. We all learned to play it in school, starting from the basic school level."

"My students played like they had been honing their skills for years," he remarked, genuinely taken aback by their talent. "I was quite impressed with them."

"You were impressed? Imagine my delight at the news! Whoever taught them did a truly wonderful job —they are definitely playing at a competitive level," she gushed, trying her best to maintain a level head despite her excitement.

"Well, I'm sure it will be the talk of this entire district when we enter the competitions—it will undoubtedly become the talk of the country," he said, his expression brightening as he looked genuinely enthusiastic about the prospect of his students putting his school on the map.

"Well, I'll make sure the head of the PE department reaches out to you tomorrow, and you two can work out all the necessary details, including how to get a proper netball court set up along with the shooting poles."

"You have certainly done some thorough research as well," she chuckled, impressed.

"Yes, I did," he replied, nodding his head earnestly as he said this. "He will meet with you tomorrow around nine in the morning. The sooner we can get this program on the road, the sooner we can join the international competitions and showcase our talent."

Marshane was absolutely ecstatic that he was taking such a serious interest in her situation. She genuinely liked this Principal; he was nice, approachable, and down to earth. His demeanor was so much warmer and friendlier than that of Principal Xue.

As Principal Huang stood up and came around the desk to her side, she rose as well to meet him.

"It was truly nice meeting you, Ms. Campbell. I can see precisely why my students speak so highly of you and liked you so much," he remarked with a smile.

"It was equally nice meeting you too," she laughed, feeling a deep sense of warmth and connection swelling within her during their engaging conversation.

They shook hands firmly, and she left with a promise to meet with the head of the PE department the following morning.

"See, there was really nothing to worry about after all."

"Yep, you're right," she sighed happily, a sparkle of optimism in her eyes. Things were finally getting

better. *"It's strange though, that he looked and sounded just like that man I sat next to on the plane."*

"It was probably just a coincidence, I'm sure," he replied, trying to ease her mind.

"But there was definitely something about his face that made me believe otherwise," she contradicted with conviction.

Something in my face? Dan wondered, feeling a twinge of unease. She was becoming far too astute for his liking.

28

THE DEMON ANGEL

That evening, as Marshane stepped inside her cozy apartment, a wave of exhilaration swept over her, making her head feel like it was about to burst from all the excitement. It was as if her life was transforming in the most delightful way, and she loved every bit of the promising direction it was taking.

The clock had just struck four, and dinner time was fast approaching. She felt utterly famished. With a sense of anticipation, she opened the refrigerator, her mind drifting to the delicious leftover oxtail waiting for her, perfectly complemented by a fresh pot of white rice cooked down with vibrant chopped carrots. She had every intention of pouring herself a glass of wine to accompany her dinner—a small indulgence to celebrate the thrilling new possibilities that lay ahead of her. She absolutely deserved this moment of self-pampering.

Rarely did she treat herself to alcohol; she usually preferred the alternative pleasures of a good movie or treating herself to a nice bottle of perfume. Yet tonight, she felt a longing for a drink, and that half bottle of wine had been sitting patiently in the refrigerator for nearly three months, just waiting for the perfect occasion.

She cooked a hearty meal, showered to refresh herself, then finally sat down to eat. After enjoying her dinner, she placed the dirty dishes in the kitchen sink for later cleaning, knowing she would tackle them when she felt more motivated. She refilled her almost empty glass with wine and carried the bottle with her to the comfortable sofa. Settling in, she propped her feet up on the center table, feeling the weight of the day lift off her shoulders, and set the bottle down beside her wine glass on the side table.

With a sigh of contentment, she picked up the remote control and began flipping through the myriad of channels, hoping to find something engaging to watch. However, after scrolling through the countless options and not finding anything of interest, she took a sip from her glass, her thoughts wandering back to the time in the principal's office. He bore a striking resemblance to that arrogant passenger who had sat beside her on the plane that fateful day. It felt like ages since that incident, so she wondered why she was even revisiting that memory. In an effort to shake off the thoughts, she took another generous sip of her wine, only to discover her glass was now empty. Reluctantly, she picked up the bottle, poured the last little bit remaining into her glass, and chugged it down, seeking solace in the rich flavor of the wine.

She decided to take a much-needed nap before diving into her research. She wanted to meticulously gather all the detailed measurements for the netball court, the shooting pole, the netball uniform, sneakers, socks, and bibs for the team, so everything would be ready for the crucial meeting scheduled for the next day. For now, she planned to clear her mind and recharge her energy, ensuring she could be fresh and fully prepared for the wealth of information she was going to present to the head of the PE department.

She let out a long yawn, closed her eyes gently, and focused on putting the principal—rather, the arrogant passenger she had encountered—out of her mind once and for all. Half an hour later, she jolted awake to the overwhelming sensation of a presence looming over her. To her disbelief, it was the same ominous black demon she had seen in front of her at the school some time ago. In a panic, she squeezed her eyes shut and turned away from the terrifying figure, her heart racing with an overwhelming sense of dread.

Suddenly she found herself sitting in the passenger seat of her cousin's vibrant purple RV. They were rocking back and forth while singing—though it was more like yelling—to their favorite song, Kymani Marley's "Warrior," blasting from the CD player.

Desert sand surrounded them in a golden sea, with only a paved road parting the vast expanse of dunes. The road weaved like a snake, twisting and turning as the RV went rolling down its path.

"I found my tribe," Purple Queen exclaimed loudly over the pulsing music that filled the air.

"What?" came the confused reply.

"I said I found my tribe," she repeated, raising her voice as she turned down the volume of the music, allowing her words to resonate.

"I thought your tribe was in Jamaica. I thought we were your tribe," Marshane said, looking perplexed and searching for understanding.

"No, that's my family; my true tribe is standing right in front of me. I'm incredibly happy that I finally found them."

"I'm genuinely happy that you're happy, but what about us? What about me?" she asked, her voice cracking with emotions, feelings of sadness and loneliness saturating her words and overwhelming her spirit.

"You never belonged with us, Shaney. You've always had your tribe in the sky."

"In the sky? What are you talking about?"

But the Purple Queen was fading, her figure blurring against the vastness of the desert landscape. Marshane stood there, watching helplessly as the Queen faded away into the distance until she was no more, tears streaming down her cheeks in silent sorrow. They had left her. Nobody wanted her. She was all alone in this unforgiving world—a lonely figure surrounded by miles and miles of harsh, desolate sand.

She found herself in a relentless desert that was so hot it felt as if it were consuming her very tear drops. Yes, she was undeniably alone, marooned in a barren desert that was eagerly drinking her tears. They had all turned their backs on her, and in that moment, the weight of their rejection sank in deep. She turned, her eyes filled with sorrowful tears, straining to see if the horizon held any semblance of hope, any sign of life, but only endless hills and valleys cloaked in shifting desert sand dunes met her gaze. With a heavy heart, she began to walk, determined to push forward while trying to ignore the scorching hot sand burning her bare feet and the relentless sun pelting down on her shoulders, each step a painful reminder of her isolation.

"Why yuh don't raas fly, how yuh lazy so likkle gal?" Her mother's sister, Netty, sharply asked, suddenly appearing right in front of her, cussing in a way that made Marshane feel embarrassed.

"But me don't have any plane fi fly, Aunty Netty," Marshane replied, trying to defend herself.

"Yuh have two big raasclaat chicken wing, pull dem out and fly," her aunt insisted, her voice filled with frustration.

Marshane watched helplessly as her aunt disappeared into the sand, feeling a deep sense of abandonment. "No, don't leave me here by meself! Aunty Netty, come back! Please come back!" she cried out desperately. "Me a guh learn fi fly, just stay till me find a plane."

Marshane sobbed pitifully, begging her aunt, who was now just a fading memory, to return. She fell in the burning hot sand, tears streaming down her face, wishing she could find a plane to whisk her away from the sweltering heat.

In the midst of her misery and despair, she suddenly felt a cool, gentle hand stroking her hair. With a mixture of curiosity and hope, she opened her eyes to find the most beautiful girl she had ever seen in all her life smiling down at her with kindness and warmth.

"Shaney, why yuh lying down here wasting time?" The beautiful girl's flippant voice, filled with a carefree lilt, did not match the gentleness of her soothing touch, nor the tenderness of her captivating smile. "Up, up, up, hurry up and get up, or else yuh wings dem a guh fry off and yuh not going to be able to fly," she cheerfully encouraged, her eyes sparkling with mischief.

As Marshane finally mustered the strength to get up, an excruciating pain suddenly blazed like lightning, searing across her upper back with an intensity that took her breath away. She screamed out in agony, her body collapsing back into the hot, unforgiving sand. In sheer desperation, she looked back at the beautiful girl, half-hoping to find her there, ready to offer some comfort with her cool hands, but to her dismay, the girl was no longer there, and all the warm sand had vanished into thin air, replaced by an air of mystery and enchantment.

Marshane found herself in an unfamiliar realm, one that resembled the majestic Garden of Eden she had read about in the Bible during her childhood. However, this version of Eden was situated within a vast, palatial-like suite that seemed to stretch endlessly.

"Is it really true that you shouldn't eat from the tree of good and evil?" she pondered, her curiosity mingling with a sense of trepidation.

"What?" Marshane asked, her voice laced with confusion and disbelief. She was no longer feeling the searing burn from the hot sand and the relentless, scorching sun above her, but instead, a killer pain had built up from her aching shoulders and was running torturously down to her waistline.

"Yuh bloodclaat deaf or sup'm?" a doctor bird interrupted, asking in a coarse and raspy voice, sounding as cross as her father usually did when he was irked.

"No, a hear yuh, but isn't dat supposed to be di snake's line of defense?" she replied, her brow furrowing in perplexity. "Mi look like a raas snake to yuh? Hurry up and nyam di fruit, me nuh have all day fi waste," the little doctor bird shouted aggravatingly at her, its tiny wings flapping rapidly in a blur that was practically invisible to her eyes.

Marshane looked around the breathtaking garden, taking in the vibrant colors and noticing that all the fruits hanging from the branches looked deliciously strange in their exotic shapes. She cautiously picked a fruit from the tree nearest to her. The doctor bird watched closely, its beady eyes gleaming with anticipation. Marshane opened her mouth to bite into the strangely alluring fruit, but instead, she suddenly shouted out in pain, her voice echoing her distress, and the fruit slipped from her hand, falling unceremoniously to the ground.

The little doctor bird hissed its tiny teeth, filled with what seemed like a deep-seated anger. It picked up the vibrant fruit with a giant hand that had suddenly materialized from its otherwise minute body.

"Me seh yuh fi hurry up and nyam di raas fruit, me nuh have all day," it commanded, effortlessly stuffing the entire fruit into her mouth.

She began chewing on it, almost absentmindedly, as the sharp pain that had been radiating across her back and down to her waist faded into oblivion. The fruit was the most sensually delicious thing she had ever tasted in her life. It was as if someone had meticulously attached a saline bag filled with crack onto a needle and injected it directly into her arm, forgetting to remove the needle afterward. Her body screamed in ecstatic response to the overwhelming assault of never-ending pleasure. It shook with an intensity that kept mounting to unprecedented heights. All the pain and anger she had ever experienced in her entire forty-two human years felt completely forgotten—utterly gone, as if they had never existed at all.

Her legs weakened and she fell down onto the soft, inviting grass below her. The grass began gently stroking her hair in a soothing manner. The touch was as cool and refreshing as the beautiful girl's presence in the desert sun. Marshane couldn't move; her body shuddered repeatedly from pure, exquisite bliss that coursed through every fiber of her being. The high seemed to stretch on forever, an endless wave of euphoria.

"Please stop, I can't take it nuh more," she pleaded in a whisper. But her neurons were unyielding, firing and firing until it felt as if her brains had exploded in a brilliant display of light and sensation. Ultimately, she lost consciousness, slipping away into a peaceful oblivion.

~~~~~~~

Marshane woke up with her entire body shaking profusely, as if she had just emerged from a terrible nightmare. She was trying hard to control it, fighting against the tremors, but it was no use; they seemed to pulse through her very being. She looked at the timer on top of the television and saw that it was well past three in the morning, a time that felt both haunting and eerie. It was far too late to begin any of her research, yet entirely too early to drag herself out of bed and get ready for work. With a reluctant sigh, she slowly got up from the sofa—convincing herself that something was decidedly wrong with the wine she had indulged in for dinner—and walked with unsteady steps to the bathroom. She couldn't seem to hold herself upright, and her back felt heavy, as if someone was sitting squarely on top of her.

Dragging herself to the sink, she splashed cold water onto her face in a desperate attempt to shake off the unsettling feeling and mentally prepare to tell herself not to drink any alcohol ever again. But the face that looked back at her through the mirror was not her own, and panic surged within her. Instead, it was that of someone as black as the depths of night, with what appeared to be grey smoke swirling ominously around it and eyes that gleamed the color of dry desert sand. Behind her, she noticed honey brown and white feathers hanging limply on either side of her, creating a disorienting contrast against the starkness of the moment. She opened her mouth to scream, but before any sound could escape her lips, the black demon figure that had been haunting her appeared with an unsettling swiftness and took hold of her. In the blink of an eye, the two vanished from the confines of her apartment, reappearing in the vast, sandy expanse of the Sahara Desert, where the sun relentlessly beat down on them and the air thick with a sense of foreboding.

~~~~~~

"Jesas! Me a guh mad."

"No, you're not. Stop being so dramatic, Moonshine," Dan said to her, his voice low and gentle, almost like a soothing balm.

It was the voice that was always present in her head, she realized, as she glanced up at the striking black angel whom she had initially mistaken for a demon haunting her distressed thoughts and dreams. He was completely jet black from head to toe, including the magnificent wings that unfurled behind him like a dark cloud. His eyes were the same haunting color as the eyes that had stared back at her from the mirror—the mesmerizing shade of the sand that now lay beneath their feet.

He suddenly shifted, transforming into Principal Huang, a figure she had thought resembled the passenger who had shared her flight not too long ago. Just as quickly, that same passenger was now standing right before her, a mere specter in the ethereal haze. Without missing a beat, he morphed into the crack-headed cousin of her friend, the one she had unceremoniously shooed away from her doorstep not so long ago. One by one, he took on the likeness of a few other faces she had encountered over the years until, in a grand and breathtaking moment, he returned to stand in front of her once again, resplendent in his full winged glory, commanding and otherworldly.

"You shanker of dark matters. It was you all this time?" she exclaimed angrily, directing her fierce gaze at him.

Dan burst out laughing, the sound echoing with a joyful resonance. The sand around them rose and twirled at the sound, forming extravagant wings that glided gracefully over their heads. He could hardly contain his happiness. She was finally here...after nearly nine hundred and fifty long years of waiting for her return. Of course, for them, it had been less than a single day, but still, it felt like an eternally long day.

She was standing there, cursing at him, just like always. He reached out to stroke her wings gently, and all the countless memories of billions of years surged back, overwhelming her with nostalgia.

"Why am I here? I thought I made it clear that I wanted you to let me rest," she questioned, her brow furrowing with concern.

"Earth is here, and she needs us," he replied earnestly.

"What? Why is she here? What's going on?" she asked bewildered, her voice revealing the curiosity and concern beneath her anger.

"We are all asking the same questions," he said, sharing the weight of uncertainty that lingered in the air.

"Okay, let's go. Oh wait, what are we going to do about the children?" she asked, a look of concern washing over her face.

"Don't worry, they'll be switched back," he consoled her, reassuring her with a calm voice.

Moonshine then lifted her face to the vast sky above and spread her enormous, wide brown and white feathered wings, resembling those of a chicken yet holding so much potential. They shot out majestically on each side of her, and she felt an indescribable relief wash over her, finally free from confinement. The transformation was as mesmerizing as it was swift; her chicken wings steadily morphed into powerful eagle's wings, and finally, they took on the appearance of the most magnificent raven-colored wings she had ever imagined. With a single, determined flap, she shifted the sand for miles around her, leaving her mark on the land.

Dan stood nearby, watching in sheer awe as she released the most beautiful sight he had ever encountered. With every flap of her incredible wings, his heart soared with excitement and admiration.

"We have to stop somewhere," she told him firmly, grounding them back in the harsh light of reality.

"Of course, lead the way," he replied, his heart racing with excitement.

He was so elated to see the return of his love that he would have conceded to anything she demanded without question. He watched as she gracefully lifted herself into the air, testing her wide, powerful wings, and then shot into the sky, vanishing from sight. Seconds later, he followed suit, both of them materializing together in the exotic country of Djibouti, located on the Horn of Africa. He observed her intently as she searched the landscape until she finally found what she was looking for. With a sudden burst of energy, she let herself go, tumbling out of the sky to the ground below, generating an explosion so loud that the entire area—from Tem'l to Caramel, across the border in Ethiopia—felt the earth tremble beneath them. She was on her feet in less than a millisecond, fanning her immense wings to awaken the raging tsunamis. Once she was finished, she performed the same dramatic act—except this time she landed gracefully on her feet rather than on her back—in Addis Ababa, then extending her reach to Tanzania, areas of Kenya, Nigeria, and numerous other major cities around the globe that had been taken over by those who were not in their rightful places.

She materialized in the vibrant City of Mexico, near the bustling Paseo De La Reforma, where she stood over her palaces that had long been covered by modern architectural structures that dominated the skyline. With a calm resolve, she slowly blew a steady breath of air, and soon all the surrounding areas began to slowly fill up with water, cascading gently like a serene tide.

"That will give them enough time to get out," she remarked thoughtfully.

He looked at her with understanding and nodded in agreement.

A few pockets of buildings scattered around the city unexpectedly caught her attention. With a flick of her wrist, she scattered some shimmering dust particles on each of them, watching with keen interest as they dissolved into nothing more than piles of dirt.

She sent urgent messages to her people, keenly encouraging them to exit the city before a certain, critical time.

Ameleki was dispatched with a solemn duty to take care of the children she had valiantly shielded. Most of these innocent ones were being tragically exploited as child prostitutes in the dark, crumbling pocket of buildings she had recently turned into mere dust. The destructions occurred in a blink, taking her no more than five minutes of Earth time to complete.

"I have a lot of important work to do, but let's go see Earth," she declared with determination. Without pausing to wait for a response or consideration, she disappeared in a swift flash.

29

SUDAN AND PURPLE QUEEN

The tribe crossed the border and ventured into Canada, on that unfortunate day they were relentlessly pursued by the KKK. At the moment, they found themselves nestled in a cozy Starbucks located in a small town in New Brunswick. They desperately needed internet access to post their videos on YouTube and to attend to various other remote working tasks.

"I had the strangest dream about my cousin Marshane in China," Purple Queen confided quietly to Sudan, who was sitting comfortably next to her. Over time, they had developed a close friendship, and it felt as if they had known each other for an eternity.

"Really, you have a cousin in China? I have a cousin living in China too," Sudan stated while putting her hands confidently on her hips and looking intently at her friend.

"What is your cousin's name?" Purple inquired with curiosity.

"We called her Shaney, a name we all loved," her friend replied with a smile.

"Really, that's exactly what we called my cousin for short," Purple admitted, feeling a strange connection.

"Where in Jamaica are you from, by the way?" Sudan then asked, eager to learn more. "My father is from the beautiful Montego Bay, but my mother hails from the bustling Spanish Town," Purple explained proudly.

"My mother is from Spanish Town," Sudan said loudly, drawing the attention of everyone else in the room.

"What's the name of your grandmother?"

"It's Myry, but we always called her Granny," Purple confirmed with a smile.

"That is the name of my grandmother as well. Sometimes she would fall asleep for what felt like hours and couldn't wake up, as if lost in a deep dream. I have an aunty named Netty and another we affectionately called Aunty Norma."

"Yes, they are my aunties too," Purple replied with a laugh, her eyes sparkling with shared memories.

"Oh my gosh, this is so incredibly weird. You mean to tell me that you two are actual cousins and you didn't even know it?" Lucas asked, his eyes wide with disbelief.

"It's freaking weird," said Sandy, who had gone all out with her appearance—she had dyed her hair a vibrant green and was sporting striking green contacts. Her ensemble included a flowing green long dress and casual green flip-flops that perfectly matched her entire look. Even her jewelry accessories were an assortment of green pieces, making her stand out even more and drawing a significant amount of attention from everyone around.

Purple looked at her bestie, her new-found cousin, and inquired curiously, "Are you Princess?"

"Yes, and you're Chunchun?" Sudan replied with a wide grin.

"That's right."

"Oh my gosh! I truly didn't think I would ever see you again, not in a million years. When your father took you away from us, Cindy and I were utterly devastated and heartbroken. So many things changed for me as well when my own father came and got me, whisking me away to the States. But despite all the changes and challenges, I never stopped thinking about my best friend over the years."

Sudan gazed intently at her cousin, the very same person who had been her dearest friend during their childhood days. She felt a wave of nostalgia wash over her as she wondered why she had never recognized her before now. Purple was completely decked out in her favorite color from head to toe, creating a striking image. Her long, flowing purple cotton dress modestly covered her from neck to toes while still allowing her elegance to shine through, and on her head rested a charming silver crown adorned with matching purple stones that sparkled in the light.

"You have not changed one bit; I should have recognized you right away." Sudan was so incredibly happy that tears of joy were running down her cheeks, glistening like tiny diamonds in the light.

"The moment I tasted that perfectly fried dumpling, I should have known it was you. You're the only one who could ever cook fried dumplings like that," Purple complimented with a warm smile. "Even when you were just that small, your talent was unmistakable."

"Yea, Sudan, when are you going to cook for us again?" Betty asked playfully, her lips curling into a mock pout that made it impossible to resist her charm.

"I kept getting up early every single day, bursting with anticipation, just to check if you were at it, hoping to catch even a tiny whiff of those delicious dumplings wafting through the air."

"Yea, Sudan, and..." I kept asking her, my curiosity piqued. Is the feast ready yet? But she kept telling me, no, nothing is there. I'm starting to think that incredible feast was all just a figment of my imagination," Tusk said, playfully imitating his wife with a grin.

"You can't tease us like that and leave us wanting more. I also kept wondering when I am going to get another one of those delicious hearty meals again,"

John said loudly, trying to make himself heard above the lively noise of the bustling café.

Every single member of her tribe shook their heads in solemn agreement. Sudan felt an overwhelming wave of guilt wash over her. She truly had every intention of cooking for them on a regular basis, frequently preparing hearty meals that would nourish them all, but she had been knee-deep in a project for her job, and it was consuming all of her time and energy.

"I'm really sorry, I've been so busy with work lately. I hardly have any time for myself as well. But I promise, as soon as I finish with it, I will be very happy to cook for all of you," she declared earnestly.

"When you're ready, just let us know so we can have all the necessary ingredients ready," Tusk replied thoughtfully. "As a matter of fact, my bus is quite spacious, and we still have a lot of empty space available. We should all come together as a community and stock up on food and water that will serve us for months on end, if needs be. That way, we won't have to keep leaving our campgrounds to buy food, which can be quite a hassle."

All the members of the tribe shook their heads in vigorous agreement, their expressions a mix of concern and understanding. They all knew, deep down, that things were undeniably changing around the world. Their recent experience a few weeks ago served as undeniable testimony to the shifting dynamics they were facing.

It was indeed a wonderfully innovative idea. Tusk was already enthusiastically designing a food storage unit in his bus specifically for them all to securely store their food.

"But wouldn't it be even better if we could buy a piece of land in some remote area and grow our own food?" Purple suggested thoughtfully.

They all turned to look at her in surprise, as if she had suddenly grown an extra head. This concept was one they had never even considered before. Lucas, ever observant, noticed that they had a few eavesdroppers lurking nearby, listening in on their conversation. So he suggested that they all finish up what they were doing and return to camp, where they could discuss this intriguing idea in much greater detail and in the privacy they needed.

They made a brief stop at Home Depot to gather essential wood supplies needed for the construction of the temporary food storage, then headed to Costco to stock up on food supplies, and finally visited the telephone company to arrange for an updated service plan, enabling them all to access internet connectivity without the hassle of leaving their camp. It took them almost three hours to get whatever they needed, before finally driving back to their boon-docking campsite located on the outskirts of New Brunswick.

They felt a surge of happiness when they discovered that nobody had taken over their beautiful green spot.

In Costco, Sudan had spotted some large, fresh snapper fish and made the decision to purchase them so she could prepare a delightful dinner for her tribe, consisting of brown stew snapper paired with steamed rice and carrots. Additionally, she planned to bake two large potato puddings and boil a generous pot of Brazilian nut porridge. While it wouldn't be the grand feast she had once, it would certainly suffice to keep them satisfied as they gathered around to discuss the land, the sticks, and the bricks.

They had all contributed in one way or another to setting the tables for the gathering. Tusk, James, and Barry were designated to take care of the drinks, ensuring that everyone would have something refreshing to enjoy. Purple expertly brought out a small butane stove and placed it carefully on a flat rock situated near the tables. Meanwhile, Lucas and John maneuvered the heavy pot of porridge and balanced it delicately on the small stove to keep the porridge warm and inviting. Sudan hurried over to turn down the heat just enough to prevent it from burning her carefully crafted masterpiece.

Once all the food was beautifully displayed on the tables, including various delicious snacks that the others had joyfully purchased at Costco, they took a moment to capture the occasion with photographs, highlighting Lucas as he offered a heartfelt blessing over the food. As they all dug into the feast with relish and enjoyment, their laughter filled the air.

When they finally finished, they found themselves too full to even think about the porridge and left it untouched on the stove.

After an hour of sitting together in contented silence, Lucas decided that he could possibly squeeze in a little bit of the porridge. He made his way to fill his porridge bowl, which Sudan had thoughtfully placed on the tables for their use, before bringing it back to his seat.

The tantalizing and aromatic smell of coconut wafted through the air, reaching their noses and tempting them even further. They lazily watched as he took a spoonful of the porridge, bringing it to his mouth, and as he closed his eyes in delight, a satisfied moan escaped him, making everyone even more curious about the delectable dish.

"Dang gosh it, girl, you really put your foot in it," Lucas complimented with an impressed grin. Sudan laughed heartily at the compliment, clearly pleased. Meanwhile, Purple got up, took her empty bowl, and headed over to the pot to fill it with steaming porridge. Sudan followed suit, eager to indulge in her craft-woman-ship. Soon, all of them were savoring the hot Brazilian nuts porridge, their contented moans filling the air as they went back for seconds.

After finishing the delicious porridge, they were all sprawled out in their camping chairs, groaning about how their bellies felt excruciatingly full from the delightful feast.

They found themselves quite content to sit quietly for the next few hours, letting the soothing melodies of Bob Marley play softly in the background. The atmosphere was serene and peaceful in Canada. The tensions and horrific killings that were erupting in many areas of the United States felt worlds away, allowing them to enjoy their tranquil time undisturbed.

Sudan had lit her bug candle, which filled the campsite with a lovely lavender scent, while Tusk had taken the initiative to surround the campsite with warm light he had cleverly hooked up to his generator, adding to the cozy ambiance.

It was a wonderfully pleasant evening, characterized by the perfect temperature that made it ideal for relaxation. A few male birds were still joyfully serenading their love interests, filling the air with sweet melodies, while the stars began to peek out one by one in the darkening sky.

Nobody had turned on their radios to hear what was happening in the world beyond, and perhaps it was a good thing for the moment. Two hours later, they remained contented, continuing to sit in their comfortable chairs and idly chatting about their days and dreams. After a few more hours had passed, about half of the tribe members eventually got up, taking the eating and cooking utensils to their buses where they carefully washed them before returning them to the table for future use. Individuals picked up their utensils, and some took uneaten snacks, dutifully carrying them back to their cozy dwellings.

"Guys, what time do you want to get up tomorrow to discuss Purple's innovative idea?" Tusk inquired, breaking the comfortable silence.

"How about nine in the morning?" John suggested, looking around at everyone with a hopeful expression on his face.

They all nodded and shook their heads in agreement, clearly in favor of the idea. A few of the group stayed outside a little longer to enjoy the night air, while others made their way off to bed after taking a moment to thank Sudan for the truly amazing meal they had just enjoyed.

"Yeah, next time, make sure to whip up two big pots of that delicious porridge. It was so incredibly good that I will definitely be dreaming about it tonight," Lucas remarked, eliciting a hearty chuckle from the others who were feeling pleasantly satisfied.

~~~~~~~

Sudan got up around six o'clock the following morning to begin diligently working on her important project. The previous day had unfortunately set her back a couple of hours in her progress, but she wouldn't have changed a single thing about her experiences. She smiled softly at the delightful memory of their shared contentment and promised herself to hurry up with the project for her job, so she could prepare a lovely breakfast for everyone.

Heading into her beautifully organized little kitchen, she expertly brewed her favorite coffee and fried a couple of golden-brown egg fritters, which she carefully plated and then took to her cozy office nestled in the corner behind her bed. There, she immersed herself in her work for three focused hours before getting dressed and preparing for her meeting with her team.

The majority of them were already gathered outside with coffee cups in hand, eagerly waiting for the others to join when she stepped outside, also holding her steaming cup of coffee. Once all the members had arrived and settled in, Tusk confidently started the meeting.

"How many of you think that buying a piece of land truly seemed like a good idea?" Lucas asked, surveying the faces around him as they all raised their hands in agreement.

"Although it may not appear that way at this moment, trust me when I say that things and time will certainly change. Within another year or so, the entire world will be grappling with severe food shortages. If we take the time to plan now, we won't have to face that daunting problem later on." Lucas cautioned warmly.

The tribe members all respected and trusted Lucas's extraordinary clairvoyant abilities. If he said something was going to happen, it was not just a possibility; it was bound to happen.

"Okay, so where do we have in mind to acquire this land?" Tusk asked, curious and eager to contribute to the discussion.

"How about Central America, or perhaps even nearer to South America?" Purple suggested with enthusiasm. "It's warmer all year round, and the climate allows food to grow continuously throughout the year."

Sandy nodded her head in agreement, clearly considering the advantages.

Barry chimed in his support as well.

"What about the option of purchasing land right here in Canada? It's relatively peaceful, and living remotely in this beautiful country would bring an even greater sense of tranquility," John, who had been the quietest in the group, suggested thoughtfully.

They all appreciated the charm of Canada, but they acknowledged that there were limitations on what they could grow. In Central and South America, however, the potential to cultivate just about anything was almost limitless.

Tusk gave them a moment to ponder this idea, then he encouraged them by saying, "Who here favors the option of Central America or moving toward South America? Please raise your hands."

Sandy, Sudan, and Purple raised their hands, eager to express their preference.

"Who among you here prefer this isolated and remote area of Canada, please raise your hands," Tusk instructed again.

John and Betty quickly raised their hands in response.

"Why didn't you raise your hand, Lucas?" Tusk inquired, glancing over at him with curiosity.

"From what I'm observing, it seems they are orchestrating a plan to break Mexico away from the United States, which would undoubtedly incite a significant reaction throughout South America, the Caribbean, and various parts of North America. If we manage to secure the land in Canada, which is further away from the looming influence of the United States, we might just be fortunate enough to avoid severe repercussions," he predicted, carefully trying to avoid alarming the others with his thoughts.

"But remember, things could change unexpectedly; the future is never truly set in stone," he continued, hoping desperately that they would arrive at the right decision when the moment came.

"But what's your choice in all of this?" Tusk pressed, seeking clarity from Lucas.

"I will go for Canada," Lucas answered firmly.

"Okay, that's four to three, which leaves me to decide. I think I'll go for Canada as well."

They shook their heads in acceptance of the choices.

"Next up, how much money are we really prepared to spend? And how many acres of land are we actually talking about?" Tusk inquired thoughtfully.

"Well, we could buy ten acres of beautiful land, one that even comes with a big fish pond. And we could raise chickens, goats, and other animals, plus grow a variety of vegetables. We could construct a spacious storehouse and a great house complete with a fallout shelter, and we could even build a few tiny houses for ourselves. Not to mention, we should also think about a huge garage where we could park our vehicles safely and securely." Sandy excitedly ran off at the mouth, filled with enthusiasm for the possibilities.

"Wow, all those were actually brilliant suggestions," said Sudan, raising an eyebrow in admiration. "But will ten acres really be enough for our plans?"

"We could shoot for fifteen to twenty acres instead," John replied thoughtfully. "Considering the addition of a pond, we're definitely going to need a lot more land to make it work."

"Okay then, let's aim for that range of fifteen to twenty acres," Sudan agreed.

"Now, the next important question is, how are we going to accumulate the necessary funds?" Tusk asked, his curiosity piqued.

"Well, since we all work remotely," Barry suggested, "We can explore the option of adding another job to our existing list of commitments. This way, we can save up quickly enough to purchase the land outright, and completely avoid needing a mortgage. In the meantime, we'll all do our own research while exploring various areas until we find something that meets all of our criteria and that we can all agree upon."

"Hear, hear, bossman Barry," Sandy hooted enthusiastically, her voice echoing with excitement.

They all burst into laughter, a harmonious blend of hope and camaraderie filling the air. It was a truly brilliant plan they had devised together. After much discussion, they agreed to dismantle their camp the very next day to embark on the crucial land hunting expedition, but not before they finished constructing the additional storage space in the bus and loaded it up with the essential food and water supplies they would need for the journey ahead.

If their efforts at the micro level collaboration proved successful, then they were confident that they could most certainly replicate it on the macro level.

The guys unanimously decided to tackle the construction of the food storage unit that very day, while Sudan excused herself to concentrate on finishing her project for her job. Meanwhile, the others eagerly brainstormed and made plans to search for online jobs that would supplement their income, allowing them to save for the purchase of the land they were all dreaming of.

An air of anticipation enveloped them; a thrilling new chapter was about to unfold in their lives.

30

ROUNDING UP THE SKY PEOPLE

Moonshine appeared suddenly in front of Roboliac and Starr as they were on their way to their practice session. She took a moment to look at the beautiful young girl with the mesmerizing silver-blue tint in her hair and couldn't seem to place her identity within her memory. The girl did not appear to be an Earth being, nor did she exhibit any characteristics typical of sky beings. "You look quite strange," Moonshine remarked, her curiosity piqued.

"She's an alien from Golealm, a mysterious planet hidden behind dark matter almost a million light years away," Starr facilitated, her voice filled with enthusiasm.

"What is she doing here? And, how exactly did she end up getting here?" Moonshine inquired, her brow furrowing with concern.

"Relax, Moonshine. She's Earth's sister," Starr reassured, her expression brightening with understanding.

"Hmm," Moonshine breathed, looking suspiciously at Roboliac with narrowed eyes, then she turned on her heel and walked off with an air of mystery.

"Wow, she acts just like one of my sisters," Roboliac remarked, now lost in thought as she recalled memories of Laliac and her unpredictable nature.

"Stay away from her until she gets the information she needs," Ameleki stated firmly as she appeared beside them, her voice carrying an authority that was hard to ignore. She had already completed her important task of restoring the abused children and ensuring they were placed in safe, loving homes, far away from the dangers of the City of Mexico.

"Okay, but who is she, exactly?" Roboliac asked, curiosity piquing her interest.

"She, my dear, Luminaire, is the powerful entity responsible for maintaining the peace on earth, but she has been resting for quite some time. Now, she's returned to find that earth has fallen into a state of deep mire and chaos. She's not at all pleased," Ameleki volunteered, her voice tinged with a mix of respect and concern.

"I suppose we will be seeing a lot of shifting and upheaval taking place all over the globe in the coming days," stated Starr, looking as if she relished the idea of witnessing it unfold.

~~~~~~

Moonshine was not feeling particularly happy today. Aliens were insidiously taking over human bodies, manipulating them, while other humans were leading their fellow beings astray in a web of deceit and manipulation. Poverty, strife, and various forms of abuse had regrettably become a part of humanity's norm, as countries clashed and overtook one another, raping both the people and the lands, and dislocating the indigenous populations from their ancestral spaces. Alarmingly, almost forty percent of the Earth's lush forests had been deforested, leaving behind scars on the planet. The people had no real understanding of who those ancient trees were, nor the profound significance they represented. She had only gone to sleep for less than a day, and already, everything seemed to be falling apart; shit was truly hitting the fan.

"*Yes, but we have much bigger problems than that*," a familiar ancient gritty voice resonated, piercing through the depths of her mind.

Moonlight instantly recognized that voice, one she had not heard echoing in her consciousness for nearly three billion years. A shiver cascaded through her entire body at the recollection. The last time that voice reached her ears, both Earth and the entire solar system revolving around it were perilously close to obliteration due to the catastrophic approach of another colliding solar system. Moon, Venus, Jupiter, and Mars found themselves perilously positioned in the direct trajectory of this impending disaster. Only a couple of these planets managed to emerge partially recovered from the chaos that ensued. Meanwhile, here on Earth, nearly all forms of life faced the terrifying threat of extinction. It took the sky people, whose intervention was crucial, hundreds of thousands of years to restore the Earth to a semblance of its former glory. But now, tragically, mankind was on the verge of destroying it all over again.

"But now we have another imminent threat, and this time I don't think we'll be able to adequately recover from it."

"But what can we realistically do?" Moonshine asked, feeling a wave of unease wash over her, suddenly.

She was always a worrier and a bit melodramatic, yet she also had a pragmatic side that often grounded her. Earth had anticipated this kind of reaction from her, which is exactly why she had intentionally left out the most crucial information. She didn't want them to believe there was absolutely no hope for a future.

"Humans have developed nuclear weapons, and with what's looming ahead, they will only exacerbate an already dire situation. For the moment, we need to

devise a strategy to get them as far away from these weapons as possible."

Earth projected all the precise locations where the weapons were hidden around the globe, along with the facilities where each and every one of them had been manufactured.

"Nuclear weapons? Who in their right mind gave them this alarming information?"

"Who do you expect to have that knowledge?" Earth replied, her tone edged with irony.

Moonshine shook her head vigorously, cussing quietly at that half-beast creature lurking in the depths of her mind. *"Okay, we'll get to it,"* she reluctantly agreed, steeling herself for the task ahead.

"And we need to ensure that everyone is returned to their proper places. We certainly don't want them killing off each other before the true enemies finally show their faces." The gritty voice sounded old and tired, filled with weariness, and Moonshine could feel a sting in her eyes as her emotions welled up inside her.

"I will, Your Greatness," she replied with determination before she turned and exited the grand palace.

"You heard that?" Moonshine asked Dan, who had materialized suddenly next to her in the sweltering expanse of the Sahara Desert. "We absolutely have to wake everybody up!" she insisted, urgency creeping into her tone.

"A lot of sky people and aliens from far and wide have taken a shine to humanity."

"Yes, I definitely noticed," Dan replied, a hint of concern evident in his voice.

"Some are genuinely good and willing to fight for our survival, but others are negative influences, seeking only to cause chaos," she explained gravely.

"That, I also noticed," he agreed, his brow furrowing in thought. "Shall we get started?"

Moonshine slowly stretched out her hands at the same moment that Dan did, their fingers interlocking effortlessly. Taking each other's hands with a sense of unity, they both closed their eyes and lifted their faces gracefully towards the vast sky above. Opening their mouths slightly, they let out a silent sound that resonated deeply within the cosmos.

This unique sound was one that only their kind could hear, echoing through the dimensions from anywhere in the universe and far beyond. They stood in that ethereal state for a full fifteen minutes, calling forth their kin. Billions of sky people, from near and far, heard the enchanting call and began to arrive. Creatures of all varying colors and shapes emerged on the warm sand, kneeling reverently in front of their beloved King and Queen.

~~~~~~~~

How can I possibly convey this to them? How can I instill fear in their hearts about the profound terror that would ultimately beset all of mankind? Lucas, the king of the Clairvoyants, was deeply concerned about the safety and future of his small tribe and the impending calamities that were destined to unfold on earth when he suddenly heard the urgent call. He was quite a distance away from his dear friends, hidden among the dense trees, lost in his contemplative thoughts, yet he still felt an unsettling urge to look around, to ensure that no one was observing. When he did not detect anyone in his immediate vicinity, he took a deep breath and disappeared. Mere seconds later, he found himself amidst the gathered throngs of the sky people, their elegantly large wings spanning wide, all situated in the heart of the vast Sahara Desert. They were all respectfully kneeling before the dignified heads of their Monarchy. As he knelt in the warm, fine sand, his massive wings vanished in an instant, blending seamlessly with the surroundings. A handful of others around him also discreetly retracted their wings, a subtle act among the assembly.

The silent sound persisted for another five long minutes, stretching into a suffocating silence that seemed to envelop everything around them. When the couple had finally finished their task, Moonshine and Dan exchanged glances and began to look around to see if everyone was still present.

A couple of individuals were notably missing from their ranks, but Moonshine already had an inkling that they would be absent. With a firm resolve, she conjured the image they had been given and implanted it in their minds.

"We need to locate all of these items, gather them into a substantial pile, and eliminate them once and for all," she informed them with urgency. "Make sure to travel in pairs or threes. The humans we are dealing with have become truly ruthless, unfeeling, and wicked at heart."

"As you wish, Your Highness," they all responded in harmonious unison. Without delay, they gathered in small groups of twos and threes before disappearing into the shadows to tend to their pressing tasks, leaving the King and Queen to confront the most wicked among humankind—Queen Elizabeth of England.

31

THE BODY THIEF

J alaniac and Laliac were deeply concerned about
their sister's well-being. It appeared she was
invested in Solstilert much more than she was in
maintaining her relationship with them. Yes, she
could no longer hear their voices or their heartfelt
expressions, but at the very least, she could have
made an effort to reach out and keep in touch.
Instead, it felt as though she had completely chosen to
eliminate them from her life entirely. The two were
seated in one of the many expansive lounging areas of
Jalaniac's underground palace, which was adorned
with intricate designs and soft, ambient lighting.

Laliac, who had never been much of a talker,
silently absorbed Jalaniac's growing concerns.

"I think Solstilert needs her companionship right
now. There seems to be something uniquely special
about our sister that positively influences her. So
perhaps we should let her be for the time being until
further notice," Laliac suggested thoughtfully.

"But it's my solemn responsibility to see that she is properly safeguarded. Since she's fully merged with humanity, if anything happens to her, we will not be able to save her from whatever fate awaits. Did you see the way she looked? She has completely transformed into a human. And to make matters worse, her Golealmness has become increasingly more obvious. How is she going to survive out there in the real world, looking like that?" Jalaniac finished with a deep sense of dread.

Roboliac was the last of the triplet and notably the most sensitive of them all. She was well-loved throughout Golealm and considered the favorite among the family members. When she had made the decision to leave Golealm and followed her sisters to the distant new planet, their father was utterly devastated, but he eventually realized that she, like her sisters, was meant to be a traveler. Now, however, she had gone and fully merged herself with humanity. What was going to happen to her in this new life? What was Solstilert's true motives for hanging onto her the way she was currently doing? What were they going to do about it? What could they possibly do to help her?

They couldn't quite figure it out. They were also extremely weary of Solstilert's incredible powers. It was the strongest force they had ever witnessed in any galaxy they had explored. Who was she, really? They sat in contemplative silence, slowly sipping on their new ackee wine, allowing their thoughts to drift and swirl around the mysteries that surrounded them.

~~~~~~~~

Jalaniac, having left her human body, Myry, who was sleeping motionless on the sofa upstairs, returned to discover it was now mysteriously occupied.

It was a bright afternoon, and to her astonishment, Myry's body had reverted back to the youthful age of sixteen. She was gyrating energetically to the vibrant rhythms of Lady Saw and Beenie Man's hit song, "Man Fi Get Cuff." The movement was spirited, with Myry's body executing the latest dance moves while singing loudly and enthusiastically along to the track.

Jalaniac and Laliac stood frozen, watching in shocked horror, their minds racing. This strange occurrence had never happened before in their experience. How was it possible that another being could breach the invisible protective barrier they had meticulously wrapped around the entire property, stealing Myry's body in the process? What was going on here?

"Who are you and what are you doing with my body?" Jalaniac asked, her voice barely above a whisper, tinged with both curiosity, anger and concern.

Myry turned and gave her a most mischievous laugh as she continued to dance, lewdly, to the pulsing rhythm of the music that enveloped the room.

When the music finally finished, she abruptly stopped all movement, and in an instant, all trace of happiness and mischief vanished from her once playful face.

"Your body?" Myry asked in a chilling, creepy voice that was more shocking than the sudden sound of a rat squeaking in the dark. "Where do you come from talking bout your body? You've chosen to abandon the body, so it's no longer yours to claim."

Laliac stretched out her right hand and summoned a flaming silver sword, its brilliant light illuminating the space between them, and pointed it firmly at Myry. "Get. Out!" she ordered sternly, commanding the being that had taken residence in the body.

"Or what? You're going to chop me up? Go aheaaaaad," it replied throatily, maintaining that eerie, screeching voice that sent chills down their spine. Once again, Myry offered them a mischievous, mocking look that seemed to challenge their resolve.

Laliac didn't bother to answer, her silence speaking volumes in the tense atmosphere. In less than a fleeting second, she had her sword raised high and stood protectively in front of Myry, her stance fierce and unwavering. With a swift and practiced motion, she swung the sword, and it went straight through Myry's body as if she were merely a shadow.

"Noooooooo!" Jalaniac screamed at her sister in utter disbelief and horror.

The blade, however, didn't have any effect on the human matter; it slid right through Myry's material form like a hot knife through soft butter, leaving the physical body completely undisturbed. Subsequently, the being that had taken residence inside Myry's body fell out onto the ground, gruesomely split in two, its essence now liberated but also irrevocably altered.

It was the most disorganized, misshapen, and grotesque looking thing they had ever encountered on Materealm. It was utterly black and resembled a living fishnet, all tangled up together, with tendrils of darkness emanating from it as if it were alive. The upper half, where the creature's head should have been, appeared disturbingly unformed and amorphous. The area where a face was supposed to exist was merely a deep, bottomless pit of inky blackness, devoid of any features. They couldn't believe what they were witnessing with their own eyes. It was a nightmarish creature from the enemy planet in their galaxy that had somehow become trapped and sucked into a treacherous black hole.

The planets in their vast and magnificent galaxy breathed a collective sigh of relief when it had finally been consumed. The creatures that inhabited it were a vile and grotesque set with no comprehension of right and wrong, causing chaos wherever they roamed. But now here it stood, defiantly in their house, as if it possessed the audacity and right to be there. They were like rat droppings scattered carelessly; if one was spotted, it usually signaled that a whole swarm of them was lurking nearby.

"Where are the others?" Laliac demanded, fiercely pointing her oversized sword at the creature, her eyes ablaze with determination and ready to swing it again, looking fiercer than anything Jalaniac had ever witnessed before in all her life.

~~~~~~~~

Dan, Solstilert, and the two beautiful, shirtless Nubians strode confidently in through an invisible door just at the very moment Laliac raised her sword menacingly toward the grotesque, misshapen creature.

"*No, not yet!*" Solstilert urged Laliac firmly, her voice steady and commanding in her mind. "*We need more information before making any rash decisions.*"

Jalaniac had inexplicably returned to Myry's young sixteen-year-old body, which had collapsed onto the ground the second the misshapen creature had violently exited it.

She had no awareness of having entered the vessel. The final merging had begun its irreversible process. With a scream filled with disbelief and deep-seated anger, she fought against the overwhelming transition relentlessly.

Laliac cast a concerned glance towards her sister, witnessing her struggle and turmoil, before turning her attention to Solstilert, who was now stooping over the creature with a look of intense concentration and purpose.

The face that Earth was showing him was not merely a face anyone had ever seen before, but an otherworldly visage that defied all logic and comprehension. It was a face that embodied the most grotesque of all grotesques in the vast and expanding sky, a manifestation of horror that seemed to writhe and distort in the very atmosphere. A face, so unknown and unfathomable, not even the Creator could have possibly known of its existence. She wielded the face to her advantage, skillfully concealing its full terrifying nature, not revealing just how truly frightful it would be to the others.

"Where are the others?" She calmly asked it in its own alien language. The fishnet creature found itself caught in a conflict, reluctant to divulge the whereabouts of its fellow beings, the ones who had miraculously survived the immense dangers of the black hole and found themselves marooned on this unfamiliar planet. However, it yearned for the nightmarish visage that haunted them in the blackhole to stop. A face that replicate the harrowing experienced within the black hole. It want it to vanish along with the spectral sword that could slice through its very essence.

Still, despite this pressing urge, it could not betray the secrets of its remaining comrades' locations. They were the sole survivors of their once-thriving planet, and it was imperative that he keep them safe from any impending threat.

Solstilert, having seen all the fragmented thoughts and precise locations of the others racing through the creature's mind, stood up decisively. She glanced over at Laliac and, without forming any words with her lips, communicated her intent. *"I want to see what that sword can truly do. He's all yours."*

Laliac, emboldened by Solstilert's unspoken challenge, swung her sword with fierce determination, slicing the creature into four distinct pieces. However, astonishingly, the creature did not perish; instead, it appeared to stretch and stubbornly reattach its fragments together as though healing from the assault. Just then, Dan vanished from sight, only to return in less than a minute, bringing Priscilla with him.

"Here, take this vial and apply its contents to your sword. Then slice him again and see what happens," Dan instructed Laliac, handing her a small glass vial that had been retrieved from Priscilla's bag.

Laliac carefully poured the liquid from the vial onto her sword, and to everyone's shock, the metal emitted a piercing scream. They observed Laliac as she whispered soothing words to the sword, which gradually calmed down. Fueled by renewed determination, she sliced through the creature lying helplessly on the floor, vertically cleaving it from head to crotch. Almost immediately, the creature began to melt away, oozing a white and grey liquid that resembled melted plastic, pooled on the ground.

Seizing the moment, Priscilla reached into her bag once again, retrieving another vial, which she hurled at the creature while muttering a powerful incantation. Instantly, the being began to bubble ominously with smoke before vanishing into the nothingness from which it had emerged.

Dan returned Priscilla swiftly and was back in the same amount of time as before.

Solstilert had stood up immediately the moment the creature had dissolved into the ether and looked intently at Laliac.

Laliac, who had never felt fear in any situation throughout her life, was now staring back at Solstilert with a heart that thundered in her chest.

"*We want your weapons and your help. Will you aid us in our quest?*" Solstilert asked, her voice steady and calm despite the turmoil around her.

"That depends on what you wish to use my help for," Laliac stated calmly, redirecting her gaze towards young Myry, who was pouting with her lips jutting out and arms wrapped tightly around her waist. Myry was tapping her right foot impatiently against the floor, her body moving restlessly, she looked like a spoiled brat with an unresolved issue.

Solstilert flooded Laliac's mind with vivid images so profound that a big "O" formed on her lips, and she suddenly swallowed hard before immediately closing her mouth in contemplation.

"When all of this is over, will I get my sisters back in their original condition?" she asked, her eyes betraying a flicker of vulnerability beneath the surface.

"That I cannot guarantee, but we will strive to do our utmost," Solstilert promised with determination in her tone.

"That's good enough for me," Laliac responded, and with that, they all walked through the invisible door leading to the grand palace, a mix of hope and uncertainty guiding their steps into the unknown.

32

THE THREE GOLEALM SISTERS

K lam had just finished a particularly tedious and exhausting training session with Starr and Ameleki. Her body was practically raining sweat, and she felt as if she could barely walk straight. What she really needed now was a long, indulgent soak in her Jacuzzi tub—a tranquil escape with absolutely no distractions.

Feeling fatigued, she made her way to her luxurious suite to pour herself a big glass of refreshing sorrel juice, hoping to quench her overwhelming thirst. After all, that kind of excruciating exercise always took a toll on her. Putting down the empty glass, she confidently headed toward her oversized bathroom, shedding her clothes one piece at a time as she walked. Upon finally reaching her huge, inviting tub, she was taken aback to discover it was already occupied by two other beings, leaving her momentarily speechless.

"What are you doing in my tub?" she asked, her tone laced with irritation and a hint of disbelief.

She was not in the mood for any kind of company at all. After all, she had made that point abundantly clear to her trainers. Of course, they had only batted their eyelashes at her, not taking her seriously. Starr even blew her a playful kiss as she turned away, completely unfazed. She had been really looking forward to some precious alone time in the comfort of her bathtub. It was the perfect excuse she needed to meditate deeply on her growing, complicated feelings for the two Nubians.

Having two male at once was culturally acceptable in Golealm, yet the question lingered in her mind: what were they to Solstilert? Why did their presence stir such wanton emotions within her? Was she simply still feeling the lingering effects of the intoxicating fruit? She was consumed by a maddening confusion. Why was she feeling this way at all? Was this sense of bewilderment simply part of being human?

"Your tub? Get your butt in and stop ruining our quiet!" Myry ordered, still feeling miffed about her merging.

Klam looked closer and saw, to her astonishment, that they were indeed her beloved sisters, a younger Myry and—"Laliac! Is that you?" Laliac was fully merged into the ethereal body of a sky person, radiating an otherworldly beauty that rivaled even that of Ameleki and Starr. Klam's heart raced as she struggled to comprehend the sight before her; she could hardly believe her eyes, overwhelmed by the rush of emotions and the longing she had carried for so long. She had missed them so profoundly.

"What are you doing here?" Klam asked, her voice trembling, with tears of joy welling in her eyes. She couldn't help it; it was a deeply human reaction that surged within her, betraying her usually composed demeanor.

"The same thing as you, Trippy," Myry replied, a teasing grin spreading across her face as she used the affectionate nickname they hadn't uttered in almost two hundred and fifty thousand years.

Despite the time that had passed, she was still pouting in that familiar way, a cheerful glint in her eyes that seemed to bridge the immense gap of time apart.

"I take it this was not your idea," Klam said, laughing happily as she settled into the cheerful atmosphere. She was positively thrilled that they were all here together.

"You're so noisy," Laliac remarked quietly, her tone revealing a hint of annoyance that was unmistakable. Klam carefully got into the tub, trying her best not to accidentally step on any of them.

Playful, she squeezed herself between the two, wriggling her body into a cozy position where she felt warm and snug. Glancing at both of them, she flashed a bright smile, but they were deliberately pretending to ignore her. With a soft sigh, she leaned her head against the tub, closing her eyes as she let the music wash over her, the familiar tune from their favorite song drifting through the air from the mp3 player someone had so thoughtfully left.

"A Luminary party, fabulous!" Starr exclaimed, bubbling with enthusiasm as she appeared on the opposite side of the tub just five minutes later.

"A tub party, what a wonderful idea," Ameleki cooed, joining in beside Starr with her characteristic warmth, adding to the joyous camaraderie of the moment.

They obviously had not taken Klam's request seriously. The two new arrivals were looking intently at the three sisters, yet they were being completely ignored. Starr, with an air of command, pushed a button in the wall beside her, and two waiters promptly appeared in response. "Darlings, could you please fix us up with some delightful drinks, will you?" she said to the waiters in a charming tone. A minute later, they returned, balancing trays laden with six exquisite gold-trimmed wine glasses, five carefully selected bottles of wine, and a large fruit tray, beautifully arrayed with vibrant colors. They placed the items on a table that had been cleverly pulled out of the wall over the luxurious jacuzzi.

"Will that be all?" one of the waiters inquired, his tone professional yet attentive."Yes, thank you very much," said Starr, giving them a surreal smile.

Ameleki poured them all a generous drink, carefully handing each of her friends a glass filled to the brim.

"To wonderful times to come," she proclaimed warmly, lifting her glass high with a bright smile.

"To wonderful times," mimicked Starr with a playful grin, her eyes sparkling with excitement.

"To whatever you say," echoed the three sisters in unison, their voices blending together harmoniously. In that moment, everyone burst out laughing, a joyful sound that illuminated the atmosphere and truly lifted their spirits.

The tub party turned out to be an effective ice breaker, filled with laughter and camaraderie. By the time all the wine was finished and all the fresh fruits had been devoured, the five emerged from the tub feeling as if they were quintuplets, bonded in a delightful experience that none of them would soon forget.

~~~~~~~

Earth and Golealm were intently observing the five children happily splashing about in the tub.

"*Do you think we can genuinely find a solution to this pressing problem?*" Golealm asked, his mind swirling with concerns about the future and the well-being of his precious daughters.

"*I'm not entirely sure, but one thing is certain: we will certainly try our very best*," Earth responded, determination lacing her voice.

EPILOGUE

WHO ARE YOU?

He walked into the Round Office with only one thought fervently occupying his mind: how in the world could he rid himself of Meloskie? She had been nothing short of a persistent thorn in his side ever since her House ascended to power and took control.

"She must go, but it absolutely cannot appear that I'm behind it," he plotted meticulously.

So intense was his focus on Meloskie's potential demise that he almost completely overlooked the stunning, dark-skinned young woman with the lustrous, voluminous, floor-length black and white sisterlocks, sitting there with an aura of calm confidence. She was comfortably perched, cross-legged, in stylish white, remarkably wrinkle-free linen pants and a chic suit. Her black stiletto pumps complemented her designer handbag, which she had carelessly tossed aside on the luxurious sofa. Just as he was about to take a seat, he suddenly realized she occupied his favorite spot—on the very sofa he cherished.

"Who the fuck are you and how the fuck did you get in here?" he asked, his voice dripping with disrespect. He quickly glanced around in search of his guards, who were supposed to be keeping watch but, to his surprise, were nowhere to be seen.

"I'll have to fire those freaking guards again," he thought to himself, his irritation rising, finally turning his full attention to the most breathtaking Nubian woman he had ever laid eyes on.

As he gazed at her, trying desperately not to stare and failing miserably, something bizarre happened — she suddenly morphed into the most grotesque creature he had ever encountered.

"What is this?" Panic surged through him, a sense of terror overwhelming him at the sight of the being sitting before him.

He continued to watch in disbelief as she shifted into a Caucasian woman, then an exquisitely beautiful Indian woman, morphing seamlessly into the very epitome of beauty from the Orients. He was entranced, unable to pull his gaze away from the ever-changing faces. Yet, just as suddenly, she took on the visage of the terrifying figure that had haunted his dreams in childhood, and he felt a wave of dizziness wash over him, threatening to pull him under.

He could no longer bring himself to look at her when she dramatically transformed into a magnificent lioness while still wearing the familiar form of a human. Confusion quickly overrode his sensibilities, and his stolen heart began beating uncontrollably in his chest. He desperately wanted his heart medicine to soothe the frantic rhythm, but he knew that taking it would be detrimental to his well-being. Turning his head sideways, he averted his gaze from her, attempting to calm himself while inconspicuously stealing glances at her from the corner of his eyes— just to convince himself that he was not experiencing some vivid hallucinations. Yes, the creature was still there, as real and tangible as he was in that moment. Terror seized hold of his heart, and he pursed his lips defiantly, refusing to reveal the extent of the effect her mere presence was having on him.

She regarded him with penetrating eyes that radiated every color of the spectrum and more, captivating and unsettling all at once. He looked away again, struggling to maintain focus as dizziness began to wash over him, the shifting, haunting faces of her transformation only intensifying his disorientation.

"You will not fire anyone else. You will not kill anymore. And you will absolutely not send anyone to do your killings for you." The otherworldly woman's words echoed ominously in his mind, filling him with a sense of dread. They were more than just thoughts; they penetrated deep into his consciousness. It was as if she possessed the uncanny ability to read his every thought and intention, revealing the darkest corners of his mind and exposing him for who he truly was.

"Who the hell are you?" he asked once more, his voice dripping with a petulant, whining tone that reeked of a weakling who was far too privileged to comprehend the seriousness of his current situation.

He turned his gaze toward the door, frustration etched on his face, "Those fucking guards, where are they?"

But instead of the expected presence of his loyal guards, two of the most stunningly beautiful Nubian males he had ever encountered materialized out of thin air. His dormant groin stirred with desire, yearning to rise, yet it remained frustratingly unable to.

He looked at them, his heart racing as he waited anxiously to see if they were going to change, like the woman had, but they didn't move a muscle. He breathed a heavy sigh of relief, his mind momentarily easing.

"Sit!" The woman commanded him with an authority that left no room for disobedience.

The voice in his head was a chaotic mix of harshness, soothing softness, gentle tones, coarse edges, low murmurs, deafening echoes, musical notes, alien vibrations, and an unwavering authoritative presence.

He shook his head vigorously, desperately trying to rid himself of the cacophony that invaded his drugged, embalmed brain, seeking clarity amidst the turmoil.

"Wh...," he stuttered, but before he could finish the word, the two beautiful Nubian guards were suddenly beside him, their presence both commanding and unsettling. They had him seated on the cold floor right in front of her, and in an instant, they had returned to their positions at the door, standing vigil like statues.

It only took a mere five seconds for his panic to entwine with a deep-seated terror. He realized with grim certainty that he was going to die here in his office while those guards were off somewhere, attending to their own pursuits. The young woman regarded him with an unsettling calmness in her features, a serenity that inexplicably reminded him of a sleeping ocean, vast and unfathomable, hiding untold depths beneath its tranquil surface.

"In just two short days, you will formally resign from the Round Office. Should you choose to outright refuse to resign within that timeframe, be forewarned that your stolen heart will experience a catastrophic explosion right in your chest. However, there is an alternative: if you comply with my directive and resign, you will endure a severe stroke, yet you will, to some extent, manage to recover from it. Do you fully understand the gravity of this situation?"

He studied her intently, nodding his head, with fear clearly illuminating his eyes and his mouth pouting like that of an old, spoilt man-child he had always been.

"And let me make this clear: do not even think about executing another person to obtain their heart. It will make no difference whose heart you attempt to wear; it will inevitably still explode."

The stunningly beautiful woman—who, in reality, was anything but—cautioned him with an intense gaze, carefully observing the blend of malevolence and idiocy—two truly disastrous traits for someone in a position of power—as they flickered in his eyes. He watched as she stood up, noticing her considerable height. His eyes abruptly widened in astonishment when she shrunk to an unassuming five feet. His astonishment grew as he saw her transform into an obese giant and just as quickly, she morphed into a slender model. She was once he, then she transitioned into she, until she ultimately settled into the image that he had observed when he had nearly sat on her.

The two exceptionally beautiful males appeared on either side of her, radiant and striking. The one on the right elegantly stretched out his hand and, with a fluid motion, opened a door that seemed to exist in a dimension beyond the ordinary. In an instant, all three disappeared through this ethereal portal, leaving him still sitting on the floor in astonishment, gazing at the empty space where they had just been. His mouth hung open in disbelief, unable to comprehend what had just transpired.

"Two days, Manny," she repeated gently in his mind, using the name his mother affectionately called him, a poignant reminder of his past.

THE END

Of Book 1

GLOSSARY

Duppy.	Ghost
Dutty/dooty	Dirty
Idiat.	Idiot
Cho.	A Jamaican Expresion
Bloodclaat.	strong Jamaican bad word
Pussyclaat.	Strong Jamaican bad word
Bumboclaat.	Strong Jamaican bad word
Raas.	Mild Jamaican bad word
Mi.	Me
Dem	Them
Dem	Plural you
Neva	Never
Yuh	You
Oonuu/onu.	Plural you
Dat	That
Puppa Jesas	Father Jesus
Jesas Chrise	Jesus Christ
Guh.	Go/to go
A guh.	Is going to
Wha.	What
Weh	Where/what/why

Wope	Hope
Nuh.	No/not
Nyam	Eat/ to eat
Nyame.	Name
Sup'm.	Something
Sumpting.	Something
Sista.	Sister
Scueem.	Scream
Dis.	This
Brekfuss	Breakfast
Yah.	Here
Inna	In a/inner/in the
Falla	Follow
Si	See
Earliyah	Earlier
Tek	Take
Not'n/nut'n	Nothing
Har	Her
Fi	For/to
Dah	That
Deh/dey	There
Duh	Do
Attaclapse	Armageddon, the end The big finale
Pickney	Child: son or daughter
Pickney Dem	Children: sons or Daughters

Tank	Thanks
Batty	Bottom/butt/ass
Shitty Batty.	Shitty butt/ass/ bottom
Shitten Temper.	Severe Diarrhea
Mawning.	Morning
Cyaan/caan.	Can't/can
Seet.	See it
Seet deh.	There it is
Kine.	Kind
Buh-bye	Bye-bye/goodbye
Teacha	Teacher
Di	The
Bawl	Ball/cry
Nut	Not
Tiyad	Tired
Wi	We
Wissle/Wissel	Whistle
Likkle	Little
Fada	Father
Mada	Mother
Draws	Underwear
Punaney	Vagina
Tawk	Talk
Crosses.	Bad Luck

About the Author

 T R Chambers was born and raised in Kingston, Jamaica. Her journey led her to the United States, where she pursued higher education with determination and focus. She earned an Associate degree in Liberal Arts, along with a certificate in  Interior Designing from Monroe Community College in Rochester, New York. After her time at Monroe Community College, Chambers transferred to the University at Buffalo. There, she excelled academically and obtained a double bachelor's degree in Psychology and Global Gender Studies, graduating magna cum laude. Her educational background reflects a deep commitment to understanding both individual and societal dynamics.

In addition to her academic achievements, Chambers has a passion for traveling. She embraces a nomadic lifestyle, cherishing the diverse experiences and perspectives gained from her journeys. Through her travels, she continues to expand her horizons and deepen her understanding of different cultures

TANYA R CHAMBERS

OLD MAN TREE PRESS

NOTE FROM THE AUTHOR

Dear Readers!

I pray you enjoyed reading the first book of the Dan series YARDIE AND THE ALIENS trilogy!

Please take a moment to leave a review and visit our website for more info.

<u>www.lazygalswofiyahself-publishingthingsllc.com</u>
www.oldmantreepress.com

ALSO BY T R CHAMBERS

THE JAMAICAN:
SOUL IN DARKNESS

The beginning of self love is self acceptance

Rena stood beneath the flickering streetlight, shadows dancing around her like whispers of forgotten dreams. The vibrant colors of Mexico City washed over her, a stark contrast to the darkness swirling within. It was here, in the depths of her despair, that she contemplated the twisted journey her life had taken.

The decision to flee Buffalo, NY had been impulsive-driven by an unbearable need to escape the chains of her struggling existence. She left behind not just her job and home, but also her ex-lover, Behanzin, who embodied everything a human male could ever possessed, until he made the mistake of propositioning her into the prostitution ring. It was so easy to walk away from, unlike her ethereal soulmate, a powerful figure cloaked in danger and allure — Jahazap. The embodiment of everything she feared and craved, a riptide dragging her into an abyss she struggled to resist.

Finding herself in a city where the air was thick with opportunity yet weighed down by despair, Rena tasted the bitterness of desperation as she wandered the streets. Being propped up by her past and present misfortunes, Rena was far from the girl who used to explore the world with passion and curiosity. Now, every glance in the mirror revealed a stranger — a dark soul, haunted by desires so intense they threatened to consume her. The very thought of embracing what resided within her pushed her toward the brink; a power she both feared and craved.

In moments of quiet, she recalled the warning from her soulmate, a being whose existence was both a blessing and a curse. His ethereal presence lingered in her mind, reminding her of the fragile boundary between light and dark. **"To gaze upon me is to risk your survival,"** he once said, a warning that had fallen on fearful ears as she let her heart drift to the physical realm, seeking the thrill of human connection.

She felt the urgency mounting—it echoed in her chest and throbbed in her veins. Whether it was the essence of danger calling to her or the allure of the unknown, she tried not to be drawn towards Luke's ultimatum. The biggest drugs lord in Rochester whose money she needed to survive. **"Find a man in Mexico, Rena. I'm tired of supporting you,"** he had said, meanest lacing his voice.

With no other options, she embraced her predicament. Rena walked the streets with head held high, determination lighting the darkness within. She would become the hunter rather than the hunted, reclaiming her power.

Rumors of shifting beings flickered through the alleyways, tales of those who danced between worlds. Rena was drawn to whispered stories of a mysterious figure—the Jamaican—who could help her understand her newfound strength and embrace the darkness brewing inside. The Jamaican was said to be a master of shadows, able to shift forms and blend into the very fabric of night.

As night fell, she found herself in a dimly lit bar filled with smoke and secrets. Her heart raced, a lure of uncertainty coiling deep in her gut. Each moment felt electric, charged with potential and danger. **"I'm here to find you,"** the shadow declared to her in the dimly lit room where she was testing the air around her.

The figure emerged from the darkness, enigmatic and captivating. His eyes glimmered with an otherworldly light, unrestrained by the boundaries of this world. Painfully beautiful, the being held a promise of darkness and desire, an echo of her own Jamaican soul.

Rena's breath caught, and she battled the urge to surrender, knowing that gazing upon him might unravel the fragile sanity she clutched so tightly. Yet the pull was undeniable; questioning everything she knew about love and darkness, she stepped closer. **"To unleash the monster within, you must first know yourself,"** he murmured, his voice a symphony that tugged at her very core.

With every encounter, Rena navigated the brink of surrender, flirting dangerously with the darkness that threatened to overtake her. Would she allow herself to harness the power she'd long hidden? Or was she destined to remain a beggar—both in spirit and in love—reflecting the remnants of the life she left behind?

The answer remained cloaked in shadows, waiting to be revealed as Rena discovered the depths of her soul in a world of chaos and transformation.

www.ingramcontent.com/pod-product-compliance
Lightning Source LLC
Chambersburg PA
CBHW020254030726
47499CB00001B/197